VERITIES

A Journey by Tracks

—Inspired by a True Story—

Randy White

VERITIES

A Journey by Tracks

Inspired by a True Story

RANDY WHITE

BELLE ISLE BOOKS
www.belleislebooks.com

ISBN: 978-1-951565-04-6
LCCN: 2019916392

Cover and layout design by Michael Hardison
Production management by Christina Kann
Cover photograph: © ROSS / Adobe Stock #154129802

Printed in the United States of America

Published by

Belle Isle Books (an imprint of Brandylane Publishers, Inc.)
5 S. 1st Street
Richmond, Virginia 23219

BELLE ISLE BOOKS
www.belleislebooks.com

belleislebooks.com | brandylanepublishers.com

For Cadence and Brooks,
And all who sing for those without a song.

Invictus

Out of the night that covers me,
Black as the Pit from pole to pole,
I thank whatever gods may be
For my unconquerable soul.

In the fell clutch of circumstance
I have not winced nor cried aloud,
Under the bludgeoning of chance
My head is bloody, but unbowed.

Beyond this place of wrath and tears
Looms but the horror of the shade,
And yet the menace of the years
Finds, and shall find me, unafraid.

It matters not how strait the gate,
How charged with punishments the scroll,
I am the master of my fate:
I am the captain of my soul.

—William Earnest Henley

"It's a gift to exist and with existence comes suffering. There's no escaping that. If you are grateful for your life...then you have to be grateful for all of it. You can't pick and choose what you're grateful for. (Through suffering) you get the awareness of other people's loss, which allows you to connect with that other person, which allows you to love more deeply and to understand what it's like to be a human being."

—*Stephen Colbert*

1

Waiting on a Sunny Day

"It's raining but there ain't a cloud in the sky."
—Bruce Springsteen

In the beginning, it was hot. The heat was absolutely miserable. It would follow you around like an older child pestering his younger siblings. Even in my sleep, sweat misted my skin as if I'd walked through a thick fog.

My house was almost a hundred years old, and we didn't have central air-conditioning. We had an AC window unit in the living room that did its best to pump in more comforting air, but its battle against Virginia's scorching summer heat was futile. The entire house felt feverish. Even the cold water was hot.

Heat molds what it touches. It can melt steel or change water into a completely different state of matter when exposed to it for too long. Imagine what it can do to humans.

My friends thought I was crazy because I loved when it rained in the summertime. They hated those days. But the only time my house cooled off was when it rained.

We lived right outside Richmond, in a small town called Verities. We flirted with the bizarre each day in my childhood

1

home. I was always on high alert for drama. Tension seemed to breed in the swiss-cheese walls of the house, along with the mice that inhabited them.

I spent most of my time in my bedroom with the door shut, alone as an oyster. I felt safe there. The only window in my room had broken long ago, and a wooden board replaced it. My dad had installed the panel so securely that no light shined through it. The only thing that bothered me was that it blocked a quick escape route. You never know when you might need to get away in a hurry.

An eerie painting hung in our living room downstairs. Its image burned into my mind like a brand. Something about the picture drew me into it, as if I were meant to be part of the scene. The picture showed a young girl looking sadly through the canvas as if bereaved. Her eyes, in their voiceless innocence, made me want to reach out to embrace her.

The girl sat barefoot with her legs stretched out straight ahead of her on the floor of a small house. The fancy cotton dress she wore suggested she would soon be going somewhere special. Two red doors—both without any knobs or handles—and a small A-frame window were placed mockingly behind her. Outside the window, a vast field of waving yellow hills expanded as far as the eye could see. A fruitless tree, its midsection rotted out, clawed toward the window, like a naked black hand with sharp nails.

One morning, I was in the kitchen near the painting, making myself a bowl of cereal, when I realized the milk was gone from the fridge.

"Mom, is there any milk?"

There was no answer.

I walked into the living room. The aroma of a freshly lit cigarette sweetened the air. I loved the initial scent of a lit cigarette, but every breath after that made me nauseous.

My mom was lying on the sofa in her usual Sunday position. Her blonde hair was pulled back in a tight ponytail, and she was in yesterday's clothes.

"Mom, do we have any milk?"

"No milk—use the tonic water," she said in her scruffy voice, which had already been rubbed raw by years of hard drinking and smoking. Her annoyance was as obvious as the broken capillaries around the corners of her nostrils. "Can you grab me some Advil, Sam?"

I ignored her and walked to the trash can to throw away my dry cereal. As I pulled back the lid, there was a loud, familiar clinking sound.

A twelve-year-old shouldn't automatically know what that sound means, but I did. Glancing into the trash can, I saw nine beer bottles and an empty container of cheap vodka filling the plastic bag inside.

Mom was hung over again. However, her alcoholism bordered on morbid, so the night before must have been a slow one for her.

A sudden rumbling, loud as the train that passed behind our house, signaled that my older brother was running down the stairs.

"Good morning, Kevin!" I said as he appeared. I was always excited when my brother was around.

"Morning, Castor!"

Any child of an addict can tell you that one of the perks of having a parent who's high all the time is having an embarrassing middle name. Kevin knew how much I despised being called by mine, so (like all older brothers) he relished in using it as often as possible.

"Shut up, Pollux!" This was my only defense: the only person with a more embarrassing middle name than mine was my brother. We were both Geminis—hence the odd names.

With a faint smile, Kevin relented at my warning shot. "Okay, okay. Good morning, Sam!"

In my duels with my brother, I savored any victory, no matter how small. Although we shared the same birthday—June 3—he was five years older than me, so I was usually on the losing end of any competition.

Kevin's victories didn't stop with me, though. He was a quiet star at almost everything. He'd been an all-state offensive lineman in high school two years in a row. He played center, and his coach said Kevin was the best he'd ever seen. He also held the record in basketball for the most three-pointers made in a season, and was an all-star catcher on the school's baseball team.

Kevin loved any sport involving balls—but his favorite was boxing. He spent hours training at a boxing gym called Vintage Boxing Club, just up the road from our house. He became a pretty skilled amateur fighter, but he never fought outside the gym. He only fought internally.

Kevin's talents didn't just pertain to sports: he was also a great student. He was near the top of his class, and was able to remember almost anything after reading or hearing it only once. He never forgot anything. In fact, many members of our family possessed the gift of a strong memory. Sometimes I thought it was more of a curse, though. The ability to forget is a blessing.

The only thing my brother didn't excel at was social interaction. It's said that Gemini is the most philosophical and communicative of the signs, but my brother barely ever spoke. Maybe there were complex ideas in his head, but he rarely expressed them. He was so shy and quiet—especially around girls—that Dad often teased him about being gay. I always found it odd that Dad's worst insult was to call Kevin a homosexual. It was Dad, in all his flattery, who focused considerable energy on pleasing men.

Dad would say some awful things, but we figured he wasn't serious. At the time, Kevin was his star—his first and favorite child, even though Dad still treated him poorly. Dad enjoyed living vicariously through Kevin's accomplishments, but still wanted him to know who was in charge.

"Kevin dear, can you bring me an ice pack?" Mom asked as he passed. She always perked up a little when my brother was around.

"Why, Mom? Hung over again? I guess if it's Sunday morning and you're lying on the couch, that's a yes, right?"

Kevin would get mad when Mom drank, but I think it was sadness disguised as anger. I guess that's what all anger is, really: camouflaged sorrow.

Unlike my brother, I didn't mind being around Mom when she was drinking. Sometimes, if she got drunk enough, she'd hug me and tell me she cared about me. When she was sober, that kind of thing never happened.

"Is that any way to talk to your mother?" Mom asked Kevin. "Don't you know the first commandment is to honor your mother and father?"

There was always something particularly annoying about hearing my mom, clothed in her hypocrisy, quote from the Bible to rationalize her lifestyle. She had to do some heavy convincing to justify her bad behavior as good and her immorality as moral.

"That's not the first commandment, Mom," I said.

"Well, what *is* the first commandment then, smarty?" she snapped back.

"I am the LORD your God! You shall have no other gods before Me!" Dad roared as he entered the room.

The sound of the word *LORD* traveled straight to my amygdala, and adrenaline stung my veins.

"Dean!" Mom squeaked as she got up to grab her ice pack. "You scared me!"

"Leda, shut the hell up! We have to go soon! Get your shit together!"

My dad ordained himself king in our house, but we knew he was more like a puppet emperor. Around other adults, he was a timid-talking sycophant. He reserved the worst parts of himself for his family, and was indifferent to the idea that we had feelings. Once you see someone as subhuman, you can justify any horrible action toward them. Sometimes he wouldn't talk or even look at us for weeks at a time. When he finally spoke, it was always something hurtful. I hadn't even realized that "son of a bitch" wasn't a term of endearment until I was in my early teens. I'd always thought it was my dad's pet name for me. Some fathers call their sons "bud" or "pal"; mine called me "son of a bitch."

When he graduated from high school, Dad had scored a union job with excellent benefits. He made good money, and Mom said he was a little nicer then. He took night classes at a local community college, all paid for by his company. He had hope for his future and what he might accomplish.

A couple years after he was hired, Virginia became a right-to-work state. The union was broken up, and his employer was able to pay him a lot less, without offering any benefits. They even stopped paying for Dad's college classes, so he dropped out. He had to work extra hours anyway to make ends meet due to his lowered salary.

When I was in elementary school, my family had been friends with people of all economic classes. Some of our neighbors had college degrees, some were managers, and some were leaders in the community. We played with their kids, participated in the same sporting events, had cookouts together, and attended many of the same school functions. But when the unions left, neighbors who could afford to leave left as well. They made their homes on the other side of the tracks. Some of our friends were even evicted from their homes because they couldn't afford to pay rent with the lower wages. They simply vanished, leaving all their belongings on the curb.

My family soon realized that everyone left in the neighborhood was pretty much alike. We no longer interacted with people of different backgrounds. Our schools got bad, and the teachers got worse. What little money our parents had was spent on food and utilities, not luxuries like books. When we entered school, we were already behind our peers, who owned children's books and had been read to all their lives.

Bad things began to happen in the neighborhood. Sometimes there were even gunshots. Many of us were traumatized by the things we saw and heard. The kids from the other side of the tracks were naturally relaxed, unless a crisis came up; but our internal defaults were programmed to stay constantly stressed.

Once, when I was outside playing with my mom, a man

passed by and told her that he'd make all our lives better if she'd let him be her pimp. I'd never seen her so scared before! She called the police, but when she did, they didn't care. Police officers had been friendly in the past, but now they looked on us with suspicion, as if we were criminals because of where we lived.

Even the local farmers' markets went away, and fast food restaurants took their places. My best friend developed type 2 diabetes when he was nine years old. He weighed 214 pounds!

It was still possible for someone on our side of the tracks to get a job, but they were no longer jobs of dignity. You couldn't hold your head high with pride when you were scraping by under crude and degrading working conditions. Employers paid workers the smallest amount they were just desperate enough to accept. Where once in the neighborhood men had spoken of their employment using words like *craft*, *honor*, and *fulfillment*, they now used words like *tedious*, *humiliating*, and *draining*. The faces of those nearby soon evolved into expressions of flat, dull anguish. It was a scary transformation to witness. It was as if a virus had infected the area and turned people zombielike. There's something about the feeling of dignity in respected work, when you don't feel like you're being taken advantage of, that causes the spirit to shine right through a person's face.

Still, we were better off than a lot of the families in the neighborhood—if only because we were the rare two-income household. My mom had a part-time job as a bookkeeper at a fraternity headquarters, but each year, her paycheck dwindled. As her pay stubs dipped to smaller and smaller numbers, she poured her glasses of vodka fuller and fuller. She'd complain to us about her salary as if it were in our power to change it. She was never consistent regarding who was to blame for it, though.

It was usually the president's fault, unless someone from her favored party occupied the Oval Office. She had always spent her days watching soap operas, but somewhere along the line, that morphed into watching cable news shows. I think it was an outlet to express her anger at what had become of our lives, a mirror of her resentment.

Kevin always referred to her shows as recreational outrage. She trusted the anchors she watched as she trusted the high-lighted words in the Bible. This meant that her beliefs were never constant: they fluctuated depending on what the latest talking head had said in an effort to increase that week's ratings on any given day. She was more informed when she sat around watch-ing soap operas all day. But Mom's commitment to her shows was as strong as Geronimo's had been to his Apaches. They were the only target of her loyalty, besides the booze.

One day, I picked up one of Mom's empty lowball glasses. As I carried it to the sink, it broke in my hand, cutting deeply into my finger and filling the bottom of the glass with dark maroon blood.

Dad was mad I had bled on the carpet, but he still gathered himself and took me to the hospital. As a doctor stitched me up, Dad explained why Mom's paychecks always diminished. He told me that each year, Mom's employers raised the cost of her health insurance. Instead of paying for the inflated costs, they took the increase out of Mom's paychecks.

Dad said it was my and my brother's fault, but I secretly blamed the president, too. Blame helps keep away the sadness you feel at wondering whether something is your fault.

"Can I ask you something, Dad?"

He shot me an annoyed glance. "What?"

"Remember when that bad man broke into your work truck?"

"Yeah, what about it?"

"You were mad because you said he got a free lawyer when you went to court. Right?"

He turned his back. "Yeah. So?"

"Was that man a criminal?"

He turned and looked at me like I was an idiot. "Of course he was. He burglarized my truck!"

"Well, if a criminal has a right to a lawyer, why doesn't a working person have a right to a doctor?"

He glanced down and away. "I don't know, Sam. I guess it's just the way it's always been."

⇌

As is often the case, the last chapters of a person's story are determined by its beginnings.

My dad had grown up in a quaint two-story house with four rambunctious brothers. They all shared one bathroom. Dad was the second-oldest child. My grandmother said that my dad was born sick. He had some kind of disease that turns your skin yellow.

All of Dad's brothers had tan skin and jet-black hair. They looked so much alike that people in their neighborhood couldn't tell them apart. Their father, my grandfather, was a residential plumber who was strong in both temper and physique. He could carry two cast-iron bathtubs up a flight of stairs, one on each of his shoulders. His five boys couldn't even make it up the stairs with one tub lifting all together.

My dad said his father was meaner than a junkyard dog in those years raising his boys. His anger got the best of him, though: at forty-five years old, he had a stroke that left him in a wheelchair, paralyzed on the left side of his body. He only had forty-five years to be a man in this world. The stroke left him not quite a child, but something resembling one.

Dad's mom was a stay-at-home mom in those days. Eventually, she developed what doctors called bipolar disorder. When I asked my dad what that meant, he said it meant she was crazy. She was frequently institutionalized when I was very young. I remember visiting her at psychiatric hospitals all the time as a kid. Doctors put her through all kinds of psychothera-peutic approaches to treat her disease, but nothing ever seemed to work. They knew little about how to successfully treat the dis-order, but they prescribed her the most effective treatment: lith-ium. She was never the same after she began taking it.

My parents left me at her house one night a few years after my grandfather died. In the middle of the night, I was awakened by loud, guttural sobbing. It sounded as if my grandmother was begging for her life!

For a moment, I thought that someone had broken into the house and was hurting her. I grabbed a pocketknife from the nightstand beside my bed and slowly cracked open my bedroom door.

My grandmother was rocking back and forth on her knees in the living room, with her arms stretched straight out into the air above her, as if she were reaching for an invisible apparition. The whole scene reminded me of an amateur exorcism. It looked like something was tormenting her. Frightened and unsure what to do, I threw myself back in bed and stayed there for the rest of the night.

When I mentioned this horrifying experience to my parents

the next day, they acted like it was no big deal. "That's how she meditates, you wimp," my dad said.

I never spent the night at my grandmother's house again.

—

Mom's childhood was a lot different than Dad's. Her young life was marked by separation, sickness, and sadness. Her mother, Anne, had named her Leda Sue. Leda was Anne's paternal grandmother's first name, and Sue was the name of Anne's favorite drinking buddy. My great-grandmother once told us that Anne was the only prostitute that had ever been kicked out of Suzanne's Place, the neighborhood whorehouse, for salacious behavior.

One night when she was six years old, Mom and her four siblings awoke to a loud banging on the front door at two o'clock in the morning. Angry shouting followed. One of my grandmother's side-men had come to the house with the intent of shooting my grandfather so that he and my grandmother could be together.

Mom always said her mother was easy to fall in love with. Taking meth and meeting up with strange men at night apparently wasn't unusual for my grandmother, who had gotten hooked on the drug after her doctor had prescribed it as a diet aid. Anne and this man had been taking meth together for the better part of the previous day, and now, he shouldered his way inside as the door latch broke under his weight.

Awoken by the commotion, my grandfather met the big man at the door as he entered. The visitor pulled a large .357 Magnum revolver from his coat pocket and aimed it at the center of my grandfather's head. Grandfather begged the stranger to wait to shoot him. He summoned each of his young children from their beds and directed them to stand on the living room couch in front of the mysterious man. Mom remembers noticing that the man was dressed in all black. She said that it made her want to play the clapping game Miss Mary Mack right there on the sofa with her sisters.

After gathering his brood, Grandpa announced that if the stranger was going to kill him, he ought to do it in front of these five small children. This, no doubt, was a strategy to incite the man to put the weapon away, as Grandpa hoped that the stranger would be unable to bring himself to murder another man in front of his young children.

But Grandpa's appeal to the morality of the man in black was in vain. Without conscience or consideration, the stranger pulled the trigger, and a bullet struck Grandpa on the right side of his skull. Blood and brain matter sprayed the children's pajamas as the man in black laughed maniacally. Pieces of Grandpa's bloody skull stuck to the small teddy bear my mom was holding.

After that incident, my mom and her siblings were sent away to live with their grandmother and aunt. They never saw their mother again. Their survival from that point on was credited to welfare programs and the kindness of strangers.

Without her parents around, something strange happened to my mom, and to her thoughts about herself and the world around her. It happened to all her siblings, really, in different manners and to varying degrees. It was the plague of her life—of all of their lives. They were life-stunted, emotionally barren, unable to comprehend the diminutiveness of the hollow feelings the absence of their parents aroused inside of them.

Mom was always a sickly child. She spent much of her adolescence in bed and missed a lot of school. A positive for her was that being sick was a great way to get the care and attention she didn't receive otherwise. Mom's aunt, Bea, didn't really interact with her very much. Bea could never relate to my mom. She was the kind of person who saw Mom's constant illnesses as an evolutionary defect, a weakness in need of being eliminated. She admired tough personalities and people who could hide their emotions—or better yet, erase them. Bea paid more attention to my mom's two older siblings, who shared those qualities. Mom's grandmother Nana, on the other hand, was much more compassionate. She tended to my mom in the way a child tends to a bird with a broken wing, and looked on my mom's siblings with concern. She worried that the toughness they possessed might make them hard to love as adults.

Mom spent most of her young life in a very poor, predominantly black neighborhood in the city of Richmond. During her ninth-grade year, Mom and her two older siblings were the only white kids who attended her high school. Although she missed a lot of school, she did well academically and was near the top of her class.

That was also the year she met Dad. They attended the same Halloween party on Brooklyn Park Boulevard. She first spotted him playing five-card stud with his brother, who, coincidentally, was also her sister's boyfriend. Dad was the only person at the table not wearing a Halloween costume. His brother introduced them, and Mom agreed to let Dad take her out on a date.

I've often fantasized about going back to that moment as an adult and talking to those two naïve kids on Brooklyn Park Boulevard. I want to tell my mom, in her untouched innocence, and my dad, in his cocky free-spiritedness, to go home, to turn away from one another. I want to tell them that the path they'll walk together leads only to pain, that what they'll whisper into being won't be the healing blaze they imagine, but a flash of fire followed by a slow burn that will wane into ashes caught in a cold wind. But if I could do that, of course, then I wouldn't be here to tell you our story.

Apparently, Dad seduced Mom by acting like someone he wasn't. For their first date, he took her to see *Swan Lake* at the Richmond Coliseum. My dad knew and cared absolutely nothing about culture or ballet. He couldn't explain the first thing about *Swan Lake*. But he wanted Mom to think he was sophisticated and classy, and it worked. Sometimes it's easier to fall in love with a lie than with the truth.

They ascended into a romance that was like a Cinderella fantasy to my mom. She had received little affection in her life. Affection can heal old wounds and show you beauty you didn't know existed. Dad's care for her was both foreign and comforting. He threw out kind words, which were in short supply in my mom's life at the time. He feigned love, which was even rarer; and with an assist from Tchaikovsky, Mom was soon another teen pregnancy statistic. A week after they found out she was pregnant, they eloped to the city courthouse.

It wasn't long after *Swan Lake* that Dad beat her bloody for the first time. She had gotten drunk and laughed at him about something. He actually knocked out one of her premolars. For the rest of her life, she blamed my brother for her choice to stay in the relationship after that first beating, claiming she had remained for the sake of the baby. Leaving is never easy, but her words were a heavy burden to place on the shoulders of a naïve child.

—

One spring day, Dad announced we were going to try out a local church that coming Sunday—Verities Baptist Church. He wanted to go, not because he was religious or curious in any way, but because his friends the Nieds were members there. My father wasn't a worshipper of God; he was a worshipper of men.

To my dad, the Nieds were the perfect all-American family. They lived an upper-middle-class lifestyle in the most prestigious neighborhood on the other side of the tracks. Mr. Nied was a dentist, and his wife was a biology teacher. Their daughter, Kim, was a star softball player; and their son Joe was the quarterback on my brother's football team. Mr. Nied and my dad had been friends since they were kids, and their friendship was one of the rare ones that had endured despite the fact that they lived on opposite sides of the tracks. Dad was always trying to impress Mr. Nied. He envied Mr. Nied's job, his clothes, his house, his wife—everything. Although Dad's all-consuming envy made him miserable, it was a true passion for him.

When he was around the Nieds, Dad turned into a completely different human being. Dr. Henry Jekyll had nothing on my father. The put-downs, screaming, and cursing with which we were inundated all day disappeared, and he became mild-mannered and pleasant. It was his most impressive trick: persuading people that the malevolent person he was at home didn't exist. It was as if he passed through a magical barrier that transformed him into an alternative version of himself whenever he exited the front door of our house. If I had been one of his peers, I would have liked the guy who walked out our front door. But since I was only his son, I knew the truth: I didn't matter to him.

As we went to the car to travel to our first church experience, walking by the many dogwood trees that decorated our property, I heard the familiar sound of a passing train.

The train tracks in our backyard were an important part of my life—so much so that when I was seven, I had painted my name on them in glossy white paint. When things were crazy in my house, I'd take a walk out on the tracks. I'd sent out more than one train-track prayer in my short lifetime.

I think my brother knew the power of the tracks as well. When it got too hot in the house, I caught glimpses of him walking contemplatively along them with his head down.

As bizarre as it might sound, sometimes I'd even talk to the tracks. They'd whisper back silently in a language only I knew, reassuring me, consoling me. Even when I lay in bed at night, nothing was as comforting to me as the sound of a train whistle.

We packed ourselves tightly into Mom's burgundy 1978 Volvo 240 and headed for salvation.

"Mr. Nied said this is the perfect church to attend—no long-noses or coons," Dad said as he drove.

I wanted to ask him how Jesus, a dark-skinned Jew, would interpret that comment. But Dad had long arms that could easily reach the back seat while he was driving, and I didn't want to taste blood that morning unless it was from a communion cup.

As we drove, we passed a silver Cadillac, and Dad let out a sharp wolf whistle. He loved Cadillacs. They were his favorite cars.

"One day, I'm going to get you a Cadillac," I said to him.

"I'm sure you will," he said sarcastically.

"No, really. I am!"

"Matchbox cars don't count," he said with a smug grin. "Do you know how expensive Cadillacs are?"

"I'll be able to afford it, I promise," I said, unable to sit still in my excitement.

"You're a dumbass. You can't even remember to put the milk back in the fridge, and you think you'll be able to buy a Cadillac? Just sit back there and shut the hell up, Sam."

⇒

We arrived at the church early to meet with the head pastor before the service began. I stepped out of the car and looked at the building in amazement. In an area with record levels of poverty, the biggest structure around was the church in front of me. On the way, we had passed a small house of prayer that was serving meals to the homeless, but it was tiny compared to this grand complex.

When we walked inside, I saw that the grandiosity extended past the outside of the building. The church's clean interior was decorated with the gaudiest furniture I had ever seen. It looked like the inside of a king's castle.

The pastor, Mr. Franks, was a tall man with a short, bumpy nose. He had the same broken capillaries around his nostrils that my mom had. He looked just as you'd imagine a Southern Baptist preacher would look. His black hair was threaded with lines of silvery gray and had been pulled back and flattened until it was slick as a rat with a gold tooth. Thick black-framed glasses protruded from his round, pudgy face, and he wore a black suit with snowy dandruff sprinkled liberally around the shoulders. His most defining feature was his unique smile. He had a devilish grin that made the hair on the back of my neck stand up.

Mr. Franks wanted to speak to us one-on-one. I waited patiently on a hard, wooden bench in the hallway for my turn to come.

As I waited, people began arriving at the church. Old ladies with bitter faces, oversized hats, and cotton dresses that smelled of urine congregated in corners. The parishioners were mostly indistinguishable from one another, but I did recognize one older gentleman who, oddly, had evicted three of my closest friends from their homes the week before Christmas.

Pray on Sunday, while preying on the vulnerable every other day of the week, I thought to myself.

As the parishioners began to crowd the space, a greasy smell permeated the air, and I noticed all the men had the same slicked-back hair as Mr. Franks, slicked so tightly that they could hardly blink. I started to wonder whether I'd have to start slicking back my hair on Sundays if we became members of the church.

A solitary Bible lay on the bench beside me. I opened it to a random page and read the first verse I came to: "God put His law on the minds and hearts of everyone. No longer would someone teach someone else how to know the Lord, they would know Him personally."

I flipped toward the back to a verse in Acts that read, "The Most High does not live in a house that human hands have built."

I wondered if Mr. Franks had read these passages. I thought that he most likely hadn't. He could lose out on this beautiful building if people believed they alone were the authorities on God's word! They wouldn't need Mr. Franks anymore.

I read another verse to myself: "But you, when you pray, enter into your inner chamber, and having shut your door, pray to your Father who is in secret, and your Father who sees in secret will reward you openly."

Hold on, I thought. *Why are people always praying out loud if the Bible clearly says not to? Are they doing that to benefit themselves in the eyes of others?* It was all very confusing.

As I was lost in thought, Mr. Franks' office door creaked open at a snail's pace. It was my turn to speak with him. My dad called me over, and I noticed the most bizarre and repulsive thing: my dad was now wearing Mr. Franks' dreadful smile.

I walked quickly past him and into Mr. Franks' office, trying not to look at my dad's face, and was instantly hit by a grassy smell that made my head ache. Bookshelves lined every wall, but they were mostly filled with pictures and church paraphernalia. None held any books.

Behind me, the heavy door shut with a loud clang.

"Well, Sam, how are you today?" Mr. Franks asked in a kind, robust tone.

"Good, thank you. You?"

"I'm great! It makes me so happy that you're here today! Do you have any questions about what it means to be a Christian?"

"No, sir," I said. This was a lie. I had a ton of questions. I just didn't know if I felt comfortable asking them to the stranger in front of me yet.

"You sure?" Mr. Franks asked. He sounded almost insulted that I didn't have any questions for him. I felt I should ask something so as not to be rude.

"Well, I do have one," I said, looking oddly at a portrait of Jesus in a gold-plated frame on the wall.

Mr. Franks' smile stretched, revealing yellow-stained teeth

and sharp incisors. "Go ahead, son! That's what I'm here for!"

"Okay, great! This is something that has always really bothered me."

"Yes?"

"Well, do you think God would prefer a kind atheist to a hateful Christian?"

Mr. Franks let out something like a snicker, and it made him start coughing uncontrollably. When he was finally able to compose himself, he said, "Well, I guess I don't believe so. I personally think God would prefer the Christian. But there's no dispute that the majority of the Bible challenges us to think beyond our own religion when loving our neighbors." Then he asked again, "Do you know what it means to be a Christian?"

He was trying to change the subject. This was a common tactic adults used whenever I asked questions they were uncomfortable answering.

"Wait," I said quickly. "In your opinion, you believe God would prefer someone who did evil things and was a Christian to a good person who wasn't?" This intuitively didn't seem just. Where you grow up has more control over your religious affiliation than anything else. It wouldn't be right to send people to Hell for being born in the wrong place.

"Sam, do you know what it means to be a Christian?" Mr. Franks asked a third time.

I understood what the questions-in-three meant. They meant he was done with my questions and wanted me to move on. He wanted to talk about what *he* wanted to talk about.

"No, sir, not really. Does it mean I have to slick back my hair?"

Mr. Franks let out a belly laugh that reminded me of a mall Santa Claus.

"Goodness no, it doesn't mean you have to slick back your hair! It means you're saved and will go to Heaven with Jesus— but only if you follow and believe in his every word." He held up a massive Bible with worn pages and hundreds of tabs sticking out of it. "From the Good Book that He left us!"

I wanted to reply, but I was afraid he'd laugh at me again. I knew that Jesus didn't write the Bible with a pen and paper himself. He wasn't even in the first half of it. So I wondered what Mr. Franks meant when he said He *left* the Bible to us.

I'd once watched a documentary on television that said the Bible was made up of hundreds of separate books, all with different authors and written at various times throughout history. No one truly knows exactly who composed each book, or who they even were, because none of those original manuscripts survived the passage of time. The stories were passed down orally. Hundreds of years after Jesus died, a group of men got together to decide what the authors intended to say and which books should or shouldn't be included in what we now consider the Bible. Unfortunately, no one could agree what the original stories were even about! They all had their own personal beliefs about what God wanted from humans.

"Now, take my biological father," Mr. Franks continued, interrupting my thoughts. "He was a good Christian man. He supported us and was good to our family all his mortal life. He made our home a safe place, and he fed us. But he never believed he had to be baptized *while immersed in water* to be saved, even though it clearly says so right in here!" He held up his oversized Bible again, with a look of disbelief on his face. "So now that he's passed on, I know he's in Hell and I'll never see him again. Yes, that pains me. But that was Daddy's choice, and he made it, and that's all there is to it!"

Mr. Franks' statement made me realize that anytime an idea is attached to religious commitment, the ability to think critically about that idea is lost. However, something else bothered me. I wasn't necessarily shocked that Mr. Franks said his dad was in Hell. I knew my dad was going to Hell. I was more shocked he'd said his home was a safe place.

"Made our home a safe place?" I thought. *He was good to his family all his life?* That alone should get a father a ticket into Heaven. As strange as it sounds, it had never occurred to me that a father could be anything but a monster. I'd assumed that was how all fathers were. It had never entered my mind that there could be such a thing as a *kind* dad. To me, the phrase was oxymoronic.

"You need to read this," Mr. Franks said, handing me a small Bible. "The Bible is the greatest gift God has given us."

Without hesitation, I blurted, "The ability to think is the greatest gift He's given us! Don't you think? This is something else I've always thought about—"

Mr. Franks interrupted me midsentence. "Oh, gracious! Look at the time; the service is about to begin!" He stood up quickly and hugged me a little too tightly. "Why don't you go find your folks in the sanctuary, and I'll see you out there!"

⇀

When I entered the sanctuary, I was awestruck. It had a beautifully rich, Gothic appearance. Large windows with high, pointed vaults surrounded the perimeter of the room. The massive windows were bordered by polished stone and filled with stained glass depicting various Biblical scenes. The sounds of the congregation talking to one another echoed off the church walls and merged into a monotone.

I spotted my family alongside the Nieds in a middle pew. I walked over and sat by Kevin.

"They should open up these walls and make it bigger," I said as I sat. "They could fit more people in here."

As we waited for the service to begin, my dad caught me staring at one of the church's walls. My staring seemed to aggravate him.

"What are you looking at?" he asked crisply.

I pointed to a frame with a Biblical verse on the wall. In large Gothic letters, the ominous sign read,

AND HE SHALL SMITE THE WICKED.

The service was interesting enough. We sang, talked, and shook hands with fellow parishioners, then sang again. When it was time for Mr. Franks to start his sermon, I sat up straight as an arrow in my seat. It made me feel special to know that the important man who was speaking in front of this large crowd of people had been speaking to me only moments before.

"My fellow parishioners," Mr. Franks began. "I come to you today with a message from the Almighty God. Today's sermon is an important one; it's a message your very soul depends on. The Lord sent us out into the world to show kindness to others and to be accepting of one another. To make a world that reflected everything positive and good that grows from our Christian faith."

I looked at Mr. Nied. He was nodding and smiling encouragingly at Mr. Franks. My dad noticed Mr. Nied doing this, too, and mimicked the gesture.

"It's the love you show your neighbors that will prove you

are a child of the Almighty God. And friends, know that it's the grace of God that will truly save you. Now, does this mean you can go out into the world and do whatever you want? Does it mean you can go out and make the world your very own Sodom and Gomorrah? Absolutely not! God's truth is everlasting and doesn't offensively change with the times! Lately, our society has begun to legitimize sinful behavior. People have tried to modernize the Bible's sacred words to suit their own sinful motivations. Homosexuals have invaded the media and the surrounding culture that our precious children inhabit. Do not fall for Satan's tricks, my friends!"

Mr. Franks' voice grew louder with each new declaration. He squeezed out certain words and syllables in thunderous, arousing booms. "All those who perpetuate homosexual behavior will go straight to Hell! We must guard ourselves against the impure conduct this society tries to force upon us, for it will lead us into eternal damnation if we let down our guard! People, do you know what makes a person a slave? It's the call for obedience! The Devil will call on you to be obedient to serve his own purposes! If good people stand by and passively witness an evil, they become co-conspirators when they keep silent in the face of it! I say, love your Christian brothers and sisters! Don't love sin! Feed one another, clothe one another, and heal one another, but turn away from evil things! The great God almighty sculpted you with His eternal understanding, and loves you! For Psalm 139, verses 13-14 tell us:

> *For it was you who formed my inward parts;*
> *You knit me together in my mother's womb.*
> *I praise you, for I am fearfully and wonderfully made.*

His voice softened and the bounce of his previous movements slowly diminished. "Now, my flock, comes the part of the service when you can make a personal decision to start a real relationship with Christ our Lord. Today, if you accept Jesus as your Lord and Savior and wish to serve Him for the rest of your life, do not be ashamed to approach me for a baptism that will wash away your sins and allow you to be born again, uncontaminated and pure. Come forward now if you wish to be saved."

I didn't really know what to think of Mr. Franks' sermon. It was theatrical, and I wasn't really a fan of theatre. I looked at my father to gauge his response, but he seemed more interested in what Mr. Nied was doing than in what Mr. Franks was saying. Mom was dozing off, no doubt due to a persistent hangover, and she seemed to be having trouble understanding where she was.

But then I looked at my brother. At first I thought my eyes were deceiving me. My strong, skilled, superhuman brother had tears streaming down his face. They were full-blown, rolling tears spilling down his innocent adolescent cheeks, and his expression was one of complete understanding. I immediately felt compassion for the tenderness of the act.

Mr. Franks' words must have moved him in a profound way, I thought.

Mom and Dad began looking at Kevin, too. When he became aware that we were all noticing the tears dripping down his cheeks, his expression grew panicked, and he stood as if he was about to run straight out of the sanctuary! But instead, he turned awkwardly but unhurriedly and began walking boldly to the front of the church. As he reached the altar, he took Mr. Franks' hand in his, and the preacher baptized him that day in

front of my family, the Nieds, and all those followers who were
gathered in the church.

⬥

Kevin's tears haunted me after that church service, not only
because of how moving the honesty of it was, but because I had
never seen him cry before. I hadn't thought he cared enough
about anything to produce such emotion.

We never talked about what happened at the church or why
it happened. It just wasn't something we did in our family. But I
felt there must have been something more going on than just a
touching sermon that had made Kevin respond in such an emotional way.

At the time, Edvard Munch's famous painting *The Scream*
adorned one of my bedroom walls. *The Scream* had always spoken
to the anxiety I felt in that home, and reflected a piercing loneliness that I believed only I understood.

Now I realized I might not be the only one who felt that way.
After all, my brother had grown up in the same house. Maybe his
tears that day were an expression of his own loneliness.

After witnessing such a dramatic response from my older
brother and seeing how much enjoyment Dad had taken in
impressing the Nieds with his faux display of religious devotion,
I was certain we would be regulars at Mr. Franks' church from
then on. But when the next Sunday came, Mom lay in her usual
spot on the couch, more hungover than she had been on the previous Sunday. Dad was downstairs, screaming over God knows
what. And so, that service ended up being the first and last time
my family ever set foot in a church together.

2
Fortunate Son

"It ain't me, it ain't me, I ain't no fortunate one, no."
—Creedence Clearwater Revival

Three years after what came to be known as "the church incident," Kevin left for college. He received a full football scholarship to a state school about an hour and a half away. He rarely called home, and the few times he visited were spent partying with his friends.

Dad spent his time at work or asleep, which didn't bother me since his waking hours consisted of sharing variations on how worthless I was. Mom still worked part-time, but had a new-found obsession with playing bingo most nights. I had the holy grail of teenage life—a driver's license, a vehicle, and parents who didn't care where I was, why I was there, or who I was with.

I spent most of my time with my friend Lynn Buchanan. We'd been close ever since we were both knee-high to a ground-hog. We were more than friends, really—even more than best friends. He was the only person I knew in the world who thought about things the same way I did. We both had wounds in similar places inside of us, and that forged an understanding. There is no greater feeling than being understood by someone else. It's on the same spectrum as love.

Lynn and I had very different lives. He lived on the other side of the tracks as a son of privilege. All the Buchanan men had gone to Yale, dating back to Lynn's great-great-grandfather—mainly as a result of the good fortune of Lynn's great-great-great-grandfather, who had been the first in their family to attain wealth. He had lived in Verities back when the roads were still just dusty, unknown paths. While dove hunting, he'd stumbled upon a stash of gold bars that a group of bank robbers had abandoned as they were being chased by law enforcement. He used the metal to start a railroad business, which had morphed over the years into a construction conglomerate.

Lynn and I were never bothered by the fact that we were from polar opposite social classes. I never questioned why our lives were so vastly different. I had always figured it was because his family worked harder than mine. But the truth was that Lynn's family was born on third base thinking they'd hit a triple—while mine had all but been hit by the pitch.

My economics teacher, Mr. Wynne, had explained how money was divided among the population in the US once. It was an eye-opening experience for me. He'd said that if the US had a population of one hundred people and the total amount of money available to share with everyone was one hundred dollars, someone like Lynn's dad would own forty-three of those dollars. The nineteen managers and friends he employed would own about $2.50 each, and the rest of the eighty people in the country would own about nine cents each. He'd also said that inherited money, like Mr. Buchanan's, was why many children from rich families had a head start toward staying rich—a state that middle- and lower-class kids had little chance of attaining.

"Let me tell you something else that might shock you!" Mr. Wynne had said. "On the entire planet, just eight men possess as much wealth as the bottom 3.6 billion people, who make up the poorest half of the world's population. In America, three men own more wealth than the entire bottom half of the American population combined. That's 160 million Americans!"

Mr. Buchanan couldn't care less about those people. He was rarely at home, but I remember him taking Lynn and me into the city once when we were kids to visit a satellite horse track. As we had walked to the entrance, an old man with two missing front teeth approached us and asked if we could spare any change so he could eat lunch. He looked like he hadn't eaten in days. Mr. Buchanan walked right past him with an irritated look on his face. As we entered the building, Mr. Buchanan told us that he despised people like the old man—people who were "just looking for a handout."

"Those people need to get a job and work for their money!" he said. "They don't want to work!"

It was a strange response, coming from Mr. Buchanan. His father had handed him millions of dollars in inheritance money for doing nothing more than winning the sperm equivalent of a fifty-yard dash. But he felt entitled to his money, so he had to do some tricky rationalization. In his mind, that money wasn't a handout; it was something he had earned.

I'd always felt that if you're focused on the powerful while ignoring the vulnerable, you didn't understand God's language. I had experienced the pangs of hunger many times in my life. We didn't know the old man's story. We hadn't walked in his worn-out shoes.

Inside the satellite horse track, I searched for something I could give him. I found a set of vending machines, and bought a bag of Doritos and cheese crackers.

As I was grabbing the items, I noticed something scurry behind the machines, and quickly moved to the side to see what it was. A chubby white mouse the size of a tennis ball was hidden in the shadows, quietly licking his dry paws. When he started moving again, I noticed he was heading straight for a mousetrap on the floor behind the machines!

The trap was out of my reach, so I opened the package of cheese crackers, picked off a few small pieces, and set them up on the floor in a line leading away from the death device. To my delight, the mouse began eating the little portions I had placed on the ground for him. He ravenously ate every teeny morsel in seconds.

It was more than enough to fill him, but the chubby little guy got greedy. He sniffed around slowly, scurrying back toward the cheese on the trap—toward death disguised as gratification. He was able to steal a bit without setting it off, but still he wasn't content. He wanted it all.

He's just like us, I thought to myself. *Never satisfied.*

The mouse continued to eat, edging closer and closer to the middle of the trap. Then suddenly—*bang!* There was a violent snap, frantic shaking, and then silence as fate came—fate just as hungry as he had been.

I shook my head sadly. *Didn't it know any better?* I thought.

I wondered if God looked down on us with the same detachment with which whoever had set that trap looked down on that little mouse. The thought scared me, made the inside of my chest shiver.

I left the still creature to serve eternity for its greed and took what was left of the crackers and Doritos outside to the old man on the street.

"God bless you, son!" he said with a kindhearted smile as I handed him the snacks. He opened the Doritos, smelled the contents of the bag, and threw a chip into his mouth. "I love that smell," he said happily.

As the man ate, I noticed a large tattoo on his forearm. It showed a prisoner next to a guard tower. "POW" stood out in big, bold letters, and the words "You Are Not Forgotten" were written below in faded ink.

"Cool tattoo! Where'd you get that?" I asked curiously.

"Little Vegas," he said. "Did it myself." For the first time, pride painted his leathery face.

"Wow, you're a great artist! Were you a professional cardplayer?"

He laughed and said, "No, son. Little Vegas was what they called a camp I spent a little time in back in '68. Hanoi, North Vietnam." He turned to walk away and yelled out, "Thanks for the snacks, kid!"

As I watched him disappear down the ghostly street, I wondered where he'd sleep that night, and where he'd get his next meal. I also wondered what had led him to his current situation. I had a feeling it was something more than just not wanting to work, as Lynn's dad had so self-righteously proclaimed.

When I walked back inside the building, I saw Lynn staring callously at me. "Why'd you give that loser anything?" he asked.

"Give the guy a break. Imagine if you passed out right now and woke up in another person's body, with a magical genie hovering above you. The genie offers you two choices. First, he says you could go back to living on Earth again, but with the caveat that you wouldn't know whether you'd end up your dad's son or that old man's son. You'd have a fifty-fifty chance of each. Or, second, the genie says you can go back and be born from one of two men who are not rich or poor, but equally middle-of-the-road. Which life would you choose?"

"The second, of course!" Lynn said. "I'm not stupid enough to take a risk like that!"

"Exactly! Now think about our world. Billions of children are destined to be born to the old man, while only a couple thousand are going to be born into a life like yours."

"But," he said proudly, "you have to think about something else. Maybe everyone in my family is harder-working and more intelligent than a lot of those people. Maybe we deserve to have more."

"Maybe. But is being born more intelligent or having the environmental makeup to be more ambitious a good reason to allow those born without those traits to suffer?"

Lynn scrunched up his face as if he suddenly smelled rotten eggs, while I continued. "Sure, you should get more, but there are twenty-two hundred billionaires in the world, out of seven billion people! Don't you think that's a bit unfair?"

"Sam, that's just the natural fallout of making money. Don't you want to have the opportunity to become one of those billionaires?"

"What I'd rather see is fairness. You heard what Mr. Wynne said in economics class. In the US, the top twenty percent of the richest people own eighty-four percent of the nation's wealth! That means that the overwhelming majority of people, eighty percent, split the remaining sixteen percent of wealth! The whole bottom twenty percent own just one-tenth of one percent! I'm not saying there shouldn't be rich people; I'm just saying there shouldn't be poor people. And the discrepancy between the haves and have-nots shouldn't be so gigantic. We shouldn't have people begging for food on the streets when someone like your dad can drop thousands of dollars on a Tuesday-night meal at a fancy steakhouse."

Lynn stared at me as if I'd just shit in his hat.

⇌

Mr. Buchanan lost five thousand dollars that day betting on horses. It didn't even faze him. That was more money than my mom had made working that entire year!

On our way back to the Buchanans' home, Mr. Buchanan stopped at a shoe store and bought Lynn three pairs of brand-new shoes.

"You can never have too many shoes," he told Lynn with a pompous grin.

I glanced down at the tennis shoes my mom had bought for me at the Goodwill—my only pair. My big toe peeked out of a small hole on top. I salivated over Lynn's new footwear, but Lynn didn't even appreciate them. Appreciation grows out of want, and Lynn wanted for nothing.

⇌

The Buchanans' home was absolutely magnificent. It wasn't the Taj Mahal, but in my eyes, it was close. Mr. Buchanan had designed it from the ground up, constructing it entirely of an elegant gray stone. The wraparound driveway was lined with tulips, and the grass was greener than a grasshopper's back.

The home's most defining feature was a set of massive metal

gates at the front of the driveway. They were hand-sculpted and stood at least twenty feet high. Decorative dragons adorned each of the two doors, their scaly bodies coiled in mirrored poses until their heads came together at the top and kissed.

The first time I saw the dragon gates, I joked to Lynn that they looked like the gates of Hell. Lynn shook his head reflectively and said that I wasn't too far off. His comment made sense to me: it had been my experience that the more welcoming a home looked, the less welcoming its tenants were.

The house itself was three stories tall, and the top floor boasted a game room equipped with a pool table, a bar, and a giant forty-inch television. The six-acre property on which it had been built sat adjacent to a popular golf club where the Buchanans had a seemingly permanent membership. Old magnolia trees, attractive gardens, and broad lawns decorated the acreage. In the backyard, an oversized pool surfaced with decorative tile sat next to a spacious blue stone patio featuring a pergola. The pool house, made of the same gray stone as the main residence, was used primarily for Mrs. Buchanan's yoga sessions. Its master bedroom was bigger than my entire home!

Yet in spite of the spacious pool house, Mrs. Buchanan always said she had never been truly happy with the place until Mr. Buchanan had built her the tennis court. It was the finishing touch on her dream compound.

Still, even with all those great amenities at his place, Lynn was always at my house. I never understood why he wanted to be at my home when he had everything he could ever want at his. He said it was because he could be himself at my house— instead of an *idea* of himself. Personally, I couldn't help but think it was because he was able to drink beer at my house without having to worry about getting caught.

In the end, though, I didn't care what the reason was; I loved it when he came over. His presence tempered my dad, who was always more concerned with appearing to have a happy life than actually having one. Dad was on his best behavior when Lynn was around, because he adored Lynn's father. He laughed at Mr. Buchanan's stupid jokes the way a middle-school girl laughs at her crush.

What my dad didn't know was that Lynn was one of the few people outside of our house who knew the truth about him. Lynn had played a role in one of the worst stories of my life.

One day, as I was out walking along the tracks, I had come upon a stray dog wandering the rails. I was anxious at the wild stranger until he ran up to me, licking my face as if it had been covered in buttered sugar. He was thin—I could clearly see the skeleton outline of his ribs—so I took him back to my house to get him something to eat.

But after I fed him, the little guy wouldn't leave. He was a purebred boxer who couldn't have been more than a year or two old. He turned out to be a really sweet dog, so I adopted him. I named him "Jessie the Tramp" because I'd found him on the tracks, an unlost wanderer just like me.

After only a week, Jessie and I were inseparable. He was the only soul who had ever come close to giving me the sort of friendship I had with Lynn. I taught Jessie all the basic tricks: how to sit, lie down, come, and even shake my hand. I fed him twice a day and took him for a walk each afternoon after school. It was a tenderhearted time, having another soul around who genuinely cared for me. In some of the hardest moments of my life, when I reached out and should have found a hand, I found a paw instead. I'd never had someone so excited to be in my presence. When Jessie saw me come home, his ears lay straight back, and his rear shook uncontrollably from side to side. This mini-quake spread quickly toward his head until his whole body was trembling. If I acknowledged Jessie in any way throughout this process, he would fly forefeet first into my midsection and dig his paws in as if he were trying to box me. I wore black-and-blue bruises on my stomach from these boxer hugs, but I didn't mind. It felt good to be wanted.

One day, I was outside playing with Jessie when my dad came home from work in one of his moods. He laughed when he saw me, and asked me why I was wearing a pink shirt that day.

From my experience with Dad, I knew that a gay joke was coming, so I ignored him. This set him to DEFCON 1. He began screaming his usual insults and reminded me that no one would ever love a loser like me—and then he blindsided me with a closed fist right to my nose.

Right away, I knew it was broken. This wasn't my first rodeo with Dad. For a moment, it felt like a burst of lightning had turned my brain off. My vision was a quick, flashing light. With every heartbeat, tiny pins pricked my cheeks, and my sinuses felt explosive. My eyes watered, which made my nose run. I reached up to wipe it and nearly threw up at the amount of blood on the back of my hand and forefinger.

Jessie had always been skittish around my dad—but loyalty leads to bravery, real bravery. Not the soft kind that bullies and belittles or draws blood out, but a reckless daring that rises up for what's right, even knowing it's doomed to do so. I watched the hair on Jessie's back stand up as he assumed a protective stance beside me. He growled angrily, displaying sharp, milky-white teeth. This sent my dad further into his rage. His face contorted into pure anger, and he picked up a maroon-colored brick lying near the driveway and hurled it as hard as he could in Jessie's direction.

The brick struck Jessie on the right side of his precious little head. He collapsed and died right away. I fell to my knees, shaking him futilely. His head was soaked with blood. I knew he was gone, but I breathed into his nostrils in a vain attempt to save him anyway.

I looked up, horrified at my dad. He turned and walked calmly into the house as I wept like a baby for my best friend, who now lay frozen in front of me.

When he was gone, I glanced bitterly at the brick that had struck Jessie. It had a black number three carved into the middle of it, and it was now dotted with thick specks of blood.

I knelt there in confusion for what seemed like hours, riddled with guilt. "I'm so sorry," I kept whispering.

Will I ever see Jessie again? I began to wonder. *Do dogs go to Heaven?*

It scared the hell out of me to think that I would never play with Jessie or receive those boxer hugs again. But at that moment, a verse from the Bible Mr. Franks had given me popped into my head. It went something like, "There is no greater love than to lay down one's life for a true friend." It gave me hope that I would indeed see my friend again.

I buried Jessie that night in the backyard near the tracks, in the middle of a cold, October drizzle that I thought would last forever. I dug a hole deeper than any I had ever dug in my entire life. It had to have been at least five feet deep. I thought that if

I buried Jessie deep enough, I'd somehow forget. But inside, I knew it didn't really matter how deep you buried something. It would find a way to come back to the surface eventually.

Jessie's blood and mine had merged to form a dry crust on my face. I wrapped him gently in the blanket that he had slept on each night at the foot of my bed. Blood-infused tears kissed the ground and consecrated the soil under which my martyred friend would now sleep forever.

"I won't forget," I whispered as the wind breathed coolly on my damp face.

When I finished burying Jessie, I went to my room and packed my toothbrush and a few of my clothes. I was sickened by what my dad had done, and I couldn't be in that house with him anymore. I wanted to get away from the pain of that place, and leave the monster behind me for good.

I drove in a zombielike state straight to Lynn's house. As I crossed over the railroad tracks, I didn't slow down. The impact when I hit the rails made a thunderous sound, and my truck catapulted into the air, scattering CDs off my dashboard and across the cabin's floor. It angered me that the tracks, usually my protection, had shown such an indifference toward my grief.

"Damn you!" I screamed out unfaithfully as I passed them by.

It was late when I arrived at Lynn's place. From the outside, the house looked vacantly cold and dark. I threw rocks at his bedroom window in an effort to wake him. After a couple of hits, his blanched face peeked angrily through the dark curtains. When he realized it was me, he pointed irritably toward the front door.

He opened the door slowly, and at first seemed annoyed that

I had woken him—but when he saw my dirty face and my blood-soaked clothes, his demeanor changed completely. Without saying a word, he sat down on the stairs next to the front door and began to put his shoes on.

"What are you doing?" I asked.

"I'm going to beat the hell out of whoever did this to you," he said.

I talked him out of revenge and made him take off his shoes. It was time for reflection, not rage. He said he'd let it go if I told him everything that had happened that day, and I agreed.

It felt odd consenting to tell an outsider what had happened inside the confines of my home. Our family had an unspoken omertà enforced by threats of violence. We were strictly forbidden by this code to tell our secrets. But Lynn took me inside and cleaned me up, and through a mixture of sniffles and snot, I told him my sad story.

To my surprise, Lynn too was heartbroken that Jessie was gone. A tear fell from his face as I told him what happened that night, and how I had buried Jessie alone by the tracks.

"Let's just go to sleep," I said as I finished, before he had a chance say anything. "I'm exhausted."

I cried myself to sleep on the hardwood floor at the foot of Lynn's bed that night, and dreamed of my heroic friend. I dreamed that Jessie and I were walking together in a dark forest. Frightening sounds echoed all around us. Thunder bellowed as high-pitched human voices wailed menacingly from the branches of the trees and hyena-like laughing came from the darkness. Quiet voices in the leaves whispered in unmelodic song that I would never escape the forest.

As we walked, three hideous beasts appeared out of the gray

shadows. Baring brown, rat-like teeth, they drifted slowly in my direction as if on water. My first instinct was to run, but Jessie growled protectively. He had a silver suit of armor wrapped around him, and the creatures backed off, cowering spiritlessly at his protest. After startling awake with tears in my eyes, I sat up straight and looked out of the skylight above me, staring at a blue moon.

Jessie showed me that love is someone who stays with you in the storm. With him gone, I felt incredibly alone. His love had given me the illusion that I wasn't on my own anymore.

As I got up, I thought to myself, *I'd gladly choose to walk with Jessie in that dark forest forever than without him in the best of light here.*

Outside of missing Jessie, the next week at the Buchanans' house was one of the best weeks of my life. We ate dinners together, minus Mr. Buchanan, at an oversized wooden dining room table. Mrs. Buchanan was a fantastic cook! My mom never made us meals, outside of heating up frozen dinners. Mrs. Buchanan, on the other hand, whipped up appetizers, salads, soups, main dishes, and desserts from scratch, like Julia Child on a bender. She didn't just make dinners, either: we had home-made biscuits and gravy for breakfast and fresh Cuban sandwiches for lunch on the weekends, with homemade crab dip and pita chips! It had never even occurred to me that these types of foods could be made at home. I thought you could only get them in a restaurant.

One of the best comforts of staying at the Buchanans' was that they owned horses. I rode them whenever I got the chance. Lynn said I handled them even better than he did! Sometimes when I wasn't riding, I watched them graze in the pasture. I admired the way they coexisted so peacefully. One horse didn't feel the need to eat every blade of grass in the field or drink every drop of water from the troughs. They realized there was enough for them all.

Something about the horses moving freely through the field touched some place deep inside me. The barbwire fence that kept them corralled bothered me, though. I wondered what they'd do if those walls didn't exist. They were completely secluded from the world outside that enclosure, having no understanding of reality beyond the boundary of the fence. There was so much they'd yet to see, and all they had to do to experience it all was jump over the comforting barrier. I wondered what kept them from taking that leap.

At night, I studied the photos on Lynn's bedroom walls—souvenirs of a carefree childhood. One photo showed Lynn, cake smeared across his face, laughing with his dad at what looked like a birthday party. Another showed him hugging his mom on Christmas Day, presents spread across the living room floor behind them.

My favorite photo was one of Lynn, no older than five, sitting on his dad's shoulders at a baseball game, spilling the ice-cream cone he was eating onto his dad's head. He seemed to have lived an untroubled, fun, and happy childhood—one every child deserves. I should have felt happy for him, but I didn't. I felt resentment, as if I were the only plant the gardener had forgotten to water.

Lynn and I stayed up late every night playing video games and perusing his rather extensive collection of *Playboy* magazines. This was the first time that Lynn told me he was a virgin.

I knew he went to church every weekend with his parents, but I also knew they were religious, not spiritual.

"Are you waiting for marriage?" I asked him.

"Hell, no!" he protested. "But honestly, I would like to be in love with the first person I do it with."

We talked about life and our dreams for the future. We discussed our parents and our childlike ideas of them. Lynn told me he had never heard his dad cuss at his mom before. This absolutely shocked me! I hadn't realized there were husbands who didn't curse at their wives. It also surprised me when Lynn told me he hated his dad.

"Why do you hate him? I've heard him tell you he loves you. If my father told me that, I'd melt into his arms like ice cream on a hot day."

Lynn looked pained. His eyes fell sadly, and his shoulders drooped. "With my dad, affection and approval is always tied into what we accomplish. You always have to be number one, at any cost. It makes it hard to coexist with anyone else in a natural way, or to find enjoyment in anything, really. And don't listen to what someone *says*, Sam—look at what they *do* to see what's truly important to them. A person spends all his time with what he really loves. Dad doesn't love us; he loves his money. Trust me: you can't fully love your family and love money. You'll always love one and resent the other for being in the way of it."

I realized that the monster doesn't only live in anger, like with my dad. It infects people where it can do the most damage. It infected my dad with anger, but it poisoned Lynn's dad with greed. Both were equally destructive to their hosts and the people around them.

"That thirst for money will make you lose yourself, man!"

Lynn added. "You become a prisoner of it in a lot of ways. The work you put into keeping it and the time you spend fantasizing about its benefits will end up eating away at your humanity like a hungry caterpillar. When my dad was our age, he was actually a pretty good guy."

While my days at the Buchanans' were peaceful, the nights were not. Each night, I had the same recurring dream. I was back in that dark forest with the storm raging all around me. As the beasts came closer, I looked desperately to Jessie, only to realize he wasn't there anymore. I was utterly alone.

Once I realized I'd have to face the beasts on my own, I tried to run, to escape—but I couldn't move. When I looked down, I saw that my legs were submerged in quicksand.

The beasts surrounded me in a triangle as I struggled to break free. Right before their final attack, I awoke in a panic, throwing off the covers violently and jumping to my feet.

Some nights, I awoke not knowing where I was. On those nights, I looked fearfully at the room's shadows, which I believed had somehow followed me from the dream.

About two weeks into my stay, Mrs. Buchanan asked me why I was spending so much time at her house. I told her I didn't want to live with my parents anymore, and a look of horror appeared on her face. She pleaded with me to return home. She assumed every child's home life was as comforting as the one she had made for her children. She assured me that my parents were worried sick about me and the right decision was to face whatever difficulties I was having at home. She gave me a long lecture, about talking out problems and finding common ground with my parents. Though I didn't mind listening, and though I liked Mrs. Buchanan, I just didn't trust *any* adult. Mrs. Buchanan didn't know what my home life was like, and I wasn't going to tell her.

Still, after that lecture, I began to think she might be right. Perhaps there was a chance that during my absence, my parents had recognized how important I was to the family. I envisioned everyone sitting around the dining room table with regret, worried sick that I had disappeared. When I walked through the door, maybe my dad would hug me and say he was sorry, and promise things would be different from then on. Mom would wipe away her concerned tears and tell me I was the most important thing in her life—even more important than her booze.

I wanted to find out the truth. I also sensed I was running out my welcome at the Buchanans'. So I packed up my things, thanked Mrs. Buchanan for her kindness, and left their manicured manor, heading for home.

Right before I left, Lynn told me something I really needed to hear.

"I'll always be there for you, Sam. I have your back to the end. Call me if you need me."

What made that simple remark so moving was that I believed him. For the first time in my life, I trusted another human being.

⌐

When I arrived home, I was confident I would find Mom lying on the sofa in her standard Sunday-morning hangover position. But surprisingly, my brother was lying there in her place, in a disturbing imitation of our mother.

"Where's Mom?" I asked him.

"Bingo," he said, so quietly I could barely hear him.

I looked around. There was nothing but silence.

"Where's Dad?"

"Outside," he said, taking a deep breath. "Hey, can you grab me an ice pack?"

I took an ice pack from the freezer and let the door shut on its own. Kevin flinched at the sound of the door slamming and rubbed his temples with his middle finger and thumb.

"You okay?" I asked. "Aren't you supposed to be back at college?"

He appeared tired, and dark hammocks carried his blood-shot eyes. "I lost my scholarship," he said softly.

It took a second for me to process what he said because he had expressed it so nonchalantly, as if he were telling me he had misplaced his car keys.

"Why? What happened?" I asked in shock.

"I received three citations for being drunk in public. The university police are dicks! After the second one, they told the coach, and he said if I received one more, I was off the team. I thought he was bluffing."

I was stunned! Kevin explained what had happened almost as if he was proud.

"Well, I'm home," I said hopefully.

"I see that," he said, and turned his head away.

I walked outside to gauge my dad's reaction to my home-coming. He was changing the oil in his van beside a group of apple trees that grew near the back of the house. They had grown to a decent size, but for some reason of which I wasn't aware, we never ate the apples that grew on them. At the end of each autumn, the bitter red and green fruits always fell to the ground, where they gradually fermented and turned into an alcoholic stew that the soil, by then turned acidly sour, soaked up faster than a thirsty Lutheran preacher.

"Hey, Dad," I said as I glanced toward the tracks at the still-fresh mound of dirt where Jessie was buried.

"Hey."

"Whatcha doing?"

"Oil change."

I stood there for a minute before deciding he wasn't going to say anything else, and began to walk away.

"Sam," he said.

I turned hopefully back to face him. His voice was genuine, sincere. He looked up at me and paused, contemplating how to express his next thoughts.

"You're going to fix the yard over there where you buried that stupid dog."

I didn't say a word. I didn't even make a facial expression. I couldn't give him the satisfaction of knowing how much his words hurt me. I just turned and walked to the house.

"Sam!" he shouted again.

I turned slowly, bracing myself. Whenever he raised his voice, my entire body winced in anticipation of what was coming.

"Can you bring me some fruit punch?" he asked with a rancid grin.

At first I was confused. "Fruit punch?"

"Yeah, from the kitchen."

"Sure," I said, holding back a sedated outrage.

I first went into the bathroom to pee. As I did my business, my attention was drawn to the trash can. Mom had left a bloody tampon sitting on top of the trash pile for all the world to see.

"Disgusting!" I said out loud.

It looked like a little tea bag with a white string attached to it. Suddenly, an idea came to me—an awful, wonderful idea. "Stupid dog?" I asked the bathroom mirror.

I used a piece of toilet paper to pick up the bloody mess by the string. I poured Dad's glass of fruit punch and steeped the tampon in the drink as if I were preparing tea. Then I took the glass outside and handed it to him with a polite, servile smile. He laughed smugly, satisfied in his supremacy, and downed the entire drink in a single gulp.

"Thanks," he said, throwing the empty cup at my feet.

"No problem!" I said, as hospitably as a waiter in a five-star restaurant. "Can I get you anything else?"

Instead of responding, he went right back to working on his van—so I walked briskly away, whistling a victor's tune.

My mom came home from her morning bingo session around noon. She never said a word, or even looked in my direction. She went straight to the freezer where she kept her vodka. No one mentioned my absence or asked why I had been gone for two weeks. I didn't think they'd even noticed I'd left.

The great satisfaction I had felt at getting revenge on my dad was quickly replaced by a familiar unhappiness. Dejected, I decided to go to my room and comfort myself in solitude. As I slowly climbed the stairs, I passed under a wooden sign Mom had bought at a local craft show. In thick red lettering on a creamy white background, the sign read, WELCOME HOME.

~

At four thirty the next morning, the sound of my phone

ringing woke me from a dead sleep.

"Hello?" I said as I picked it up, still mostly unconscious.

"Sam, it's Lynn! What are you doing?"

I wasn't sure if I was awake or dreaming. "Just waitin' for you to call me," I said groggily.

Lynn laughed. "Wake up! I have to tell you something!"

I looked at the clock on my nightstand. "It's four thirty in the morning. Is everything okay?"

"Everything's great! And it's about to be even greater! I got a question for you." He paused for dramatic effect. "Want to go to the beach with me today?"

"What? How?" I asked, now fully awake.

"My dad rented a beach house in the Outer Banks for the week, but some business came up and he can't go. He said we can stay there all week if we want."

Waters always seemed to part like that for Lynn, as if he were Moses.

"Holy shit! When can we leave?"

"Go look out your hallway window!"

I ran to the hallway and pushed the curtains aside—and there in the first gray of daylight was Lynn, suitcase in hand and a big smile on his face.

———

The beach house in the Outer Banks was three hours from Verities, but it felt like we made it there in twenty minutes. That was how it always was with Lynn and me, whenever we made this trip. We never needed the radio; we'd just talk the whole ride down, without ever missing a beat.

As we drove through the Hampton Roads Bridge-Tunnel, I was reminded of our families' last trip to the Outer Banks. Mr.

Buchanan had rented a large oceanfront cottage for both of our families. One morning, my brother went out to buy some ice and passed by the Surfside Inn, the most expensive hotel on the peninsula. As he stopped at a red light across from the hotel, he looked over and saw Mr. Buchanan going into a hotel room with a woman. Kevin had worked for Mr. Buchanan earlier that summer, and he immediately recognized the woman's long straw-colored hair. It was Mr. Buchanan's executive secretary!

Now, I wondered whether Mr. Buchanan hadn't been able to make this trip because business had truly come up—or because his secretary couldn't make it this time.

"Dude, this is going to be awesome!" Lynn said happily as we rode past a blue sign with "Welcome to the Outer Banks" imprinted on it in bold white letters.

"What time is it?" I asked.

"A little after eight."

"Let's go to the beach house and drop off everything. Then we can hit up our place!"

Lynn knew exactly what I meant. Whenever we reached the Outer Banks, the first restaurant we stopped at was Art's Place. They had the best hamburgers I'd ever eaten!

We arrived at the house and unpacked. The place was absolutely beautiful. It had three big bedrooms, all with cable TV, and it was only a thirty-yard walk to the beach! But to me, the best feature of all was the crow's nest that sat atop the roof. It offered a spectacular view of the ocean and surrounding area.

Once we had fully inspected everything, we jumped back in the truck and headed to Art's for loaded burgers and french fries. After we finished eating, we stopped at a small convenience store next door to Art's Place called Winks.

"I should get some of these for emergencies," Lynn said, pointing to a rack of condoms.

"Go for it!" I laughed. "You can never be too prepared."

We headed back to the beach house to relax and digest our meals. We played three games of Spades, and Lynn won all three. He seemed to have luck embedded into his DNA.

Around eight o'clock, I decided it was time to jump in the shower. That night we were going out to Kelly's, a popular local bar and dance club. We had been there before, and they didn't ID us, so we figured we'd try to get in again.

When I stepped out of the shower, I heard a faint knock at the door. I pulled on some boxers, wrapping my towel around my neck as I walked into the living area, where I saw Lynn asleep on the couch.

"Lynn!" I shouted.

He startled awake. "What?"

"Someone's knocking on the door!"

"Well, answer it!" he hollered.

I cracked opened the door, and a short chipmunk-faced woman stared at me with an empty expression. She wore a dull white polo shirt and simple khaki pants, and appeared to be about my mom's age. Her deep-set cat-green eyes seemed lifeless and tired under eyebrows that were plucked to almost nothing. I thought she was the manager of the property we were staying in and was embarrassed at my underdressed state.

I pulled the towel from around my neck and quickly tied it around my waist as she stared at me, not saying a word.

"Is something wrong?" I asked nervously.

"No," she replied. "The manager of the property sent me."

"We parked in a no-parking area, didn't we?"

"No, you parked fine," she said, smiling.

"Well, what can we do for you?" I asked. I was becoming politely annoyed.

She placed a finger to her lip, while her tongue touched the corner of her mouth. "Nothing at all," she said, her other hand poking my bare skin above the towel on my waist, "but there *is* something that I can do for you."

I wondered uncomfortably, *Is this woman propositioning me?*

"Oh, okay. I see," I stuttered. "I don't need anything right now, but my friend here would love some company!"

I escaped out the door and closed it swiftly between us, leaving the strange woman inside with Lynn while I stood outside, still in my boxers. It was my way of playing a joke on Lynn. Leave him to handle getting the old lady out.

Only, the door didn't open right away as I had expected it would. I walked down the stairs to the driveway and looked up at the living room windows. The lights inside the beach house had been turned off, and the curtains pulled shut. Only the faint, flickering glow of the TV was visible, throwing light shadows on the windows.

"There is no way that Lynn is trying to hook up with that woman," I said to myself.

But half an hour went by, and still there was no movement in the windows.

"Maybe they're playing Spades," I said to myself. Clearly, my joke on Lynn had backfired. "This is crazy," I said out loud.

I climbed the stairs, sat in an Adirondack chair by the front door, and waited for one of them to come out. It wasn't long before the mystery lady finally appeared.

"You must have had a good time in there," I said, smiling.

"I don't know what you're talking about," she replied, "but I can show *you* a good time if you'd like, for a price." She rubbed a finger down my bare chest, making me jerk back awkwardly. Her long nails were brown and dirty.

"Oh, no, no, no, thank you, but I have a girlfriend and she'd kill me!" I lied.

"I understand. No problem," she said respectfully. Then she walked down the street to the sound of waves splashing on the beach and disappeared into the evening, protected by the night.

I stepped into the living room with a smirk on my face, knowingly gazing in Lynn's direction. He was sitting in a desk chair by the sofa, with a worried expression on his face and a large, black Bible in his hand.

"So," I said, holding out the "o" way too long. "What happened?"

Lynn barely let me finish the question before he shouted, "Oh my God! She just gave me a blowjob!"

Laughing, I asked, "Is that why you have the Bible out? Are you worried?"

"Shut up, Sam! It's not funny!" he shot back.

"Well, good work, my man!" I said, trying to cheer him up. "I'm happy that at least one of us is getting some." I looked around the room and studied the scene. "Did you have to pay for it?"

"Twenty bucks," he said reluctantly, without looking in my direction.

We sat there in silence for a good minute before he broke like a dam and burst out, "Dammit, man, I can't lie to you! I had sex with her!"

It suddenly occurred to me that Lynn had just lost his virginity to a prostitute in the Outer Banks for twenty bucks. "Oh . . . my . . . gosh," I said slowly. "Are you serious?"

I could barely get the words out before he jumped from his chair and raced to the bathroom. I heard the rusty squeaking of the shower knobs turning as water began to flow.

I lay down on the sofa and grabbed the remote. I was changing channels on the TV when a dense cloud of what I thought was smoke seeped into the hallway. I jumped up to inspect it, thinking something might be on fire, before I realized that the cloud was hot steam coming from under the bathroom door.

When Lynn came out, I told him I had never seen so much steam coming out of a bathroom before.

"I was scrubbing myself as hard as I could with scalding hot water and soap," he said. "It felt like I was sandpapering myself."

"You think that kills infection, huh?" I asked sarcastically.

He continued to worry for the next hour and a half, sitting in shamed silence as he rocked back and forth. His arms wrapped around his knees, which pressed against his chest. His lips moved silently, as if in prayer.

"Well, that does it! I'm definitely going to Hell," he said suddenly.

"Shut up!" I tried to reassure him. "How's she any different than someone like your dad? He prostitutes his principles for money; she prostitutes her body. It's the same, if not worse in his case! Lynn, you're a human being, and human beings have needs. You don't have to feel ashamed about being human."

He thought for a second, staring into space, searching for a way out of the mess he had just put himself in. "You know what? You're right!" he said, as if forgiving himself. "Thanks, Sam. But *please*, keep this between us, okay?"

"You did use the condoms, right?"

"Yes, of course I did! I'm not stupid!" He picked up a small trash can and pointed to the condom wrapper inside. "Can we please just skip Kelly's tonight and go to Duck Donuts? I want to gorge on some donuts and pretend this night never happened."

"Prostitutes and pastries?" I said. "That's a hard night to forget!"

He shook his head, but allowed a smile to sneak through. "Shut up! But that's a good one."

"I thought you said you wanted to be in love with the first person you had sex with," I said.

Lynn stared straight ahead to some place deep inside of himself, his adolescent eyes as wide as the sea outside our beach house. Slowly, and deeply contemplatively, he softly said, "I think I was . . ."

3
Whiter Shade of Pale

"And although my eyes were open,
they might just as well have been closed."
—Procol Harum

As the leaves changed that fall, so would all our lives—for this was the season when Newman first came into our story.

Newman was a seventy-three-year-old Korean War veteran who had gone through both a triple and a quadruple bypass surgery on his heart. He was a tall man with greasy gray hair that made him look like a wise old professor. Raised Catholic, he wasn't fond of going to church every weekend, having grown tired of its ritualistic nature.

Newman had grown up in Verities, and had been a Richmond City police officer before squad cars had radios. He'd retired fifteen years earlier after his first heart attack, living off a combination of his pension and Social Security checks. His wife had passed away from complications due to alcoholism. She'd been in and out of rehab facilities before it was fashionable. Newman told me she used to hide bottles of vodka throughout their house like Easter eggs. Even years after her death, he'd find half-filled bottles stashed away in the attic or vents around their home.

Newman didn't have children, or any family living nearby. His closest relative was a niece living in Maryland whom he only saw occasionally.

To me, the best thing about Newman was the rambling, philosophical stories he'd tell. If you didn't stop him, he'd go on for hours. I think he believed he was Socrates or some other great philosopher reincarnated.

Newman was a lifetime member of the VFW, the Veterans of Foreign Wars, America's largest organization serving war veterans. They hosted bingo games each Wednesday evening, Saturday night, and Sunday morning. Sometimes Newman worked the events, and sometimes he played bingo himself. One day, he and my mom sat next to each other while playing, and halfway through the first jackpot, they struck up a conversation. Even though Newman was thirty years older than my mom, they hit it off and developed a unique, if peculiar, friendship. It began with Mom bringing Newman to the house after bingo for drinks. Because Newman was so much older, Dad didn't mind. With his poor health and grandfatherly appearance, Newman didn't come off as threatening in any way. My dad actually looked at him as a father figure.

Newman rewarded my parents' hospitality by paying for trips to Atlantic City or Charles Town, where they'd play the slot machines. He eventually became a fixed member of the family, going on vacations with us and spending holidays at our house. I didn't have grandparents around, so it was nice to have a grandfather-type figure in him.

Newman even took me to lunch for my seventeenth birthday. We went to Northside Grille, a couple miles from my house. I felt pride in the way people looked at us as we entered the restaurant. I could tell they thought Newman was my grandfather, and somehow that made me feel more normal.

About halfway through the meal, Newman slid a small gift-wrapped box across the table.

"Open it," he said.

"Really? For me?"

"Of course!"

I unwrapped a golden Citizen Eco Drive watch. It had a black, silky face that made it look space-age. He'd had it engraved with my name and birth date. It was the perfect size for my wrist—not overly bulky like most watches were on my skinny arms. I'd never been given a watch before, and I didn't receive any other gifts that day, so it meant a great deal to me.

The stories Newman told me at that lunch captivated me. He said he'd worked as a lifeguard on a beach in New Jersey when he was in his twenties, and had saved thirty-three people from drowning.

"I could never be great like that," I told him.

"Anybody can be great if they're good," he said sincerely.

"Trust me, I don't see myself getting the opportunity to change lives like that."

A pained look appeared on Newman's usually cheerful face. He squinted softly and looked directly into my eyes. Deep wrinkles, formed by years of working in the sun, touched one another and outlined his forehead.

"You don't have to change the entire world to be great. If you change one person's life for the better, you're in the company of the saints. It doesn't have to be as dramatic as saving someone from drowning in an ocean. It could be something as simple as gifting a smile to a stranger. A small act like that could save someone from drowning in their own loneliness."

"You think?" I asked.

His eyes lit up. "Oh, yeah! And all those small acts end up becoming world-changing when they're all combined. Think about it! One small raindrop can barely satisfy the thirst of a chrysanthemum. But when millions of drops come together, they can form a mighty river that can transform the very surface of the earth!"

"I don't know," I said. I was thinking about the differences between Lynn and me. "I think some people are fated to change the world and some aren't."

"You guide your fate through the choices you make. In reality, there's no such thing as fate. You're in charge of who you become. And I agree that we spend most of our lives drifting through chaos, but there are things we can do to tame it."

"Like what?" I asked.

"Like living in the moment and looking at every single situation in a positive way. That can make all the difference in the world! We really define the world as *we* are, not as *it* is. Everyone thinks Heaven or Hell are places you wait your entire life to get to. But you can live in Heaven or Hell right now, on Earth, just by the way you define what's in front of you! And when you're living in Heaven, you naturally end up bringing Heaven to others."

"I agree with that," I said, "but I think chance plays a huge role in the opportunities you have in life. That's all I'm saying."

Newman contemplated for a second. A barely noticeable smirk lifted the right corner of his lip. "You remind me of my pops. He always said we were like feathers blowing at the mercy of the wind. Sometimes the wind blows you beyond the tracks, and sometimes it blows you to the debris."

"Sounds like a wise man," I said proudly.

"He also said not to lose your goodness and become cynical while being carried through the chaos." He looked adoringly out a window to the sky, as if it was the last time he'd see its beauty. "And to be grateful for the magnificent ride."

—

Soon after my birthday, I noticed my brother was going through a peculiar phase. He started wearing camouflage shirts every day, but he never hunted. Then he put fishhooks on all his baseball caps. Using his entire life savings, he had a lift kit installed on his pickup truck. His truck sat so high, I had to do a giant bunny hop to reach the seat.

Kevin also started paying NRA dues and got an NRA license plate. This was bizarre because Kevin had never owned a gun. In fact, I had never even seen him shoot a gun.

"I can't believe you support the NRA. It's so commercial-ized now," I said to him.

"What do you mean?" he asked as if I'd just insulted one of the apostles.

"They're not interested in gun *rights* anymore; they're inter-ested in gun *sales*," I responded. But Kevin just scoffed and turned away.

Kevin also began watching NASCAR and got a job fill-ing boxes with horse feed for customers at a farm supply store called Southern States. When he brought home a friend who said he aspired to be a fat guy wearing an American flag T-shirt, I knew something weird was going on with him.

Kevin's whole demeanor had changed. He talked differently and carried himself differently. His formerly witty jokes were now facile and targeted at my manhood. They weren't funny anymore; they were just mean. He would call me a girl or a homo if I did anything outside what he and his new friend defined as "macho." This new persona, combined with his increasingly worrisome drinking habit, made me not want to be around him anymore.

I asked him once if his new personality had anything to do with the way we lived and the way we were treated. He looked at me as if he was insulted. "What do you mean?" he asked.

"I mean the stuff with Mom and Dad; our lives. Does it weigh on you?"

He looked away silently. "We're lucky," he finally said.

Kevin had a sort of childhood Alzheimer's. He believed that if only he ignored our past, he wouldn't be defined by it. Of course I understood why he wanted to forget. But I also knew he couldn't forget. We needed to remember to have any chance of healing. We needed to face the hurt and the ugliness and talk about it with each other. We needed to share our pain so we could learn how to defeat it together. You can't win a battle, much less a war, against an enemy you're trying to pretend isn't there.

"Lucky?" I asked, contempt dripping from the word.

He wouldn't even look at me as he spoke. "Yeah. It could be a lot worse. At least we have a roof over our heads!"

"That's a pretty low bar, isn't it? That's like saying Nero was a good son because he sent his mom on a Bay of Naples cruise. Do I need to remind you that you're missing two of your adult teeth because of him?"

"It is what it is," he said impatiently. "Now get out of my room, wuss!"

"Hold on," I interjected. "I came in here to ask you something." He looked in my direction with an annoyance that would make a teenage girl blush. "Why do you have a Confederate flag hanging on your truck?"

"Because I love the US of A, that's why!" he shouted, as if the answer should have been obvious.

"You realize the South was trying to secede from the US?"

"That's irrelevant," he said. "Flying the stars and bars is the most patriotic thing you can do."

"Wait a second. Are you saying that the most patriotic way to honor America is to fly a flag that represents a fight to renounce it and form a new country?"

"Yes, that's exactly what I'm saying!" he said, his head raised confidently.

"Is this who you are now, or who you're trying to be?" I asked incredulously.

But Kevin didn't answer. He wasn't the person I had known and looked up to for so many years—not anymore. Something had changed. Either that, or he was trying to pretend he was something he wasn't. And one day, it occurred to me I hadn't seen my brother walking down the tracks in a long while. Instead, alcohol was becoming his new set of tracks.

—

One warm Friday night, Lynn and I decided to fight our boredom and spice things up by heading to the city to participate in a weekly event called Friday Cheers. We had gone twice before and had a great time. It was held at a big, grassy park on an island in the middle of the river. There were live bands, beer trucks, delicious foods—and most importantly, cute girls!

"What's playing tonight?" Lynn asked as we drove there in his brand-new Jeep Wrangler.

"Jazz," I said with a smile.

"Awesome! Chicks love jazz. They'll be all over the place!"

When we got to the venue, we pulled up to find the parking lot flooded by a sea of cars—but somehow, Lynn was able to find a spot right next to the front entrance.

"How does a space like this open up for you?" I asked.

"It's talent!" he said. Then he barked excitedly, "Let's do this!"

We headed for the entrance. Walking through those front gates, I had no idea how much my life was about to change.

We walked leisurely through the crowd, checking out girls and looking for anyone we might know. Lynn recognized a buddy of his in the distance.

"Hey, Scott!" he called out to his burly friend.

We walked over, and Lynn said something about jazz music to the guy. I stood beside them, people-watching instead of participating in the conversation. I noticed a group of attractive girls near us, all dressed in chic clothing. You could tell they'd spent a lot of time on their hair and makeup. I was never a fan of caked faces. I always believed that people who are dirty on the inside feel like they have to decorate themselves on the outside. They hope the decorations will take attention away from the mess.

There was one girl who wasn't plastered in makeup, though. She was tall and slender, with long, black hair as slick as silk. A bell-shaped black skirt wrapped tightly around her waist. She wore a white T-shirt with the words "Five Card Stud" written on it. A picture of five ace cards divided the words and clung firmly to her body.

I still have no idea what came over me next. I'd never had courage with girls before. But something forced me through the entire group and straight to this black-haired beauty. When I was close enough, I reached out and took her hand in mine.

"I'm Sam," I said confidently as her friends eyeballed me strangely.

"Ryan," she replied in the most beautiful voice I'd ever heard.

"I feel like I know you from somewhere."

She looked at me curiously. "I don't think so. Where are you from?"

"Verities," I said.

"Me too!" she smiled. "We've probably passed each other at some point." The sound of her voice was like a cool breeze blowing.

I grinned teasingly. "I would have known if you passed me by."

"Oh, yeah?" she asked, holding her mouth open to reveal her cherry-red tongue and a small wad of green gum.

"Yeah," I said sharply.

There was a silence as we stared easily at one another. I looked around to see if anyone was near us. "Want to dance?"

She laughed and self-consciously said, "Are you joking?"

"Absolutely not!" I replied firmly, taking her soft hands in mine and pulling her close to me.

We danced right there, with her friends watching in caked-faced envy. We were the only two people dancing in the crowd. We stared hungrily into one another's eyes, and, for a moment, we became the only two people at the event. I had never believed in love at first sight before, but in that moment and on that day, I believed. I felt awakened! There was spark, a fiery particle alight from ashes, that flared as if our stone bodies had struck together to create a glow.

"You have a boyfriend?"

"No," she whispered, her breath tickling the hairs on my ear.

"Want one?" I asked boldly.

She smiled, raised her thick eyebrows, and said, "That depends."

Right then, one of her friends yelled, "Ryan, come on, it's time to go!"

"Oh, shit. I have to go!" she said. "This was fun, though! Want my number so we can do it again?"

"Of course! Write it right here." I pointed to the inside of my forearm. She wrote her number as I stared at her magnetic, lime-green eyes. They seemed to radiate in the venue's lights.

"There you go, babe! See you later, Blue Eyes." She leaned in and kissed me on the cheek. "You better call me!"

I watched her walk away as you'd watch a cotton-candy-colored sunset, mesmerized by the wonder of it. Just before she reached the exit, she turned around, looked back at me, smiled, and blew a kiss in my direction. The hairs on my arm stood up, and chill bumps covered my skin.

"Lynn, let's get out of here," I called to him. "I'm ready to go."

"We just got here," Lynn protested. "Why do you want to leave so early?"

I didn't want to admit I was anxious to go straight home to call Ryan.

"The music. I'm just not feeling it tonight."

He smiled as if he were a detective and I had just been caught lying about a crime. "Bullshit. You want to go home to call that girl, don't you?"

I stared blankly at him, my mouth wide open. It always amazed me how well Lynn and I knew each other.

"Just one more hour?" he asked innocently.

"Okay. One more hour," I said, looking at my watch.

It was the longest hour of my life. I watched impatiently as Lynn talked to a couple girls and the crowd slowly receded. The entire time, my mind was drunk with reflections on the tall girl I had met that night. When fifty-nine minutes and thirty-three seconds had finally elapsed, I dragged Lynn by the arm toward the exit.

As soon as I got home that night, I raced to my room and dialed the number written on my arm. And so began my addiction.

➤

Ryan was something I'd never experienced before. She was kind, smart, successful in school, and unbelievably gorgeous. Her family lived in a huge home near Lynn's house, beyond the tracks. I had never dated anyone from beyond the tracks, or even contemplated the idea that the two sides could mingle romantically. When it came to relationships between people of differing economic statuses, the families from Ryan's side of the tracks held an unspoken but otherwise obvious taboo against the practice.

For our first date, Ryan and I went to a fancy Cuban restaurant called Havana '59. I felt so comfortable with her, I instinctively reached out and held her hands across the table when we sat. She seemed caught off guard by the gesture, and eyed me awkwardly.

"What's wrong? I asked.

"I've never held hands with anyone in public before," she said as she looked nervously around the restaurant.

"Should we stop?"

She smiled and mouthed, "No."

I wanted to lean over and kiss her right there, but instead I said, "I wish I was your boyfriend."

"There's no reason not to be, I guess; but I thought you already were," she teased.

"Well, let's just make it official then," I said. "It's going to happen eventually anyway."

She smiled fearlessly and looked deep into my eyes as if she were looking through a window to the inside of me. "Done," she replied softly.

⤙

As I drove Ryan home that night, we passed a blood-red neon sign:

Psychic

$10

Reader of Your Future

I pointed excitedly at the sign. "Let's do that!"

"I've never been to a psychic before, but I always wanted to try it! Should we, though? My grandmother would kill me if she found out; she's super religious!"

"We're doing it!" I announced.

"Oh my gosh, this is crazy!" Ryan said as we pulled sharply into the parking lot.

"It'll be fun," I assured her. "Come on!"

We parked and walked into an old house. The living room had been converted into a grand reading room. It smelled of incense and old-lady perfume. A moment after we entered, a short woman glided into the room through a curtain of rainbow beads that clinked like marbles bouncing off a concrete floor as she passed through them.

"I am Madame Trixie," she announced in a low, eerie tone. Her glassy eyes looked us up and down questioningly.

Her smile was as crooked as her teeth. She had way too much makeup on her chubby face, and wore massive earrings that hung all the way down to her broad shoulders. Short, bristly hair the color of cinnamon peeked out from under a golden bandana that covered her apple-shaped head. It matched the purple-and-gold outfit she wore, which resembled a king's robe.

"Would you like me to read your future?" she asked sweetly.

"Yes—uh—please," I stuttered.

She turned off the lights and lit three white candlesticks.

"Please have a seat." She gestured toward two wooden stools positioned at a small round table in the center of the room. In the middle of the table, a crystal ball sat atop a blanket of bright white rabbit fur.

We sat, and the chubby woman gazed deeply into the mysterious orb, placing the tips of her plump fingers on the ball. In the room behind us, a fish tank filter was running. I smiled and peeked at Ryan, whose eyes were wide and focused on the psychic.

"Your love is pure and unafraid, I see," the old lady declared in an accent that reminded me of Cruella de Vil. She massaged the crystal ball. "Your first encounter was written in the stars long ago by the old magicians. Oh, how very sweet! I see the loyalty you possess for one another will receive the attention of the gods."

Ryan looked at me and smiled, and I took her hand in mine.

"I see you growing old together, always by one another's

side. You are old, but still very much in love!"

I pulled Ryan closer to me, and she gently put her head on my shoulder, smiling in Madame Trixie's direction.

"Oh, how wonderful this vision is!" She moved her face closer to the crystal ball, looking deep into our future. "Oh! Your children, they are so beautiful!" Looking at us warmly, she paused for a moment and said, "You have found what the old ones called 'the pascual,' the purest of all loves. In fact, you knew one another before birth, when you were only pure drops of light, before even the advent of time." She glanced at a large grandfather clock that ticked on the wall behind us.

"I am so sorry, children, but your five minutes have expired. Madame Trixie must end."

"That was quick," I said.

"Madame Trixie can continue for five more minutes for only twenty dollars!" the old woman offered.

"No, thank you," I told her politely. "I think we're good."

We stood and thanked Madame Trixie as we walked out the door.

"Come see me again, my dears!" she called out as we left.

"Wow, we're really meant to be together!" I told Ryan as we walked back to my truck. "I'm glad we did this!"

"Me too, babe," she said, laughing. "I can't believe we'll receive the attention of the gods!"

—

Ryan and I continued to call each other every day. We talked well into the night, sometimes falling asleep on the phone together. We were attached at the heart, like a burr on wool clothes. I first told her I loved her a week and a half into our relationship. She asked what took me so long.

I was like a dried-up flower in the middle of a desert; she provided the nourishment that brought me life. We were young, but there was no doubt that I truly loved Ryan. We gave all of ourselves to one another before we knew the agony of heartbreak, before we could comprehend the misery that can be placed on a trusting heart. Because of this, we loved fully, without pride or guarding against pain. It was dangerously wondrous to leave ourselves unprotected like that. I discovered a whole new side of myself. I wrote her soft lines of poetry and mailed her multipage love letters. I even had flowers delivered to her at random locations. Once, I bought her a fifteen-foot stuffed caterpillar! The caterpillar's head had been embroidered with the words "I Love You"; and each round segment of its body featured the word "Very," except for the final segment, on which was embroidered the word "Much." I put the mammoth insect on her front porch, to her parents' dismay, so she'd see it when she came home from school.

I can't fully describe the way I felt in words. It's like trying to describe the way you feel when you're snorkeling in the Great Barrier Reef. You only understand if you've experienced it. I was drawn to her the same way someone can be drawn to the heat of a fire. It warms an aching coldness felt deep inside of you.

Ryan's parents thought we were insane. More specifically, they thought *I* was insane. They didn't approve of such a passionate love affair between two people they considered to be children. They weren't thrilled about their only daughter dating someone from the wrong side of the tracks, either. They told Ryan we couldn't continue to see each other until they met me, so we all had dinner at a Mexican restaurant called El Azteca on their side of the tracks.

Ryan's dad was the vice president of Pluto Training Solutions, a company that lobbied the Pentagon for military contracts. He was a walking cliché, just like Lynn's dad. When I first saw him, I winced, because he was wearing a purple tie. I'd always had a pathological aversion to ties. They reminded me of a leash placed around your neck so your master can force you to go places your instincts warn you not to.

"Mark Johnston. Nice to meet you, son," he said after Ryan introduced me. He held his hand out for me to shake, and I extended my hand in return.

"Nice to meet you, too, Mr. Johnston."

His handshake was unnecessarily forceful. He squeezed until the tips of my fingers turned purplish-red.

"Please, call me Mark."

Because Mark knew the restaurant's owner, we were seated at our table right away. As soon as we sat down, the questions began to fly.

"So you're the boy who's been flooding our home with flowers and gifts?"

"Yes, sir," I said as I nervously rubbed the side of my cheek.

"What church do you go to?" he asked unexpectedly.

It was his first trap in a test to gauge my social acceptability. I sensed a trial by fire was on its way, and did my best to think on my feet.

"We don't have a set church, necessarily, but I'm definitely curious about Christianity and feel like I have a relationship with God."

"Dad's a deacon at our church!" Ryan said proudly.

"That's cool!" I said. "I actually have a lot of questions about faith." Since Mark was a deacon, I thought he'd be knowledgeable about his religion. I found out later that church was more of a social networking club for him.

"What kind of questions?" he asked.

"Well, I don't understand what the Bible means when it talks about forgiveness. How do you receive forgiveness? Like, what do you say? Or is it something you do? I know the Bible talks a lot about it, but I've never really understood it. I guess I try to forgive, and it doesn't seem to work sometimes."

"I don't need to ask for forgiveness, so you're asking the wrong guy!" he said, laughing. "I have great instincts and always make the right business decisions!"

I thought he was joking and said, "No, I'm talking about your personal life."

"Yeah, me too," he quickly replied.

I could see that he was serious. "You always make the right decisions?" I asked, surprised. "You never change your opinion on anything?"

Mark stabbed his pointer finger passionately against the table. "A real man *is* who he *is*. He doesn't change what he believes. He's decisively strong!"

"I change my beliefs about things all the time, if experience teaches me something I didn't know before," I assured him.

"You don't consider it weak to change your mind about your beliefs all the time? I think of that as being indecisive, which can kill you in my world."

"I don't always change my mind, but I look at it as growth if I do. I think wisdom doesn't come with age; it comes with an openness toward growing. Comfort is probably the biggest impediment to that, so I never want to rest in what I believe. I want to be better today than I was yesterday and better tomorrow than I am today. Even God changed his mind; he regretted that he'd created humans. That's why he sent the flood to destroy them."

Mark shook his head in disgust. "You'd never make it in the business world, kid."

Mark's wife didn't speak. I wondered if he'd forbidden her to say anything. I could tell by the way he looked at her that he had a certain disdain for women, or at least for their opinions. Ryan told me he still lived in a world that told females to sit down and shut up. He believed men were a superior species, and he was somehow sly enough to make his wife believe it as well.

About halfway through the meal, Mark's face lit up. "I got a joke for you, Sam!" he announced, looking pig-eyed at me.

"I love a good joke! Go for it!"

"What's a word starting with *N* and ending with *R* that you never want to call a black person?"

Oh, God, I thought. "I don't think I want to know," I said.

"Neighbor!" he snorted with a mouth full of food, more amused at his joke than anyone else at the table.

Great, I thought to myself. *He's racist, too.* He was trying to convince me of his greatness, when there was little evidence he even possessed basic goodness.

"My neighbors are black," I said politely. "So are two of my cousins."

There was an uncomfortable silence while Mark digested what I'd said.

"I guess that's how y'all do it over there on that side of tracks, huh?"

I was surprised at how comfortable Mark was in making these kinds of comments. We had only just met, yet he was at ease with his bigotry as a baby with a pacifier. But he didn't believe he was a bigot—he just believed he was right. Nothing is as blinding as self-righteousness.

"Dad, enough with the jokes," Ryan said, embarrassed.

"Okay. Want to talk more about my job, then, dear?" he asked sarcastically.

Ryan closed her eyes and shook her head. "I hate your job! You were at a work party the day I was born, remember? You said it was your *duty*."

"Sweetie, that job puts a roof over our heads."

Ryan crossed her arms. "A roof over *our* heads, Dad," she said pointing to herself and her mother. "You're never home!"

"Somebody has to pay for your mom to sit at home all day long doing nothing," he shot back.

"I'd love to start working again," Ryan's mom said quietly, speaking for the first time that night. I realized I had barely even looked at her throughout the evening. Now, I turned to her, and saw that her hair looked like a coffee-colored bush sitting atop her head. "I miss it."

Mark ignored her. He was staring at a nickel that a woman had dropped near the table, and apparently waiting for his chance to snatch it without her noticing him. After a moment, he swiped the coin and looked up.

"So, Sam, what are your career ambitions?" he asked.

I knew I should have prepared an answer—but I hadn't. "I've never really thought about that question before, to tell you the truth," I said. "I don't really have any career ambitions at the moment."

Contempt pasted itself on his fat face. "Well, what are you going to do with your life?" He laughed like a hyena. "You won't hold onto Ryan very long if you're poor, kid, I can tell you that!"

"I'm not really sure what I'm going to do, sir. Right this moment, I'm working on making your daughter as happy as I possibly can each day."

Ryan's mom smiled at Ryan and me. There was a longing, a lost dream in the way she gazed at us, as if she was looking back on a moment that had escaped her.

"That's the stupidest thing I've ever heard in my life," Mark said.

"Dad!" Ryan snapped.

"Well, it is, sweetie! Sam, you have to think about your financial future. The most important thing in your life will be your career."

Ryan and her mom looked down at their laps, as if the air had just been let out of their lungs.

"Well, sir, for me personally, I believe there are more important things in life than a career."

"Yeah, you'll grow out of that one day." His face perked up like a cat that's just spotted a dove. "Maybe you could come and work for me? I could pay you a nice little salary!"

My first thought was that any amount of money Mark was willing to pay me would probably cost me way too much. But I politely replied, "Yeah, that'd be great."

"Are you a hard worker?" he asked.

"What do you define as a hard worker?"

"I guess you could just look at me. I work over eighty hours a week sometimes!"

"If you're so successful, why are you working eighty hours a week?" I asked.

"I don't understand the question," he said quickly. "But I have a more important one for you anyway. Do you think you could be a manager?"

A burning irritation had traveled all the way up into the top of my throat, but I tried my best to suppress it. "I've never really thought about it."

"Do you know how to motivate employees?"

"No, sir," I said. "I've never been in that type of situation before. How do you do it?"

"Well." He leaned back confidently in his chair and put his pudgy hands on his stomach. "First, when I'm hiring new employees, I try to recruit insecure people. The more insecure, the better—believe it or not, they make the best workers! Their low self-worth is what drives them to overachieve. They have this compulsive need to please others—which works out great for us! We're always recruiting these types.

"We also constantly promote the idea of *work culture.* Really, it's bullshit psychobabble to get them to conform. We even tell them that we're all a *family.* These dumb-asses long to feel like they're special, so we try to exploit that. Yeah, we're a family— but we keep secrets from you, and don't tell you anything!"

He laughed sanctimoniously before continuing his rant. "But really, when I think about it, the best thing to do is to tell them there's a Mexican who'll come in and take their job in a heartbeat. Or even just fire one of 'em. After you fire one, they all get in line like cheap cattle. It sounds harsh, but that's what it takes to be a businessman!"

The difference between a business-focused person and a

good person seemed as plain to me as the difference between a broken shard of glass and a diamond. Ryan had warned me about the kind of man her father was: for him, everything was transactional. He was the kind of guy who couldn't act purely out of goodness—he did things so you would *owe* him something in return. Now, I saw firsthand that Ryan had been entirely truthful in speaking about her father.

"What about kindness?" I asked. "Is that a good motivator?"

He scoffed. "Kindness is weakness in a businessperson."

When her dad got up to use the bathroom at one point, Ryan whispered, "I'm sorry. I know he's being mean to you."

"Don't worry about it," I said. "It's like playing a video game to me. If you're encountering opposition, you're going the right way."

When the waiter came by with our food, Mark complained that his meal wasn't cooked properly, and belittled the waiter for not providing him with enough salsa. The server apologized profusely, but for some reason, his atonement seemed to inflame Mark's anger.

I was embarrassed, and felt terrible for the guy. I'd always thought the best measure of a person's character was the way he treated someone who served—and anyway, I thought the food looked great.

When I got home after dinner that night, Newman was at our kitchen table drinking a rumrunner, the house's newest go-to cocktail, with my mom. I talked to him about the dreadful experience I'd had meeting Mark that night. Resentment ripped right through me, and I spoke way too fast. "He's racist, misogynist, and pretty much despises anyone who isn't like him—and I was nothing like him," I said.

"If he's going to make judgements, it's best he do it in humility," Newman said assuredly, raising his head and eyebrows high. "None of us knows where we'd be or how we'd respond under the same circumstances as our neighbors. Some people need to feel superior to something, especially when they're insecure about who they are. Bigotry allows someone like him to take a group of people and convince himself he's better than them. That makes him feel better about himself. He obviously has a fragile ego; he wouldn't need to do that if he didn't."

I had never heard adults speak the way Newman did. "He thinks I'm a loser because I don't have my career planned out yet."

"Sam, don't worry about what some random guy thinks of you. If you don't think like him, that's okay. Maybe you hear a different cadence in life."

I sat down at the table beside them. "He says that the most important thing in life will be how much money I make. If that's the case, I don't think I'll be feeling too good about my adult self."

"I need to make myself another drink," Mom said as she stood up and walked to the refrigerator.

"Listen," Newman said taking a sip of his drink and straightening his back. "I went through two open-heart surgeries, and I was what most would call successful career-wise. I can tell you this from experience: the most important thing in life isn't going to be your career status. Maybe the reason so many people are addicted to drugs or alcohol or ambition is because society as a whole has lost its sense of what's truly important." He took another sip of his drink before he continued. "Somewhere along the line, we were fooled into looking out for others' interests before our own. We make other people rich at the expense of *our* energy! They've tricked us into thinking that everything on the outside is what will make us feel complete. But it's what's on the inside that gives our lives meaning."

"He's one of those guys who thinks he knows what he's talking about, but just spouts clichés. For being such an eminent businessman," I said bitterly, "he wasn't an insightful thinker. He just parroted the same old ideas the crowds always do."

Newman smiled proudly. "You're a smart young man! My grandpa always said that when you're on the side of the masses, you need to rethink what you might be doing wrong!"

I couldn't believe Newman had called me a "smart young man." It was intoxicating to hear someone describe me that way.

"Ryan said he kisses the butt of anyone with authority, but treats everyone else poorly."

Mom sat beside Newman. "Who else do we know who's like that?" she asked acidly.

Newman became serious. "You know, Dante reserved a circle of Hell for sycophants and flatterers, even deeper than the circle for murderers and tyrants. Sycophancy is just another type of fraud. I find comfort in Dante's description of Hell's punishment for this particular sin: immersion in shit! Those full of shit in life will literally be plunged into it in death!"

"I love that!" I said, smacking Newman on the back of his shoulder.

"Do you really like this girl?" Newman asked sincerely.

"Oh, yeah, very much! I actually think I'm in love with her."

Newman became serious. "Well, Sam, I have some bad news for you, but you deserve to hear the truth!"

My throat tightened, and my shoulders slumped as I imagined what he might be about to say. I was afraid he'd say Ryan and I were too young to be in a relationship, or that we didn't understand love, or whatever adults always say to young people.

Newman cleared his throat and looked at me sternly, the way a father looks at his son before he lectures him on a serious topic. "Sam." He paused and let out a hard breath. "It sounds like your future father-in-law puts the 'bag' in 'douchebag'!" Newman grabbed his stomach and burst out with a thunderous belly laugh. My mom thought it was hilarious, and began snorting like a pig. She laughed until tears came to her eyes, which made me start laughing as well. It was a great end to the night!

—

One of the sweetest days of my young life ended up being a cold, snowy day that December. Ryan came over, and we headed straight for my room. As we walked past the living room, Ryan stopped at the painting of the young girl in the house with the doors with no handles and stared silently at it.

"Where'd your parents get this?" she asked without taking her eyes off the piece.

"I'm not sure. I think it's always been here."

Ryan placed her hands on her stomach as if she felt pain. With a subtle tremble of her chin, she said, "Her eyes. They're so lonely, so sad."

"Come on," I whispered, pulling her toward the stairs.

No one was at my house except for the two of us. While we were both virgins, a sexual tension always tinged the air whenever we were together, and it was especially palpable that day. We had been together for six months, and were full of an adolescent passion that was a spark away from becoming a blaze.

When we entered my room, Ryan pulled me close to her and put her arms around my waist. She steadied her fierce green eyes on mine, burning desire into my retinas, and whispered into my ear: "I'm ready."

My young, impulsive mind went into overload. I felt like ginger ale bubbles were popping on my brain.

I laid her gently down onto the bed. She stared nervously at me as I undressed her piece by piece. We were soon lost in a place unknown to us both, satisfying a raw hunger that opened a secret place for the other inside ourselves. We were travelers down an untraveled road, but all that mattered was that we were together. I felt as if I were underwater, flying through a cool sea—no sound, no direction; only the sensation of weightlessness and wonder. But there was also an unease at being there, as if I were being pulled toward an unknown place I wasn't yet sure I was ready to go.

After it was over, we lay bare and glowing with sweat before one another, cocooned in nothing but silence. We had tasted a new power, an untouched freedom. The world shrank to just the two of us, and an innocence we'd one day wish returned to us slipped quickly away. I looked down at Ryan and saw tears moistening her flushed cheeks.

"What's wrong?" I asked.

"I love you, Sam," she said innocently. "More than anything."

The words went straight to my heart and shot out to every nerve in my body. As we held one another, it felt as if our limbs were roots entwining secretly underground and becoming one.

Ryan was soon asleep. As she slept, I held my hand against her delicate skin. I wanted to feel the warmth of her body. I peered out the window, reflecting on what we'd done and what would come next. As I contemplated the future before us, the soft white snow that had fallen just moments before changed quietly into a cold, hard rain, and I fell gently asleep.

⇌

For reasons I never understood, soon after, Ryan told her mother she'd lost her virginity to me. This did absolutely nothing to improve the relationship between Ryan's parents and me. Ryan's father was understandably upset, but also told her she was acting like a whore. In his anger and uncertain desperation, he forbade her from ever seeing me again. Ryan's mother, on the other hand, panicked and set her up on dates with her brother's friends in an attempt to get her to forget about me.

In spite of their disapproval, I continued to fall deeper in love. At first it was a passion, then a comfort; but in the end, it was a drug. Mark forbidding us to be together was like an aphrodisiac for our sex life. For Ryan, every insult he hurled was like ordering an extra dozen oysters! I came to encourage his disapproval. The more he condemned us, the harder it was for me to walk the next day.

⇌

As Lynn and I were eating lunch together a few months later, I noticed a jewelry store next door to the restaurant and said, "Let's check that place out."

Lynn looked at me like I was crazy. "Check out what, exactly?"

I pointed at the jewelry store.

"I hope you're not thinking what I think you're thinking," he said suspiciously.

We walked into the store, and the employees looked at us like we were cows walking into a butchers' market. "What are you in for today?" an attractive, meticulously dressed saleswoman asked.

"I want to check out engagement rings," I told her as Lynn shot me a death glare.

The saleswoman showed me every diamond ring in the store, starting with the most expensive. When we finally made it to the cheapest rings, my eyes lit up as I saw a tiny, lone sparkle next to a sales tag with a reasonable price written on it.

"That's the one!" I announced, pointing to the smallest rock in the store. "That's the one I've been waiting on!"

I paid for the ring using money I'd gotten by selling my old baseball card collection, and the disappointed saleswoman placed it in a blue felt-covered box.

"You bought the smallest rock they had! I don't even think that's a real diamond!" Lynn teased as we left the store. His words didn't matter to me, though. The treasure was in what the ring represented, not the ring itself.

Two days after I bought that ring, Ryan came over to my house. I made her chocolate-covered strawberries and watched her as she lay in my bed, eating each one.

"You're the best boyfriend ever," she said with a content smile.

I rolled beside her and retrieved the ring from one of the slats under the bed. I lay inches from her face, still half on top of her. Then, stumbling nervously and feeling as if my every breath had led to this moment, I placed the ring on her finger.

"Will you marry me?" I asked softly.

She looked down at the ring in disbelief, seemingly unable to speak.

"Will you?" I asked again.

"Yes," she said cautiously, as if trying to determine the authenticity of the moment.

She said yes, but apprehension lurked in her pale eyes. I didn't blame her. I was nervous too—the kind of nervous you feel before you get on the largest roller coaster at the theme park.

Ryan was only seventeen, and planned to go away to college after high school. She had worked her entire life for the opportunity to go to a major university. I didn't have a real job or any future academic aspirations. It had never even occurred to me that college was an option for people who lived on my side of the tracks.

To make matters worse, Ryan's parents still weren't huge fans of our relationship. They worked on Ryan like a mollusk that attaches its tiny suckers to its prey and slowly rips it from what it's connected to, trying to coerce her to break it off with me. But we knew we were in love and wanted to be together. In our eyes, marriage was the only way to make that happen.

I told Kevin about the engagement. He said I was making a huge mistake marrying so young, but he was still happy for me.

I told Newman too, and he was excited for us! He said that one of his biggest regrets in life was ending the relationship with his first love because his mom hadn't approved of her. When he told me about it, Newman took a long breath, and a fragile warmth came to his voice. "If I could do it over again, I'd have fought for that one! That love was the purest I've felt in my lifetime. I never had anything close to it ever again," he said regretfully.

"I can't believe your mom did that to you," I told him.

Now he spoke with a heaviness in his words, pausing several times. "Parents can be that way. Their fears sometimes blind them to the hurt they inflict on their children, even unintentionally."

Life was the best it had ever been for me! I was a cartwheel closer to what I felt I had always wanted. My dad wasn't bothering me as much, because I was rarely at home. The end of the school year was approaching, and Ryan would finally be turning eighteen, meaning we could legally get married without her parents' permission.

We spent our time fantasizing about the apartment we'd rent and how many kids we'd have. Ryan even created a two-page list of baby names for our future children. We dreamed of staying up making love late into the nights, and of growing old together, just as the psychic had predicted after our first date. Ryan joked that I would be an old, gray-haired man fixing the sink while she planted red dahlias out in the garden and waited for our grandchildren to arrive for a visit.

I felt so much hope! I'd never realized how wonderful hope could be. Nothing could really bother me, or get me too down, as long as I had hope to cling to. For the first time in my life, I felt I could see more light than darkness. I felt like everything was finally going to be okay.

4

Brilliant Disguise

"Is that you, baby, or just a brilliant disguise?"
—Bruce Springsteen

One cool Sunday afternoon, Newman came over after bingo to cook us what he called "the best chili in the continental United States." He said it was his mother's old recipe, passed down in his family for generations. I leaned against a counter in the kitchen and watched as he masterfully combined the ingredients.

⇌

"Don't spare the chili powder or the cumin, and use a mix of both ground beef and cubed chuck steak!" he said excitedly. "Don't tell anyone this," he whispered, "but the secret ingredients are cinnamon and pickle juice!"

"Pickle juice?" I asked, my nostrils raised in disgust.

"Yep! You would have never guessed it! What's your favorite food?"

"I love fried fish! Flounder is my favorite."

His eyes sparkled as if joy had taken hold of him. "Fish is my favorite food too! Do you like to go fishing?"

"I don't know. I've never been."

Newman looked shocked and leaned backward. "You've never been fishing before?"

"Nope; have you?"

His eyes lit up like a small child's on Christmas morning. "Oh, yes. I love to fish! In fact, I'm going tomorrow. You want to come with me?"

"Really? I'd love that! But I know absolutely nothing about fishing. I don't even have a rod or anything."

"Don't you worry about that! I have everything you'll need, and I'll show you the ropes."

"Great! I can't wait!" I said. "Do I need to wear anything special?"

Newman walked over to the fridge, took out some hot sauce, and began sprinkling it liberally into the pot. "Yes, you do," he replied. "Wear clothes you don't care about. We're most likely going to get soaked and covered in mud."

"Really?" I asked. "I didn't realize it would be like that."

"Fish can be mighty fighters! If you try to stay clean and dry, you're going to lose 'em. You'll find you're going to have to take risks sometimes to pull 'em in, especially the big ones! You have to go where they take you in the moment, and fight like hell while you're doing it! You're going to get dirty, and maybe even a little cut up, but the reward of reeling one in is worth it!"

I was getting more and more excited. "What kind of fish do you think we'll catch?"

"That's one of the best things! We have no idea what we're going to catch. The pond is full of a variety of fish, and you never know what's going to nibble at the end of your line at any given moment."

"This is going to be great!" I could barely conceal my delight. "I hope we catch some big ones."

"Just keep this in mind: one day you can go fishing and catch nothing at all, and the next day you can go and catch a bag full of whoppers! Prepare yourself for that now. You have to be okay knowing you might not land anything good on some days. That's when you just sit back hopefully and enjoy nature and the time spent with whoever else happens to be there!"

~

The next morning, I woke up early and put on warm clothes. It was chilly, and I hated the cold, so I dressed in multiple layers. Newman picked me up around seven. He had a rod and reel ready for me, and we stopped and picked up some bloodworms and crickets to use as bait. Then we drove twenty minutes to a pond he said he'd been fishing at for years.

When we arrived at the pond, I was so excited to throw out my first cast, I sprinted down the steep hill that led to the water. The scene was breathtaking! The pond perfectly reflected the cloudless sky above, tinting its calm surface baby blue. It lay in the middle of an open field with smooth, golden hills surrounding it like a shield. The smell of fresh water mixed with honeysuckle to sweeten the air. Croaking frogs flirted loudly, and water skaters skimmed the surface of the pond. A chorus of birds singing and bugs fraternizing overrode an otherwise peaceful silence that kissed the air around us. Occasionally, a soft plop of water echoed around us, as if a small stone had been dropped into the pond. By the time I turned to investigate, though, all that remained were waves resonating outward in all directions, the water's skin hiding its secret.

When Newman finally reached me at the pond, we settled

in, and he showed me how to bait my hook and put a bobber on the line.

"What's the bobber for?" I asked.

"It'll show you when a fish takes your bait."

He showed me how to push down the button on the reel before casting out the line sidearm like throwing a baseball. On my first attempt, the line flew behind me and landed in the branches of a nearby tree. Newman didn't laugh, though. He said the same thing had happened to him when he'd tried to cast for the first time, back when his dad was teaching him how to fish.

My second attempt at casting was a success! The line zipped out and flew about thirty feet before dropping into the water with a low-pitched *clunk*. Tiny ripples hurried quickly away from the red-and-white bobber and spread out indefinitely. The tiny sphere danced gingerly on top of the water for a moment, and then was still.

"This is great!" I said to Newman. "It's incredible out here!" Being there, alone with only the sounds of nature around us, was like communicating with something divine.

"That's part of fishing for me," he said. "Just enjoying the serenity of it all. Close your eyes and listen for a second."

I shut my eyes and tilted my head back slightly. The harmony of nature's life-sounds and the wind blowing softly through the trees around me gently touched my ears.

"When I was little," Newman continued, "I used to think the sound of the wind blowing through the leaves was the trees speaking to God in prayer."

As he spoke, my bobber dipped briefly beneath the surface of the still water. Newman whispered hurriedly. "Now, just wait and be patient until he pulls it all the way under for a couple seconds, and then give it a little tug."

When the bobber disappeared completely, I jerked the rod hard. The line snapped like a twig! It broke with a sound like a flyswatter slamming down on a hard surface. I looked at Newman, disheartened.

"It's okay, Sam!" Newman said, smiling. "You just got a little too anxious. If you snap your line or if the fish takes your bait off the hook, just go back, bait it again, and keep on trying." He put down his rod on the bank of the pond and walked over to his tacklebox to hand me another hook and bobber. "Learn from whatever mistakes you made. It's the failures that eventually make you great."

Newman was absolutely right! About fifteen minutes after snapping my line, I had caught my first fish! Newman said it was a crappie. At first I thought he was making fun of me because the fish was so small, but he said that was its actual name. Even though the fish was tiny, that didn't matter to me. I was thrilled with my first catch!

Newman explained how to slip the fish off the hook, and after a bit of careful maneuvering and some unfortunate yanking, I got the hook out of the fish's tiny mouth and looked at the crappie as proudly as if it were a two-thousand-pound marlin.

Newman took a picture of me posing with my prized catch. To me, I had caught his elusive whopper!

"He's too small to keep," Newman said. "We're going to have to throw him back."

I gently placed the fish beneath the water's surface. He didn't move for a second, and I worried I had accidently killed him. Then, with a quick jerk of his tail, he darted away, disap-

pearing forever into the muddy water. I felt my hand stinging after he swam away. Looking down, I saw tiny droplets of
blood between my fingers.

"Be careful of those sharp spikes on the fish's spine; they
can easily cut you," Newman said as he inspected my hand.
"Take your time to smooth down the spikes next time before
you try to handle him."

Thirty minutes passed. I hadn't seen any action since I had
caught that first crappie. I was doing all the same things I had
done when I landed the first one, but I hadn't felt so much as
a nibble.

I looked to Newman for guidance. "What am I doing
wrong?"

Newman was pulling in his sixth catch at this point, a small-
mouth bass. He talked to me while he took the slimy creature
off the hook.

"You can stand in the same exact place, using the same
bait that you caught a fish with previously, and never catch
one in that spot again! Don't try to recreate the past. Move
around or use a new type of bait. Be nimble. Do what works in
the moment! You probably thought that spot was special, but
sometimes it's just about luck."

I moved all around the pond and used different kinds of
lures. I caught four more fish that day before we left: two cat-
fish, a bass, and another crappie! We took them to Newman's
house, and he fried them all up in a cast-iron skillet. We ate
them with a homemade tartar sauce he whipped up using
Duke's mayonnaise, relish, and onions.

That day is still one of my top ten all-time favorite memories. Newman graciously told me to keep the rod and reel he'd

let me borrow, and from then on, I never bought fish from a store again. I ate all the fried fish I could catch whenever I wanted!

⇀

A couple weeks after the fishing expedition, my mom brought home a telephone from her work and said I could put it in my room. It was one of those see-through phones, so I could see all the tiny parts inside that made it work. When there was a call, the whole phone lit up in sync with each ring, like caution lights. The ringer on the phone didn't work, though, so I had to physically see the phone flashing in order to answer a phone call.

I put the phone on my windowsill, the one place I could see it wherever I was in the room, turned out the lights, and waited for it to shine. When it started flashing later that night, I dashed to the windowsill and hurriedly picked up the receiver. After I said hello, an unexpected recording began.

"This is a collect call from the Richmond City Jail. You have a call from—" At this point, the recording paused, and a real woman's voice came on the line and said, "Anne." Then the recording continued: "Do you accept the charges? Press 1 if you accept and 2 to deny."

I didn't recognize the name or the woman's voice, but I pressed "1" out of curiosity. A scratchy voice broke through the silence.

"Hello? Hello? Leda?" it said.

"This is Sam."

"Sam? Is Leda your mother, dear?"

"Yes, Leda's my mom."

The mysterious voice became animated, its tone changing to a high squeal. "Well! Hello Sam! I'm your grandmother!"

There was a hard silence while I attempted to process what I had just heard. She gave up on receiving a response and asked, "Is your mother there, darling?"

"Yes, she is. Hold on a second and I'll go get her."

I put down the phone and darted downstairs in search of my mom. I found her lying under a blanket on the sofa looking disheveled.

"You're not going to believe who's on the phone right now," I said.

She looked at me with a cautious curiosity. "Who?" she asked.

"Anne." The unfamiliar name felt strange coming out of my mouth.

"Anne? Anne who? My mother Anne?" she asked, sitting up quickly.

"Yeah, she called collect from the Richmond City Jail."

Mom shook her head scornfully. "Of course she did."

She walked to the phone in the living room and cautiously picked up the receiver, as if it were a delicate vase. I went back to my room and put my hand over the other phone's transmitter to listen.

"It's been a long time. I thought you were dead," I heard Mom say.

"Yes, it has." Anne paused and stammered as she said, "I've been, I've been messed up for a while, but I'm alive, if you can call it that."

"How long have you been in jail?" Mom asked.

"Just came in yesterday."

"What for?"

"Stealing cigarettes and violating the terms of my probation."

"What were you on probation for?"

"Stealing cigarettes." Anne stopped talking for a moment before she continued angrily. "I think the cops set me up! I might sue!"

Mom sighed heavily. "So, what do you want?"

"I wanted to talk to my daughter, and I knew you still lived in the area."

Obviously irritated, Mom asked, "How come you've never called before now, then?"

"I told you, Leda, I've been messed up for a while. I'm sorry I haven't called."

"We're *all* messed up, Anne. Wonder why that is?"

"Listen," Anne cut in immediately, "would you want to come and visit me here?"

There was silence as Mom processed the request. "What for?" she finally asked.

"I'd like to see you, and maybe see that son of yours too."

"I have two sons, actually. You sure you want the first time they meet you to be in a jail?"

"I don't think it matters. I'm their grandmother!"

Mom snickered. "You're not their grandmother. You don't even know them."

"Well, I'd like to change that. Would you please come to see me, sweetheart?"

Mom thought about it for another moment before quietly saying, "Sure, I'll come."

It was the word "sweetheart" that beat her. I knew how she felt. Hearing something positive like that coming from a parent, especially a neglectful parent, is like kryptonite to a child's bitterness.

At that point, I had heard enough of the conversation, and carefully hung up the phone. Moments later, Mom came to my room—something she rarely did—and knocked clumsily on the door.

"Come in!" I shouted.

I could see an unease poking at her face. "Sam, I'm going to see Anne tomorrow. Do you want to go? Kevin said he's not going, and Dean doesn't give a shit."

It was an odd request. *Do I really want to go meet this person?* I thought. Relatives we'd never heard of before were always popping up in our lives. We'd meet them once and never hear from them again. Kevin was tired of it, but my curiosity again got the better of me. "Sure," I said. "I'll go."

Mom's expression melted into relief, as if she were a toddler who had just found her security blanket. "Okay, good! We'll go tomorrow morning. Visitation is at nine."

Mom drank a lot that night, even for her. I got up to use the bathroom in the middle of the night and saw that the lights were still glowing downstairs. This was usually a caution sign in our household. I went to investigate, descending each step slowly and quietly. When I turned the corner to the living room, I initially didn't see anything out of place. But as I scanned the area, I found Mom passed out under the dining room table, naked from the waist down.

I hurried over to her, and a puddle of foul-smelling vomit beside her head made me instantly gag. Strands of her hair mixed with the chunky mess. *I guess this is how she expresses what she's feeling on the inside,* I thought.

I pulled gently at her legs and slid her out from under the table. She didn't move or even make a sound. For a moment, I thought she might be dead. I looked closely at her chest, and to my relief, I could see that it was still rising and falling, like the ocean's surface.

A washcloth lay on the counter near the kitchen sink, and I walked over to retrieve it. I turned the hot water on and waited patiently with my hand under the faucet as the water slowly changed from cold to lukewarm. I placed the rag under the water and soaked it before squeezing out the excess liquid. Kneeling beside Mom, I wiped small pieces of vomit away from her mouth and out of her hair. Then I picked up her half-exposed body like a pitiful child and placed her gently on the sofa.

I cleaned up the dining room floor, almost throwing up a couple of times because of the stench, before I tiredly climbed the stairs and went back to bed for the night.

The next morning, I headed to the jailhouse with my mother to meet my grandmother for the first time. I wore flip-flops with black basketball shorts and a Washington Redskins hoodie. It was unseasonably warm, and there wasn't a cloud in the sky.

We arrived at the jail fifteen minutes before our scheduled visit. When we pulled into the parking lot, we were stopped at a medieval-looking guard station. The officers gathered around it resembled a group of stern, misfit police rejects. One of them studied us suspiciously and asked to see Mom's driver's license. While he spoke to her, another officer walked around our car with a huge German Shepherd that sniffed at the doors. I smiled and whistled to the dog, but the guard angrily jerked at his collar and told me not to interact with him.

The guy with my mom's license asked us to step out of our vehicle so that a third guard could pat us down to make sure we didn't have anything we weren't supposed to.

"Hi!" I said to the third guard. He looked like a boy I knew from up the street. His face was dotted with pimples and red patches of blemished skin. He didn't respond to my greeting or even change his facial expression—but after patting us down, he tapped me playfully on the shoulder.

"Kid, what do you want to be when you grow up?" he asked.

"I'm not sure," I said. At this distance, I noticed he had bits of tobacco in his stained teeth. His breath smelled like mint and trash-bag juice.

"Did you know that the US has five percent of world's population, but twenty-five percent of its prisoners? One out of every four people who are incarcerated are locked up in the Land of the Free! You should think about becoming a prison guard when you grow up. There's job security in it!"

This time, it was me that didn't respond. I just shook my head politely, and jumped back into the car.

Once we entered the facility, we were told to prepare for another search. I caught Mom's irritation when they told us, and started to get nervous. I felt like I wasn't just a visitor anymore. Somehow, it seemed that in the guards' eyes, we had become the criminals. They had come to associate us with the prisoners, and the line between visitor and criminal had blurred. I pictured myself in a black-and-white striped prison uniform and began to worry that they wouldn't let us leave.

We walked through a large metal detector and were patted down by two husky female guards. One of them even searched through my mom's purse! After that search was over, a sickly-looking receptionist with a stone face that seemed to radiate cynicism asked my mother to fill out a couple pages of paperwork. She looked like she hadn't slept in days.

We took a seat in a dimly lit waiting room that reminded me of a post office. Mom filled out the papers. A television hanging from the ceiling was showing Family Feud reruns, but I didn't watch. My eyes were focused on the guards, as sharply as a rabbit watches a hawk. Their hate for us was almost tangible in the room.

An old black man with a *People* magazine in his hands sat next to me. He had a magnificent long white beard and wore a paperboy hat that made him seem harmless. He smelled like Old Spice and lavender, and a homemade wooden cane rested between his legs. I sensed he was staring at me out of the corner of his eye.

"You a Christian?" he asked as I turned toward him, his voice raspy.

"I think so," I said nervously.

He eyeballed me questioningly, as if he couldn't decide whether I was good or not. "Is that why you're here? You a Matthew Twenty-Fiver?"

"I'm sorry?"

"A Matthew Twenty-Fiver."

I looked away for a moment, then quickly back at him. "I don't know what that means," I said, confused.

"Jesus—God bless him—prioritized concern for those incarcerated at the start of his public ministry in his initial sermon in Nazareth." The old man spoke like an old-timey preacher, stopping only to cough loudly. "He made it clear that one of the signs of faithfulness to him was whether his followers visited folks in prison."

"Oh, I see. But no, sir, I'm just visiting my grandma," I answered timidly.

The old man smiled, and his face seemed to radiate warmth. "Well, God bless you, son!"

I looked around nervously. I didn't want anyone to hear our secrets! Then I whispered to him, "The inmates scare me."

"You can't love Christ and not love the prisoner!" he said assuredly. "Some of these folks are just down on their luck. Crime is conceived in poverty and born from environment." He stroked his milky-white beard gently in thought. "You know, a poor and innocent man has more chance of going to jail in America than a rich and guilty one. American justice is expensive! And if you got a mental illness, Lord! Then you're really in trouble!"

I could sense a genuine love in the old man. It impressed me, as Verities was a mostly Christian town. I'd found love for the vulnerable is sometimes most scarce in Christian towns.

Just then, they called Mom up. She handed her paperwork to the lady with the bad attitude, who didn't look up or say anything as Mom gave her the papers.

A tall, muscular guard with a deep voice and a no-nonsense manner said mechanically, "If you have any contraband, get rid of it. We won't ask questions about what you put in the trash can right now, but after you go in, you'll be charged with a felony if you have anything you shouldn't have in your possession." He stared stonily at Mom.

"I don't have anything," she said, glancing awkwardly out of the corners of her eyes.

"Me either!" I added, my hands in the air.

The guard slid an oversized key into a heavy metal door and opened it as he motioned us to walk through. After passing the entryway, I hurried to a second door to open it for everyone. The guard called out for me to stop, and I froze.

"Every door must close behind you before another one can open," he said sternly.

I shook my head and smiled nervously. As the first door slammed shut behind us, the booming sound startled me, and I jerked toward it. The guard laughed. It was the first time I had seen one of them smile.

"It's okay, son. That door really bangs shut, doesn't it?"

He opened the second metal door and gestured for us to walk through it in front of him. We entered a small, unusually cold room that smelled like pee and burnt bread. From floor to ceiling, a creamy yellow paint flaked erratically off the cinderblock walls. The awful pattern seemed to laugh at us as we walked into the room. Two large cameras positioned high in separate corners watched over us like big, black, mechanical crows. A honeycomb-colored plastic window with small round holes drilled through it divided the area.

It wasn't what I had envisioned a prison visitation room would look like based on what I had seen on TV. For one thing, there were no chairs. Second, the wall had no phone through which to talk to the inmate. I had looked forward to talking on a phone like that.

An older woman entered the room on the other side of the honeycomb plastic. Her skin was a dull, discolored gray. Her shoulder-length gray hair was pulled back in a small ponytail, and she was dressed in an orange jumpsuit that looked way too big for her. I didn't think she looked anything like my mom.

When she spotted us, a huge smile lit up her face. I'd never seen such deep-set wrinkles around a person's eyes before.

"Hello, all!" she screamed out, avoiding eye contact with us as if she was trying to hide something.

"Hi, Anne," Mom replied in a drab, uneasy tone.

Anne looked at me and did her best imitation of a grand-motherly smile. "Is this Sam?"

Mom nudged me forward as I pushed back against her. "Yes. Say hello, Sam."

"Hello," I said breathlessly. For the first time, I noticed Anne was missing a front tooth.

"Wow, he's a good-looking man, Leda!"

Mom rolled her eyes and took a deep breath. "How've you been?"

"I've been good, sweetheart," she said. She looked back at me, and frowned like she'd just bitten into a bitter piece of fruit. "I've missed you guys so much!"

"Bullshit. You didn't even know he existed," Mom mur-mured. She raised her voice, so that her words echoed off the hard yellow walls. "So, what's it like in this place?"

"To be honest, it's an absolute nightmare!" Anne's speech transformed into a loud rant. "I'm only allowed out of my cell for three hours a day! Can you believe that? One hour is spent outside, and the other two are spent in the common area or showering. The rest of the day, I'm locked in my little cage like a canary. It's so small, I can stand up in the middle of it and touch both sides! I've never been so damn bored in my life!"

"Do you have a TV?" I asked, fidgeting with my fingers.

They both looked at me as if they were surprised that I could speak. Mom rocked on her heels with her hands clasped behind her, like a pine tree swaying in the wind.

"They sell them here, but I don't have the money for one," Anne said. "That's one of the things I wanted to ask you, Leda. Could you put some money on my commissary account? I'll pay you back when I get out, of course; but it's tough in here with no money. I figured you're the kindest of all my kids, so I thought I'd ask."

With a percipient grin, Mom raised her eyebrows. "How much?" she asked.

"A hundred would really hold me over and make things a bit easier."

Mom didn't respond. She just rubbed her forehead with her left hand, and looked at her feet.

"I'll be really happy once I get out of here," Anne piped up. "I'm going to start fresh and change my life for good! I'm putting all the bullshit behind me. I want to start spending more time with y'all! Sam, is it okay if I start sending you a card once a week? We could be like pen pals!"

"Of course! I'd love that!" I said as Mom rolled her eyes again.

"How long are you in for?" she asked.

"At least a month. Being in here really makes you miss the simple things. I've actually been more productive in here than I am at home! There's so much time to spend just thinking. I've been writing a lot, and reading too."

"Have you made any friends?" I asked.

"My celly is really nice, and I met some sweet girls in this addiction class they have me going to. There's all these special codes in here you have to follow to get along with the inmates. You have to live by the rules of the prison *and* the code of the inmates around you. You can never be who you truly are. You're constantly changing depending on who's in front of you. In that way, it's kinda like being on the outside. You have to keep reinventing yourself in order to survive."

One of the guards appeared from around a corner and stood against the wall of the room we were in.

A little too eagerly, I asked Anne, "Have you seen any fights?"

"A few, but it ain't like what you see on TV. They're usually broken up before anything good happens."

Suddenly, a loud voice barked out, "Time's up, ladies!"

"Damn, we just got here!" Mom protested in the man's direction. He didn't respond or even look over.

Anne smiled at Mom, missing front tooth and all. "It was great seeing you! Thank you so much for coming! And it was a pleasure meeting you, Sam honey!"

"You too!" I said, relieved that it looked like the guards were going to let us leave.

Anne turned around and began to walk slowly away.

"Mom!" Mom shouted. I had never heard the word "mom" sound so peculiar coming out of someone's mouth before.

Anne spun around and smiled again, this time triumphantly.

"I'll put the hundred dollars in your account on the way out."

"Thanks, dearie. You're the best. I'll see you soon, sweetheart. I love you, Leda!"

After Mom reluctantly wrote out a check for a hundred dollars and put the money in Anne's account, we made our way back through the prison maze to the exit. As we walked to the car, bored, I asked Mom, "What *is* a prison, exactly?"

"That's an odd question. What do you mean?" she said.

"Isn't it just somewhere you don't want to be? A scary place you've punished yourself into?"

"I don't know. I guess so," she said shortly.

"I know people who do that to themselves, all alone at home in their own heads."

Mom didn't respond. She just stared at the ground with a troubled gaze —or maybe she was actually looking someplace far inside herself. Either way, I could see she wasn't in the mood to talk.

"How long until we'll see Anne again?" I asked after a short silence.

"We won't," she groused. "I know her. This is what she does, and she's a pro at it. We won't see her or that hundred dollars again, trust me. She'll probably spend it all on cigarettes."

We climbed into the car and drove home in what felt like wounded silence.

Mom's words turned out to be prescient. She knew her mother better than I'd realized. There were no more collect calls from Anne, and I never received one of the weekly letters she had offered to write. In fact, we never saw or heard from her again.

⤙

That winter had an awful, bitter chill. It snowed every other week, so we missed a lot of school. At one point, a huge snow-storm rolled through our town, the result of a nor'easter. It blanketed the landscape in over sixteen inches of pure white snow, making the outside look like a more innocent version of itself.

Ryan just happened to be at my house as the storm began. We had planned this, of course, and our scheme worked out perfectly. When about two inches of snow had fallen, Ryan called her parents and theatrically told them she was snowed in at a friend's house. They were as concerned as she sounded about her driving in the storm and agreed it would be safest for her to stay off the roads. She ended up staying with me for four days straight!

We spent that incredible time making love and talking about the future while cocooned under a comforter, the heat from our stripped bodies helping to keep us warm as the snow piled deeper outside. It was like dreaming while awake.

I made Ryan breakfast in bed every morning. She'd awaken to me standing in front of her with a tray full of food, and a content smile would paint her face. We were experiencing a glimpse of what our upcoming marital life would be like, and that life looked amazing to me. Just being in her presence felt like home. All the promises and colors I saw when I looked at her made all of my future doubts disappear. I wanted to hold onto her forever. As long as I had her beside me, I knew everything would be okay.

While we were together on those snowy days, the clock seemed to tick by too quickly. I knew she'd eventually have to leave, and I tried to wring out every drop of time we had together, but time seemed jealous and uncooperative. I held her snugly against my skin, inhaled her warm, healing breaths, and let myself melt into her soft body. I had been lonely for so long, and now I felt I was finally in a place where I belonged.

When the army of awful snowplows came and the roads were cleared, I sadly realized it was time for Ryan to go. As we said our goodbyes, I sensed the storm had brought us more than just frozen rain. I noticed an unmistakable change in Ryan's eyes—a softening, maybe. It was as if we had become something else, or she had become something else. I wondered if Ryan noticed the same turn in me.

"You know you'll always be my love, right?" I said as I hugged her one last time out by her car.

Her eyes ran away to somewhere high in the clouds. As she considered the sky, I held her closely, my hands clasped behind her back. Her nose was the color of a beet, but her skin was as pale as white stone in the wintry air.

"I'll always love you," she said soberly, her teeth chattering as she looked up at me.

I glanced at the sky to where her eyes had gone. For the first time, I noticed a dark cloud in the distance. I turned back to her and smiled.

"What's wrong?" she asked as a frigid wind blew and made us clutch one another tightly, seeking warmth.

"Nothing," I said. "I just love you. Do you *have* to leave?"

She leaned her head toward me and softly kissed my bottom lip as she let me go. I opened her car door, and she sat down and pulled it shut. Then she started the engine, rolled her window down, and turned the radio off.

"I wish you could come with me," she said honestly. "I'll call you when I get home. And I love you more!"

She slowly dissolved into the road ahead as I stood there, watching her car drive away in the bitter cold. A shadow in the corner of my eye made me look toward the horizon. A black dot drifted in slow circles high above.

It had been only seconds, but I already felt lost without Ryan there with me. I'd never believed I could love someone so much.

The day that changed who I was and would become forever fell a couple months after that cold nor'easter's visit. The weather had warmed quickly after that last snowfall, and plants already wore their first blooms.

I was sitting in my room when I heard what I first thought was the sound of a rat chewing on wood in the eaves. When I listened more closely, I realized someone was knocking gently on my bedroom door. It wasn't a usual knock, the kind that begs for an answer. It was a soft, apprehensive one, the kind you make when you hope the person on the other side of the door doesn't hear it, so you can excuse yourself away.

I opened the door to see Kevin looking apprehensively at me. His shoulders slouched, and his face revealed his obvious concern.

"I need to talk to you," he said, seemingly afflicted.

My eyebrows scrunched and pointed at my nose as I looked at him oddly. "What's up, Kev?"

He walked over to my bed, sat down, and looked at the carpet. His body was motionless and his mouth pursed as he tried to think of the right words to say.

"I'm your brother. I don't want any secrets or weirdness between us, so I feel like I need to tell you something."

This prologue was strange because Kevin and I never really talked about things that were bothering us. It was part of the family's omertà.

I knew what he was about to tell me was something serious, but I couldn't imagine the destruction that was about to be unleashed. I sat on the edge of the bed next to him, and we both looked at the floor as he spoke.

"I want you to know I slept with Ryan," he said in a low, troubled tone. "I know you two aren't together anymore. She told me. But I still thought you should hear it from me."

I sat stunned. I couldn't even move. I could only look stoically at the floor. I became like a duck on water: on the surface I seemed calm, but underneath, my mind was paddling a mile a minute. I felt as if my brain were dissolving inside of my body, into a mixture of anger, sadness, hate, and self-pity. Memories of things Ryan and I had been through together, and our hopes for the future, began fading to an awful black, stained by what I'd just heard. For a moment, I hoped I'd heard wrong, or that Kevin was merely playing a cruel joke on me.

I took a deep breath to compose myself. "She told you we weren't together?" I said.

Kevin just stared blankly. "You had sex with her?" I continued in disbelief, as if asking the question could somehow change what had been said.

Kevin stood up, pressing his hands so firmly against his knees to push himself up that his fingertips became a pale white. "I'm really sorry. I was drunk. I shouldn't have done that."

His gaze fumbled around the room for a moment before he got up with his head hanging and left, closing the door gently behind him. Before it could even latch, the significance of the moment washed over me with an ache that my naïve heart had never felt before. Tears drizzled down my face like a slow-moving rainstorm, as if trying to rinse away some of the hurt in the rawness of the moment. How fast the brightest and most precious of things can fade.

I didn't know what to do besides sit there and cry. A part of me was terrified of what my life would look like without Ryan in it. My hands began to tremble as the gravity of Kevin's words pulled powerfully on my understanding. I had always believed Ryan and I were beyond something like this—as if our love was so special, nothing could ever touch it.

With my heart racing and my blood darkening inside me, I picked up my transparent phone—the same phone on which I had stayed up all night, every night, confessing my love to Ryan—and dialed her number.

"Hello," she answered happily.

The words exploded from my mouth like a cannonball. "Ryan, I need you to be honest with me right now! Have you messed around with anyone else?"

"No! Why would you say that?" Her voice sounded apprehensive and shaky.

"Tell me the truth! Do you swear on your life, and on your family's lives, that you haven't messed around?" I shouted, half hoping she would lie to me.

"Yes, of course I swear! What's going on, babe?"

"My brother just told me what happened with you two! I loved you, Ryan! How could you have done that? We're engaged!"

I was shocked and innocently angry, but there was also a new feeling of betrayal that was burning away pieces of me. I had never felt so miserable before. She had told me so many times that we were for keeps!

The room began to feel sickly and unreasonably hot. Sweat condensed on my forehead, and I began to worry that the bubbling hostility I was feeling was immolating my insides.

"Oh, God, Sam, I'm so sorry! I don't know what happened! It didn't mean anything!"

Why did you just say that? I thought. *Now it's real. There's no going back now.* Angrily, I asked, "What *did* happen? Did you tell him we were broken up?"

"I saw him at a party, and I was drinking. One thing led to another and—"

"When did you go to a party?" I shouted fiercely. "You never told me about a party!"

I had always trusted Ryan with the deepest parts of my soul. I gave her the key to places in me that no one had ever visited before. Now I asked myself, *Why did I make myself so vulnerable to her, to something I couldn't control?*

She continued, "It was last Saturday when—"

"You told me you were hanging out with Christin!" I interrupted loudly.

"It was a mistake, babe! It was a mistake! It just happened."

"A tumor just happens. This was a choice you made!"

She was now weeping uncontrollably, but her sobs had transformed. They were different from anything I had ever heard from her before. They weren't tears of guilt or regret. It wasn't a hurt cry, or a cry begging to be forgiven. It was an honest one. The type you hear at a funeral, hushed moans filled with mourning and sorrow and what-might-have-beens, when you know that the person you loved isn't going to return again.

"It *was* a mistake," I said, my voice shaking madly and my own eyes welling up with tears. "It was *my* mistake to ever trust you! I—I loved you. I loved you, Ryan!"

"I'm so sorry. Please forgive me. I want to be with you forever."

What could be done now? The white flag had been raised. The battle was over. And as with most battles, there was no real winner. There was only destruction, death, and a haunting regret. In the time it took for a heart to beat, something precious had been lost.

"I have to go," I snapped.

I hung up the phone and headed straight out the door, almost unconscious in my anger. When I reached the driveway, I stopped and looked out to the tracks. They stretched out on a blue-gray horizon as far as I could see. The dogwood trees that lined them had just started blooming, their long branches stretching out openly as if offering an embrace. Dogwoods only bloom for a short while, but when they do, it's a spectacular sight that words can't adequately express. The branches birth perfectly formed, chalky-white flowers with petals that resemble teardrops.

White is a reflection of all of the colors you've ever encountered—an amalgam of everything you've ever glimpsed, good and bad. Viewing the petals can be a haunting experience; and for a moment my anger retreated as I contemplated the scenery, my world on fire and tears still dripping down my face.

I need to get to Lynn, I thought. *He'll help make this better.*

I drove away, heading for Lynn's house and trying to comprehend how someone I had loved so deeply could hurt me so badly. The pain was beyond anything I had ever experienced, and I had lived my entire life with the wrath of Dean! I'd believed Ryan and I were living in this strong, secure place, when we were actually perched dangerously on a sword's edge, unaware that one slip could sever our relationship forever. I felt helpless. *How could I have been so blind?* I asked myself over and over.

Lynn was outside working on his Jeep when I passed the dragon gates and pulled into his driveway.

"Lynn! Oh my God!" I said, rushing up to him. "Ryan cheated on me with—"

"Your brother?" he interrupted. "I know. I saw them at the party last week."

A sudden coldness hit me right in the stomach. "Are you serious?" I asked in disbelief. "Why didn't you tell me that?"

"I didn't want to hurt you, Sam. Plus, she begged me not to tell you I saw her there."

My hands began to shake. I was shocked that Lynn, who was supposed to be my best friend, whom I also completely trusted, wouldn't have told me something so critical. I felt stupid, like I was the only one who hadn't known Ryan had cheated on me.

My brother, Ryan, and now Lynn—all had betrayed me. All of a sudden, the entire world was collapsing around me. And inside of me, walls were being built, brick by brick.

"I can't believe you!"

"I didn't want to upset you. I'm sorry!"

"You aren't a true friend, Lynn! That's not what friends do!" A wave of furious hostility rippled through me. "I have to . . ." I paused, unable to comprehend my own thoughts. "I have to leave here!"

I jumped back in my truck and sped off, unsure where I was heading, with Lynn shouting my name in vain as I peeled out of his driveway.

I found myself back at the tracks near my house, seeking answers. I walked them for hours, contemplating the meaning of it all—and wondering if there was any to begin with. Teardrops dotted the steel rails beneath me as I walked sullenly along.

A part of me wished for the ability to forgive Ryan so that the pain I was feeling would just go away and we could be together again. I felt as if I were trying to hold our love in the palms of my hands as it dripped through the seams between my fingers. No matter how hard I tried to hold onto it, there was no stopping it from slipping away. It had become a cold, shattered prayer.

I made a promise to myself, right there on those tracks, that I would never allow myself to feel that kind of pain again. I would protect myself at all costs from such harm.

A part of me began to wonder whether Ryan had purposely sabotaged our relationship. She was about to graduate high school and had been accepted into a few colleges she had applied to before we became engaged. Undoubtedly, in her heart were secret wishes of which I wasn't even aware. Because of our relationship, she was living through a civil war in her home, and I knew that had taken a toll on her. I wondered whether she had done what she had as a means to end our relationship because she couldn't bring herself to end it outright. Sometimes, when our conscious doesn't have the courage to do what needs to be done, the subconscious steps in to protect us.

My reasoning didn't dampen the pain at all, however, and at first, I couldn't believe it was all real. It made no sense to me that Ryan could hurt me the way she did.

I cried for nine straight days, until anger began to well up in me.

Really, there's no such thing as anger. It's always fear or hurt in disguise—so in retrospect, it seems only natural that it wasn't long before I began directing my hurt onto my brother in the guise of passive anger. I didn't speak to him, or even acknowledge his presence in the house. I despised him as intensely as I did Ryan for what they'd done to me. They were both supposed to love and protect me. Instead, they had brought me more pain than I felt my fragile heart could handle.

Their betrayal was part of the reason I felt I couldn't talk about the feelings I was experiencing with anyone. They were so powerful, I was scared of what would happen if I released them onto someone.

One red-eyed morning, I passed by my mom in the hallway.

"What's wrong with you, Sam? You look terrible."

"The psychic," I said, looking colorlessly into her eyes. "She lied."

Mom tilted her head and frowned. "What are you talking

about?" she asked. But I felt no need to answer, and I walked away.

I even considered briefly whether I could go on living. I truly believed I would never escape my sadness. I was convinced it was now my new life. Ryan's memory coiled like a snake around my neck and choked the happiness right out of me. Life didn't feel like it had value anymore. The betrayals—Ryan's, Kevin's, Lynn's—had made both it and me feel meaningless. When I closed my eyes, I could hear my dad's voice echoing against their words, screaming: *"You're nothing! No one loves you! You're worthless!"*

⇁

After six painful, emaciating months, I began to come to grips with the fact that the whole awful experience with Ryan was real and wasn't magically going to go away. I was becoming bored with depression. I wanted to have some semblance of a life outside my sadness. The walls of my room, which usually offered such comforting solitude, inched closer in on me each day. I felt just as Anne had described feeling in her jail cell: trapped in a cage, a prisoner of my own grief.

I hadn't spoken to Lynn since the incident. I ignored all his phone calls and messages. But I eventually decided it was in my best interest to forgive him. After everything we'd been through over the years, he deserved a get-out-of-jail-free card.

The truth was, I really needed someone to show me how to live again—and there was no better person to do that than Lynn. I needed him to wake me up. So one day when he called, I finally picked up the phone.

When Lynn heard me say hello, he blurted out, "I'm an asshole, a major asshole. I'm so sorry, Sam."

And so, in a flash of forgiveness, we jumped headfirst back into our friendship, as if nothing bad had ever happened.

Lynn called me one night soon after our reconciliation and told me to drive to his house as soon as I could. He wanted me to go with him to a party a friend of his was throwing.

"I don't think I'm up for that tonight," I told him. This had become my response any time he tried to get me to go out.

"Get your ass over here!" he responded. "I'm sick of all this moping. You're going out!"

He was right. I needed something to lift my spirits. I was sick of my moping too. So, after changing out of my pajama pants and spraying on some cheap cologne, I reluctantly headed his way.

On the way to the party, we picked up Lynn's friend Ramsay and Ramsay's girlfriend Becky. Ramsay lived in the same neighborhood as Lynn, and their families had been friends since Lynn and Ramsay were kids.

Weirdly, the couple didn't talk to each other during the drive. They were polite to Lynn and me, but appeared to have a disdain for one another. Becky in particular seemed angry at Ramsay, and stewed the entire way.

We arrived at the party around nine, only to find a bunch of people already there. Vehicles choked the driveway leading up to a two-car garage that was attached to a large Colonial style house. The doors to the garage were open, and people hovered around it like flies around slop.

As we entered the garage, I saw beer-filled coolers lining the unfinished walls. Despite my mom's and more recently my brother's attraction to alcohol, I was a virgin to consumption.

Nevertheless, I came in the door that night aching to forget, and I was ready for a drink! I'd been told alcohol was great at scaring away the ghosts for a little while, and that was just what my tired mind needed.

Lynn reached into one of the coolers and smoothly pulled out two beers. He twisted off both bottle tops, and the air escaping the containers hissed like a snake. He handed me one of the brews. It felt cold in my hand and sent a raw shiver throughout my body.

We clinked the bottles together in a toast to new beginnings and threw their bottoms back at the warm night sky.

The first taste of the beer was god-awful, as if I'd just swallowed vinegar and horse piss. I almost spat it out. But I figured forgetting had a price, so I choked back a few more unpleasant swigs, willing to suffer temporarily through anything that would aid in dissolving the memory of Ryan.

It didn't take long before I had acquired a taste for the beverage and decided it wasn't quite so bad. Soon I found myself on my fourth beer in under an hour.

"Take it easy, dude!" Lynn shouted, cackling like a drunken hen.

"Chill out. Let's have a good time!" I said, raising my bottle as if proclaiming victory.

Suddenly, I stuttered, "Lynn. Lynn. You know what?"

"What?" he asked, his face within an inch of mine.

"I want to try a dip!"

Lynn had always dipped tobacco. It was kind of his trademark. I had never tried it before, because I thought it looked disgusting. But in that moment, I had a confident curiosity, and I was ready to experiment.

"You sure about that, Sam?" he asked reluctantly.

"Of course I'm sure! Give me a little pinch."

Lynn reached into his back pocket and pulled out a small green can with a picture of a Kodiak bear's face on its top. After he opened it, the fresh smell of mint pleasantly filled the air.

"It smells great!" I said.

I took a little pinch and placed it between my cheek and gum. Not even thirty seconds later, I began regretting that decision. I started to feel terribly woozy, and developed a nauseating headache.

As I endured the changing sensations, I noticed a guy coming by with a large bottle half-full of a translucent brown liquid.

"Want a shot?" he asked cheerfully.

"Give it to me, bro!" I told him without hesitation.

He poured the brown liquid into a clear shot glass, and I quickly threw it into my mouth. It was the second decision within a minute that I would come to regret.

"What was that?" I asked Lynn.

Aghast, with his mouth open wide, he said, "Jim Beam."

I stumbled out of the garage and straight toward a holly bush, where I began puking all over the perfectly manicured shrub. Its spines stabbed my skin in protest as I leaned against its shiny leaves. Their color immediately made me think of Ryan's damned green eyes.

"Screw you, plant!" I shouted before throwing up on it again.

Lynn walked up behind me and asked, "What's wrong, my man? You okay?"

Slowly, I stood straight up. "Never take a shot of Jim Beam," I told him, my mouth open and my watery eyes closed painfully, "with a dip in your mouth!"

Lynn doubled over and sat on the ground next to me, laughing, as I painfully spat out the horrible taste in my mouth.

"I have to pee!" I abruptly announced.

I made my way inside, grabbing another beer on the way. I stumbled around the home, searching for a toilet. I tried walking down a flight of stairs, but on the second step, I lost my balance and slid right to the bottom of the staircase. A couple who had been making out at the foot of the stairs jerked their heads toward me in shock.

"Hello!" I said as respectfully as possible. They both smiled, more out of confused politeness than anything. "Didn't spill a drop, professor!" I happily proclaimed.

I stood up ostentatiously, looked at the guy, and in a bad British accent, said, "Proceed, sir!"

The couple looked at one another, shrugged, and continued kissing as I slowly stumbled into a bathroom nearby.

—

The party ran out of beer shortly after my bobsled run, so I told Lynn I was going to comb the house for more booze.

"Good plan!" he told me, giving me two thumbs-ups that looked more like four thumbs-ups to me.

I soon came across a large two-door refrigerator in the basement. I opened both doors and searched its contents. To my delight, I spotted a large bottle of champagne way in the back. Someone had written "Save for Anniversary" in old, red Sharpie across the face of the label.

It took me a while to coax the cork out of the dark green bottle, but when I finally got it free, I was highly amused at the powerful *pop* it made. The champagne fizzed toward the rim, threatening to overflow, so I took a swig straight from the bottle.

Needless to say, I was a drunken mess. I had passed the point of stumbling and was now walking around with one eye closed, trying to decipher my surroundings without knocking into anything.

I found myself leaning against a window in the basement, and noticed that it was now raining hard outside. Through the downpour, I couldn't see anything clearly. The rain tapped rapidly on the window as I peered morosely out, and again, I thought of Ryan. I felt tears welling in my eyes, and the champagne bottle slowly slipped through my fingers and broke on the unforgiving cement floor.

As I was inspecting the broken pieces, Lynn burst through the basement door.

"There you are! What was that sound?" he asked as he studied the broken glass around me. I was unable to answer him coherently, and he laughed as he said, "Lord almighty! You're tore up from the floor up. We need to get you in the bed."

Lynn put his arm around me and helped me to a room on the second floor. There, we found Becky lying on the only bed in the room. She sat up quickly when we entered, as if we'd startled her. Lynn asked her if she was drunk, and she said she hadn't had a drop. She was just tired, and had decided to go to sleep.

"Can you help me with him? We need to get him to sleep!" Lynn said.

"Of course; no problem!" she told Lynn, making the sort of face someone might make at a sick baby.

Becky stood up and helped lay me at the foot of the bed. She placed a blanket over me, while Lynn put a pillow under my head.

"I'll sleep over here on the sofa," Lynn told her as he closed the door and lay down on a couch in the opposite corner of the room. "Where's Ramsay?"

Becky turned off the lights and lay back down on the bed. "He was called up to the rescue squad. He volunteers, and they were short-staffed tonight."

"Do you guys know how much I love you?" I interrupted from the dark.

"Yes, we know, Sam. Now go to sleep!" Lynn said.

"Will you sing me to sleep, Lynn?"

"No," he said, laughing. "Go to sleep!"

"I can't sleep by myself. Can I sleep in the bed with you?"

"I'm not in the bed."

Becky giggled in the darkness and offered, "Sam, come on up here, and lay your poor little head down with me."

She helped lift me into the bed and placed her blanket over me so that we spooned under the same cover together. Soon, snoring rang out from Lynn's direction.

Lynn's snore was like an eighteen-wheeler blowing out a tire along the interstate. As it echoed painfully in the room, Becky began to rub my back. My eyes began to adjust to the dark room, which had a teal tint now from the faint glow of an alarm clock beside the bed, and I turned toward her as my eyes focused in the dim light.

"You know, I noticed your eyes on the way here," I said to Becky in a hushed tone. "They're beautiful."

I reached out and rubbed my fingers through her shoulder-length hair. It felt soft and silky, like a smooth piece of delicate fabric.

"Aw, thank you," she whispered. "They're green!"

"You're welcome," I whispered back, my lips almost touching hers, "and it's true."

"You're so sweet," she said, touching the tip of my nose. "Would you rub my back for me? It's killing me."

"Sure."

My hand floated down her back, and for the first time I realized she wasn't wearing a bra. I brushed against the side of one of her breasts, and a tingle spread across my body, causing me to shiver.

"I like that too," Becky giggled.

Confidently, she took my hand and placed it between her smooth legs. I unbuttoned three clasps on her shorts as she raised herself on her knees and climbed on top of me. She used her foot, fumbling at first, to slip my boxers off. Her dark shadow projected onto the wall beside us, interrupted only by brief flashes of lightning.

Rain tapped out a song on the roof above as I watched the shadow beside me undress. With a quick flicker of light in the electrical darkness of the room, a mix of lust, intemperance, and pain won. Becky and I were having sex as Lynn's snoring scratched painfully against the walls around us.

At one point, I noticed the snoring had stopped. I peeked in Lynn's direction and a devilish smile lit like a burning candle on his face. With both thumbs high in the air, he mouthed, *You the man!*

That was the last thing I remembered before I blacked out.

⌒

The next morning, the wonderful feeling the champagne had brought me the night before had vanished. The sweet tang of carbonated grapes was gone. In its place, a dreadful flavor had developed. It tasted like cat shit.

My head pounded like a vibrating drum. I couldn't focus my thoughts on exactly what had happened the night before.

As the fog steadily thinned, the sins of the previous night began to appear. Slowly, I turned my head toward the spot next to me on the bed, expecting to see Becky—but she wasn't there.

I immediately thought about her boyfriend, Ramsay. The thought made me feel even sicker, and produced a repentant shame.

How can I have done that to someone, after what I've been through? I asked myself.

I stood, taking a moment to steady myself, and walked out of the room. I followed the sound of laughter down a long hallway and found Becky lying on a couch in an adjacent room, watching TV. I stood in the doorway until she noticed me.

"Good morning, sunshine!" she said cheerfully. Her response aroused an instant relief that warmed my insides. She was going to ignore what had happened!

Seeing Becky sober was enlightening. She wasn't the attractive girl I remembered from the night before. Deep, premature wrinkles encircled her crocodile-like eyes. Her face drooped as if it lacked the energy to hold itself up. I wondered what had happened in her young life to cause her face to evolve into such a sad expression.

"Good morning! How are you feeling?" I almost whispered as I held myself against the doorway for support.

Becky sat up and rubbed her stomach in circles with both hands. "Hungry!" she shouted back.

"Want to grab breakfast?"

"Absolutely! You're a lifesaver!"

I rubbed my eyes hard with the palms of my hands. "I'll go wake up Lynn, and we'll head out."

"Perfect! I'll meet you outside," she said as she turned off the TV.

I walked back with heavy feet to the sin-filled room, noticing when I entered that it smelled like gangrenous marsh water. Lynn still slumbered peacefully on the couch, his mouth forming a perfect "O" as he snored like a short-nosed bulldog. I tapped "Reveille" on his head as if rapping on a drum, shouting, "Wake up, Lynn!"

His eyes opened in thin, groggy slits.

"What the hell, man?" he protested.

I patted his knee and smiled. "It's breakfast time, buddy. Come on; let's go!"

We ate breakfast at a Burger King up the street from the party house. I ordered a sausage, egg, and cheese croissant with hash browns and told Becky her meal was on me.

We sat in a mostly awkward silence before Lynn crudely blurted out, "Hey, Becky! How was the pull-out last night?"

Lynn flashed me a playful grin, acknowledging his misbehavior. I was speechless. I looked at Becky, and her eyes met mine in shared dread.

"The pull-out couch in the room next to us?" Lynn continued. "I saw you moved to the sofa bed."

"Yeah, I couldn't sleep through your snoring," she said before quickly going back to eating.

When I was sure Becky wasn't looking, I mouthed the word "asshole" silently to Lynn, and he smirked like a kid sneaking a bag of potato chips after dinner.

We dropped Becky off at her house right after breakfast.

"You going to my place or yours?" Lynn asked me after she hopped out of the vehicle.

"I better get to my own bed," I said. "I want to go back to sleep."

On the way to my house, Lynn smiled rascally as he drove. "What's with the stupid smile?" I eventually asked.

Lynn stiffened and smacked my shoulder with his right hand. "What the hell did you do last night, Sam?"

"Not a damn thing, as far as you're concerned. I feel horrible about it! Let's get something straight right now. What happened last night does not leave this vehicle, and we never talk about it again."

Lynn laughed. "Okay, no problem! It's forgotten."

My irritation flared. "Do I need to remind you of your own deflowering with your seaside princess that I've kept secret?" I asked.

"Don't worry," he said. "I'm putting it in the vault. And good work, stud!"

We pulled into my driveway to an all-too-familiar scene: my parents fighting angrily in front of the house. Lynn looked on uncomfortably.

"Don't worry, Lynn," I said. "The difference between this side of the tracks and yours is that we do our fighting on the outside." He wasn't amused. He just stared painfully. "Call me later," I told him. "I'll go see what this is all about."

I met Mom as she was getting into her car. "What's going on?" I asked her. Lynn peeled out into the street and disappeared.

"I can't take it anymore!" Mom shouted. "I can't take it anymore! The years with that man have taken a toll on me physically and mentally. I'm not the person I once was. He's made me into something I despise!" she cried out. "I'm leaving!"

"Mom," I said, "calm down for a second. Where are you going to go?"

It didn't occur to me that she'd have an answer. "I'll be at Newman's house until I can find a place of my own."

"Newman's? You're going to leave us alone with Dad and go to Newman's house?"

"Life will be different for me there. I can stop all this drinking and live a decent life for a change. I can heal! Life will finally be better!"

A raw anger shot through me. "What about my life? What about Kevin's life? Will that be better? Listen, just calm down. If you're serious, why don't you make him leave and you stay?"

"I'm sorry. I can't," she said, casting her eyes down as if ashamed. "Tell your brother where I'll be and that I'm sorry."

I suddenly realized something truly damning, something that startled me into a cold awareness: I couldn't smell alcohol on her breath. Mom was sober. This wasn't another one of her drunken outbursts. She was serious this time.

Mom slammed her car door shut. As she prepared to pull away, she rolled the car window down and looked shrewdly in my direction, squinting in the hard morning sun.

"Sam, I never told you this, but . . ." She hesitated as if willing herself to say her next words. "Your dad, he wanted me to have an abortion when he found out I was pregnant with you." Satisfied, she rolled up her window and flew out of the driveway like a bird escaping a cage.

I stood motionless while her words bubbled up to my awareness.

"Thanks for telling me that as you leave!" I yelled as she drove away. I could still see the rosary hanging from her rearview mirror, swinging like a pendulum. "Not one tear," I said under my breath.

She hit the gas hard as she passed the tracks and rode into a new story. I stood there for a while, half in shock, half expecting her to turn around and come back. But she never did. She had finally escaped.

It quickly hit me that all was not right with the world. An understanding began to rise in me, like gray smoke from a chimney. The reality of my world, of my mom and dad, was also turning out to be just shadows. Though life had always been chaotic in that home, it and the people in it were all I'd ever known to be real. Mom leaving made me question once again whether anything was absolute anymore. *Is there anything that's safe?* I thought.

I walked up to my room to the sound of my dad banging a hard tune on the wall with his angry fists. He didn't even realize he was playing a requiem.

Before I could step into my room, I noticed Kevin's door was open. He stood just inside, and as I looked over, our eyes caught one another's.

"Mom left," I said dryly.

"What?"

"She's going to stay at Newman's. She's leaving Dad."

"Wow. It kind of hurts that she didn't even say goodbye," he said as he walked toward me.

I stared into his eyes, mirrored reflections of mine, and snapped, "If you haven't been betrayed by someone you trusted, then you don't know what hurt is."

5

Brothers in Arms

"In the fear and alarm, you did not desert me,
my brothers in arms."

—Dire Straits

om had abandoned the nest. She'd flown north
to a better neighborhood and what she believed
would be a better life.

Dad seemed upset that she was gone, though he would never
say so out loud. He was still terrible to us—even more so, to make
up for Mom's absence—but now he carried an added sadness
with him. He'd taken her for granted, never believed she'd have
the courage to leave him. Now he was left alone to contemplate a
life without her. I think it began to dawn on him how irresponsi-
ble he'd been, holding onto that fragile gift.

Thoughts of Ryan came a little less each day, but I still felt
empty. When a love that can't be replaced has been lost, you feel
perpetually hollow, like an uninhabitable desert. It was exhausting
to feel lonely all the time. I even felt alone when I was in rooms
full of people. My heart had been touched by fire, and now I was
spending my days fearing I would feel that awful burn again.

I didn't let myself get close to anyone. I had lost twenty pounds since the breakup eight months earlier, and my clothes barely fit me. In the darkness, my thoughts became like a bed of nails. Insomnia was an unwelcome visitor, painting dark bags under my dispirited eyes most nights.

"Don't you be taking drugs in this house!" Dad snapped as I passed him one day going out the door.

I wasn't taking drugs; but I did feel numb, and helplessly unsteady. I was becoming used to the fog of depression, even finding a thin comfort in it. But I recognized I couldn't take up a permanent residence there. I had to get back to feeling alive again.

Kevin and I rarely spoke or even acknowledged one another's presence in the house. Even when we did speak, a quiet angst stretched between us. Our war had paused, but with an unspoken agreement that a demarcation line split the hallway and separated our existences—an invisible wall between brothers.

As is often the case, the greatest healer is a friend. I latched onto Lynn as much as possible, and rode his horses until sunset almost every evening. My mind was distracted as I rode away from the thoughts that seemed to burn somewhere deep inside me.

One warm, starlit night, I met Lynn outside his house with a six-pack of beer. His presence always made me feel like everything was going to be okay. We sat on the tailgate of my old pickup truck, talking about life and philosophizing about our worlds.

"Have you ever thought about how light is always there?" I asked Lynn, looking upward. "Darkness is just us turning away from it."

"I've never thought of it that way," he said.

"Me neither, until just now."

I opened the first beer and took a heavy, cleansing swig. Its coldness numbed my front teeth.

Lynn smiled mischievously. "I had an old man on the golf course today tell me that us kids today are brats who are ruining the country!"

I laughed. "Who does he think raised us? It's no wonder kids have no integrity nowadays. They're raised in a society where success is found through being intellectually lazy, vain, dishonest, artificial, and two-faced in the competition for money, power, and titles! Who do the old-timers think handed our generation those tools of exploitation?"

Lynn nodded and looked around as if he was searching for something. "I'm getting hungry," he said.

I reached into the cab of my truck and pulled out a package of peanut-butter crackers left over from my last supper.

"Lynn, thank you for your friendship, and for always being there for me." I broke a cracker into two pieces and handed him half. "You're the only person who doesn't make me feel like an outsider."

Lynn threw the half-cracker I gave him into his mouth and took a swig of beer. "You're closer than a brother to me, Sam, and that's the God-honest truth!"

I savored his comment as if it were a fine wine. Friendship was family to me. I threw my half of the cracker into my mouth and chewed. Peanut butter stuck to the sides of my gums, and I used my finger to loosen it.

"How've things been going with you?" I asked. I'd been so busy with my own feelings that I'd neglected Lynn's.

Lynn sat with a pained look on his face. "To tell you the truth, my dad has me worrying all the time about everything. He's dreamed up this whole nightmare that leads to me working for his company, and I don't want to work for that bastard!"

I shook my head. "Why do parents put that on their kids?" I asked him.

"What?"

"Worry—there's so much worrying! They got us walking around every day of the year with a snow shovel, waiting for it to snow, even when it's a hundred degrees out."

Lynn laughed. "I like that."

"You know what?" I asked, sitting up straight as an arrow. "We should get an apartment and live together! Get away from them all! Can you imagine?"

Lynn's face lit up like a Christmas tree. "Let's do it! We could start a business and work out of the apartment!"

"What would we do?"

"I don't know." He thought silently for a moment. "My dad could probably hook us up with something."

I looked at Lynn, confused. "Aren't you supposed to go off to Yale or something?"

"Screw that!" he shouted. "I'm not like them. I'd be miserable there!" He handed me the beer.

"I know how you feel."

"He's so tough," Lynn whispered, staring into the distance. "He doesn't care what people think about him, that's for sure. He's nasty to everyone."

"Who?"

"My dad."

"You think he's tough because he's like that, huh?"

"You don't think so?"

I thought silently for a second. "I think it's a mask, to be honest with you. I feel for people like him," I said as I grabbed another cracker from the package.

"What do you mean?"

I looked at him with my eyebrows raised high, preparing him for discomfort. "You want me to be honest?"

"Of course I do!"

"You're not going to get mad?"

"No way!" he burst out as he affectionately smacked my shoulder. "Lay it out for me. There's nothing you could ever say that could get me upset with you!"

I took a lasting and uneasy breath. "I think people who feel unloved act like that. They cover the truth with toughness as a kind of self-defense mechanism." I stared into the moonlit heavens for a moment and saw a dull glimpse of myself.

"Why are people like that?" Lynn howled.

"I think it's easier for them to say 'They don't like me because I'm tough' than 'They don't like me because of me.'"

"That's deep," Lynn said, wrestling to process my words.

"I think everything's about love—you know, the love we feel but are afraid to show."

"You're starting to sound like a chick," Lynn said, laughing.

"Screw you!" I shouted, punching him in the shoulder. "You said you wouldn't get mad!"

Lynn laughed. "I'm just playing with you."

"You know, in all seriousness, my dad's like that: scared to share who he is with the world. People like that, their wounds stay fresh. They think they're the only people life has hurt."

Lynn looked as if he were in court and a life sentence had

just been read. "So, if someone is like that, you think there's no hope for them?" he asked.

"No, I don't believe that at all. On the opposite side of the tracks are the people who choose to live openly, knowing the risks. It's like they want to protect others from the pain they've experienced."

Lynn perked up. "You know what? That's how I'm going to be!"

I smiled. I could see that Lynn was buzzing pretty well.

"That's why I look at those you think of as *tough* as fragile people. It's easier for them to become embittered and cynical."

"You know what? Screw those people!" Lynn said.

I took a sip of beer and half-smiled, biting my lip. "Those people probably need love the most. Doesn't it seem like our whole existence is all about that? Love? Think about it. Just look at us, and how much time we spend trying to hook up with girls."

"True, but it seems like we're always searching for love in shapes it can never take. You know what I mean?"

I flashed a wry smile. "Now who sounds like a chick?"

"Why are we even sitting around talking about all this shit? How'd we get on this topic?"

"I really don't remember. But we have to sharpen one another, brother!"

"That's right!" Lynn shouted, a big smile on his face as he held up his beer. "We have to protect each other and watch one another's backs. You never know when the Devil's coming!"

"You know what?" I said, contemplating the fiery sky above us. "I bet when the Devil comes, he's not going to look anything like the Devil."

Lynn hesitated, then spoke gravely. "We probably won't even see him coming."

There was a long pause. Finally, Lynn broke the silence and asked, "How are we able to sit here and have a great time with nothing but crackers and beer?"

"Probably because we're both losers," I joked. "But there's no other loser I'd rather be hanging out with."

Like flipping a light switch, Lynn's demeanor suddenly became sober. He looked at me as a soldier looks at his fellow fighters before rushing into battle. His half-lidded eyes moistened. "We're brothers, man. Even though we live in different worlds, and no matter what happens." He squeezed the tops of my shoulders and shook me. "We're brothers," he declared again.

—

I had almost forgotten about my experience with Becky when Lynn called me a couple of days later. He didn't even wait for me to finish saying hello when I picked up the phone.

"Sam! I have something I have to tell you."

"What?" I asked.

"Ramsay found out about you and Becky, and he's pissed!"

"Shit!" I said miserably. "I knew that was going to happen. How'd he find out?"

"I don't know. He was going to break up with Becky, and she freaked out! She told him . . ." He paused uncomfortably before he finished his thought. "She told him you forced her!"

"What! Are you serious? Oh my God!" My face began to feel like it was on fire with anger. I couldn't believe she would say something so awful.

"I know. What a bitch!"

I waited for Lynn to say something more. When I only heard

silence, I asked, "Did you tell him that's not true?"

"No, I haven't talked to him. Scott just called and told me."

"Well, thank God you were there! Hopefully when he finds out the truth, everything will be okay. At least as okay as things can be when you've had sex with someone's girlfriend. What the hell was I thinking that night?"

―

The next day, I awoke to a hard knock on my front door.

I opened it to find a man in a cheap suit. "Hi, son. Are you Sam?" he asked, with a sharp, rigid smile. I was sure he was a neighborhood salesman.

"Yes, sir," I said, noticing small, sugary flakes across the breast of his jacket.

"I'm Investigator Harris with the Verities Police Department. I'm investigating a possible sexual assault and wanted to ask you a couple of questions." He showed me his badge and handed me a business card.

Panic swept over me. "I can't believe this. You need to call my friend Lynn! He was there, and he can tell you everything."

He looked at me, bug-eyed. "Is this Lynn Buchanan you're referring to?"

"Yes, sir," I said, relieved the cop had already spoken to Lynn.

The investigator eyed me suspiciously. "I've already spoken to Mr. Buchanan. He claims he was not present during the alleged incident."

I didn't know what to think. My mind was racing. *Is Investigator Harris lying? Has he spoken to the wrong person? Lynn was there that night; he saw everything that happened. Surely he'd tell the investigator what he witnessed.* "There's no way he said that," I protested.

"I'd like to ask you a couple questions, if I may," he said, this time more forcefully.

I could see now that Investigator Harris wasn't there to question me. Instead, he was there to persecute me. He had already made up his mind that I was guilty, and it didn't matter what I said. He had taken one look at my house and where I lived, and had chosen not to hear anymore. The truth didn't matter.

"I'm not answering any questions without a lawyer," I said.

Exercising that particular right seemed to prove my guilt in his eyes. He smirked and said, "If that's how you want it, I can come back with handcuffs and a warrant."

"That's how I want it," I told him as I shut the door.

I ran to my room and called Lynn. The phone rang and went to voicemail repeatedly. I knew Lynn worked out at Mount of Olympics Gym some mornings, so I headed that way to try to catch him.

I pulled into the gym's parking lot and immediately spotted Lynn's orange Jeep. When he came out a couple minutes later, I stalked up to him, my anger threatening to boil over into rage.

Lynn saw me, smiled, and embraced me as if nothing was wrong. He squeezed me so tightly that his lips pressed against my cheek. I pushed him backward. "Did you tell an investigator that you weren't there when Becky and I had sex?"

Lynn studied his feet and pressed his lips tightly together as he shook his head. "I'm sorry, but—"

"What the hell, Lynn?" I asked loudly.

His face reddened. "Sam, I'm sorry."

"Sorry for what, exactly?"

"You know that Becky's dad is a business partner of my father's, right?"

"Okay. So?"

"Well, I told my dad what happened at the party that night. He told me I can't get involved in this shit. He said if I embarrassed Becky's dad by telling them what happened, her dad might stop contracting with his company." He had a pained expression on his face, and chewed on his bottom lip. "It means a lot to him. He even ordered me a 30PO silver Porsche Turbo for keeping my mouth shut. You know you'd do the same thing."

I embedded my pointer finger deep in his marshmallowy chest. "Screw your dad and that car! The officer told me he was coming back to my house with handcuffs. This isn't some game. I could go to jail! This is a felony. I could go away for a long time."

"Sam." Lynn put his hands on my shoulders and started rubbing. They felt just like his dad's hands did when he'd pet you as he was trying to sell you on something. "You don't understand. My father is pissed! They do hundreds of thousands of dollars in business together every year. He told me he'd write me out of the will and drain my trust fund if I said anything!"

I quickly swatted his hands off my shoulders. "A trust fund and a new car? Is that the going rate for purchasing a slave nowadays? I thought you didn't want to become like him."

Lynn stared at me intensely. "I have no choice."

"Listen to yourself! You can't do this to me. You're my best friend. How can you be silent? That's worse than anything anyone has ever done to me."

Lynn wasn't fazed. "Becky's dad gives thousands of dollars to the police foundation every year. You're screwed either way!"

"Don't let your dad corrupt you, Lynn. You can't buy another friendship like ours, and you certainly can't buy integrity."

I turned my back to him and took a few steps away.

"I love you," Lynn begged. "You're like a brother, but—"

I interrupted him forcefully. "When you love someone, you'll do absolutely anything to protect them."

Lynn stepped toward me, looking desperately into my eyes. "If you were my friend, you—"

"Friend?" I barked. "Friends show up, and not just in good times. If you do this to me, we're done! Don't come to me apologizing again."

"I'm watching out for my future," Lynn pleaded.

"No. You're destroying your future. And you're selling your soul away. This is your test!" I pointed to a tall oak tree that stood close by. "You might as well hang yourself from that tree right there if you do this. You'll become what you despise."

His face twisted, and he looked away in thought before turning to face me again. "It's the way it has to be," he said. "I don't know what I'd do without that money."

I became quiet, and began to feel an almost tangible sense of sadness. "All this for money?" I said dismally. "I feel like I never knew you. It's not worth sacrificing yourself for that."

I stared at him with unbroken intensity. He didn't look like Lynn anymore—not the Lynn I had known. His face had changed somehow; he had become somebody I didn't know. I had always thought his innocence was stolen away in that beach house escapade in the Outer Banks, but the truth was that the beginning of its fall was in this moment. It's the times we least expect that we allow our spirits to falter.

I turned around, tears threatening to mist my eyes, and walked sadly away. There was nothing more to say. All hope was gone.

I climbed into my truck and drove away toward nowhere.

I rode around, directionless, until the lonely sun went softly to sleep. I knew, brokenhearted and full of regret, that the daylight wasn't the only thing ending.

⇌

Everyone experiences at least one serious betrayal in his life. But in a short amount of time, I had experienced more betrayal than most people do in a lifetime—or so my young mind believed. Just months before, the world had seemed so much simpler—more innocent. Now, out of an instinct for self-preservation, my brain began to injure the part of me that trusted. They say not to let a betrayal extinguish your faith in others, but if I wanted to survive, I couldn't hold onto that part of me anymore.

When I reached the tracks later that night on my way home, the crossing gates plunged down, signaling the approach of a train. The red warning lights twinkled like small drops of blood, piercing the blackness around me. I waited for the train to pass, but it never came. I assumed the sensor was malfunctioning and crossed the tracks with the gates still down, red lights blinking wildly. When I got home and stepped out of my truck, I saw that the night was unusually dark, and realized the moon had hidden its shadowy face.

I went straight to my room and thought about everything that was happening. I felt an icy sense of hopelessness. Fear crept gradually up my spine and straight to my brain, and I soon began to tremble.

I thought about how scared I'd been when Mom and I visited Anne. I imagined spending the rest of my own life in a jail cell. The police already believed I was guilty. Becky was from the *right* side of the tracks. They'd have no issue with tossing another poor kid into jail to defend the honor of a rich man's daughter—not on my side of Verities.

I was close to breaking down when I heard a loud banging at the front door. The sound scared me straight from sadness to panic. *They're here!* I thought. *The police are here to arrest me!*

I heard my dad answer the door downstairs.

"Your son raped my daughter!" an angry voice shouted. "Where is he?"

"Which one?" my dad asked.

"That piece of shit, Sam!" the voice roared.

"He did? What an asshole!" Dad said. "He's upstairs on the left."

Before I could think about what to do next, Becky's father was at my bedroom door, forcing it open.

"Are you Sam?" he asked when he got into the room. A pale blue fury lit his eyes. His hands shook violently, and he reeked of Wild Turkey.

"It's not what you think, sir! I didn't force her to do anything! I swear to you!" I raised my hands in front of me, chest-high, the palms facing outward.

"You're going to pay for what you did to my little girl!" he shouted. Spit crusted the corners of his mouth. With every other word, the top of his body jerked back, as if an invisible apparition were yanking at his face.

The man reached into the pocket of his coat and pulled out a small black pistol. It reflected a cold, metallic light, like the skin of a rat snake.

The man pointed the gun directly at my face. I could see straight down its barrel. The cylinder was like a dark, never-ending tunnel. An empty, cold darkness surrounded us as sweat collected on my forehead and dripped like tears down my cheeks.

The scene skipped quickly from frame to frame, as if I were watching someone else's dream. Time became confusingly slow. Sound softened until there was only a vacuous silence. A kaleidoscope of emotions overwhelmed me, until I couldn't feel anything at all.

Gradually, I became aware of the heavy rumble of a passing train. It shook the house ominously and rattled the pictures on the walls.

A figure was creeping up behind the intruder's broad shoulders. It slowly came into focus, and I realized it was my brother. My blank mind had no idea what he might have been doing there.

Becky's dad closed one eye, steadied his gun, and prepared to impose judgement. Reflexively, I spun away, anticipating a gunshot.

As I turned, Kevin leaped forward and grabbed the gun by the barrel. At the same moment, a loud *pop* echoed off my bedroom walls. The gun flashed, burning a lingering charcoal image of a bright light and two dark figures into my retinas.

Kevin collapsed hard on the floor, pulling my would-be executioner down on top of him. I was panicked. I didn't know if Kevin or Becky's dad had been shot.

"What's going on up there?" I heard Dad yell cautiously from downstairs.

The man stood up and viewed my brother, who was lying limp on the floor. He gripped the gun loosely in his hand as the barrel exhaled wispy, cirrus-like clouds of smoke. The acrid smell of freshly burned gunpowder polluted the air.

My heart was pounding. A cold wash shot down my back.

"You shot my brother!" I screamed.

Becky's dad felt awkwardly at his torso. Warm blood had collected around his midsection. He pulled up his shirt, exposing his pale white stomach, and blanched, seeming to realize that the crimson liquid on his palms wasn't his own.

I waited for the him to make his next move. He looked down at his hands, and his eyes opened wide as he began to comprehend what he'd done. Then he made a loud, guttural sound, turned, and ran down the stairs and out of the house. The whole way, he bellowed as if panic-stricken: "I did not do this! I did not do this!"

"Kevin! Kevin! Are you okay?" I screamed as I dropped to the floor.

I grabbed Kevin's hand firmly in mine. It felt cold and leathery. For the first time, I noticed a dark red puddle expanding against the white carpet, and a thick glob of blood near Kevin's stomach.

"He shot me," Kevin whispered through fading, forced breaths.

I grabbed the phone and dialed 911. After three slow rings, a man answered.

"911. Do you have an emergency?"

In panic, I cried out, "Yes! My brother's been shot. I need help."

"Okay; calm down, sir," the operator said calmly. "Can you tell me where he's been shot?"

I looked down at the red spot on Kevin's shirt, but I didn't want to touch it.

"Somewhere near his stomach."

"Do you know who shot him?"

"I don't know his name, but I know his daughter's name is Becky."

I could hear computer keys tapping rapidly in the background.

"Okay, sir. Is the suspect still in the vicinity?"

"No, he's gone. He ran away!"

The operator paused, and I thought that the line had cut out. Then he asked, "Okay, are there any weapons in the home?"

"No!" I said frantically. Kevin's eyes struggled to focus. His face had become ashen. "Is someone coming? He's bleeding really badly. I think he's losing consciousness."

"Yes, sir, I have the rescue squad en route to your location. The police will have to make sure the area is secure before allowing the ambulance to enter. Can you make sure your doors are unlocked when they arrive?"

"Yes; hold on," I said, carelessly dropping the phone.

I raced downstairs and unlocked every door in the house. As I got to the living room, my dad appeared from behind his recliner, as if he'd been hiding there.

"Why'd you let him in here, Dad? Are you crazy?"

"Shut your stupid mouth, talking to me like that! This is my house, you piece of shit. That's what you get for messing with the man's daughter."

I suddenly became still and stood within a foot of him, glaring madly into his eyes. Through clenched teeth I said, "Your son is up there bleeding to death on my bedroom floor. Do you care about that, or maybe want to help?"

For a moment, Dad looked concerned. But he quickly snapped out of the trance and said, "My son is a worthless drunk, just like his mother. Since he lost his scholarship, he's nothing to me."

He had always resented anything that intruded on his deity status—and in that moment, it enraged me. I clenched my fist and leaned into him before deciding it wasn't the right time. I had to get back to Kevin.

I pushed past Dad and rushed up the stairs.

"Don't worry, Kev. You're going to be okay. I got you," I said trying to feign calm in my growing distress. I held one of my balled-up T-shirts to his stomach. "You're doin' good."

In that moment, I wished I knew what to do. I desperately wanted to help Kevin. But all I could do was be there—although sometimes that's the best a person can do. It didn't even occur to me that the 911 operator was still on the phone that was lying on the floor across from me.

"I love you, Sam," Kevin said softly. "I'm sorry about what happened with Ryan. That was shitty of me. I shouldn't have done that. I was trying to prove—"

I stopped him midsentence as sirens screamed into our driveway. "Save your energy. Don't think about that now. I got you. I love you too."

It was the only time we had said "I love you" to one another that I could remember.

Kevin's blue eyes turned gray, and his lower lip trembled. Tiny, remorseful puddles glistened in the cups of his eyes.

"Do you remember that day in the church when I was baptized, back when we were kids?" Kevin asked. The flat sound of his words was like an evanescent hum.

"I do," I said, forcing a smile through the limpid terror I was feeling.

"Do you remember what the preacher said that day?"

As I was about to respond, a voice called out, "Where is he?"

"Up here! Here!" I screamed.

Three paramedics wearing dark blue short-sleeved uniforms came hurrying through the door, shoving me to the side. Two of them carried oversized bags full of supplies on their shoulders. The third, a woman with a stethoscope hanging from her neck, stared at a clipboard in her hands and began barking out orders.

"Thank God!" I said as they began to cut Kevin's shirt off his body. It felt like it had taken an hour for them to reach the house. A paramedic later told me they touched my brother within five minutes of my phone call.

After the paramedics tended to Kevin, they loaded him onto a stretcher and quickly carried him out to the awaiting ambulance. My dad ignored the whole scene, closing his bedroom door as they passed.

When the paramedics slammed the rescue squad doors shut, an overwhelming sense of dread overtook me. For the first time, I wondered, *Is Kevin going to die?*

I realized my hands were shaking. I forced myself to put the thought aside and jumped into my truck, waiting for the ambulance to pull away.

I followed the ambulance all the way to the hospital, running every red light along with them. I parked in a place I wasn't sure was legal—but I wasn't even thinking about parking tickets.

I dashed through the automatic doors of the emergency room and frantically told a nurse at the front desk that I was there for my brother. She checked her computer and told me they were preparing him for surgery.

"You can have a seat in the waiting room, baby," she said.

Everything suddenly calmed down too quickly. I began to feel nauseous, and my skin started to burn as if I were standing too close to a fire. Memories of things Kevin and I had been through together filled my thoughts. I could see our lives replaying themselves in my mind's eye.

I had always felt like I lived in Kevin's shadow—but in that moment, thinking about what he had done to save me, I felt that maybe I had lived in his light all those years. I forgave him for what had happened with Ryan, and turned all my physical, spiritual, and emotional energy into begging God to let Kevin live. I realized how much I cared for him and needed him in my life. The time we had wasted being angry now seemed so absurd.

Siblings are like that sometimes, though: you don't appreciate how much you love one another until it's too late.

Mom and Newman showed up at the hospital about thirty minutes later. They had been playing bingo, and a neighbor who had seen Kevin being loaded into the ambulance through her living room window had called the VFW building to tell them what had happened. They came as quick as they could.

I sat with them in the waiting room, still in shock at what had transpired that evening. As they both sat in numb silence, I explained everything. After I finished, Newman took out his rosary, kissed it tenderly, and knelt in prayer as my mom cried.

Unsurprisingly, my dad never even bothered to show up.

As I sat frozen in the waiting room, a familiar face drifted through the emergency room doors.

It was the investigator who had visited me the day before. He spotted me in the waiting room and walked gingerly in my direction.

I stood up, spent and drowsy, and held my wrists out to allow him to handcuff me.

"Just take me," I said. "Becky's dad shot my brother. I don't care anymore. I have nothing to say."

"It's okay," he said coolly. His demeanor seemed to have changed drastically since I had met him the day before. "Put your hands down.

"I'm not here to investigate you. We have Becky's dad in custody. I told him the same thing I'm about to tell you. The owner of the home where the reported sexual assault occurred came forward and told us everything."

As he continued, I learned what had happened after I blacked out at the party on that regrettable night with Becky. The woman who lived in the house had come home and became concerned when she heard moaning coming from the bedroom we were in. She went to check on the noise, and when she opened the door, Becky was on top of me, clearly in pleasure, while I lay there half-conscious.

"I'm sorry! I am so sorry!" Becky had kept repeating.

"Yes, you are sorry," the woman had told her. "Now go sleep somewhere else!"

"Thank God!" I said, taking a deep breath and impulsively reaching out to hug the investigator. "At least I have one piece of good news today!"

He shook his head lightly as he pulled himself awkwardly from my embrace. "For what it's worth, Becky's dad wants to apologize. He's very torn up about all this."

"How did all of this even happen?" I asked.

"You know, America has five percent of the world's population and forty-two percent of its handguns! A hundred people a day die of gunshot wounds. I have to believe that easy access to guns when people are lost momentarily in anger is a big reason we have such an epidemic of shootings. This is just another example of why we need some kind of change. Anyway, I'll come by and take your statement after all this is over. You take care of yourself, Sam. Good luck with your brother."

The investigator walked away just as a doctor came out to speak to us. I rushed over to him, almost pushing him backward into the wall behind him.

"He's recovering from the anesthesia and should be awake soon," the doctor said. "When he wakes up, you can all go back and see him. He's going to be okay. The bullet went through one of his kidneys, and we had to remove it. He can live without it, but it will take some years off his life expectancy."

I let out a sigh of relief that felt like twenty pounds of air. I was so fatigued, I didn't even realize I was talking out loud when I jokingly said, "Gosh, I always thought that Kevin was immortal."

The doctor grinned. "Well, son, I'm sorry to inform you that he's immortal no more."

I turned to Newman, my mind overloaded and numb, and solemnly whispered, "He gave that up to save me."

Newman just stared blankly, a perplexed look on his face. "It's okay, kid," he said, rubbing my back. "Everything's okay."

6

Comfortably Numb

"There is no pain, you are receding."
—Pink Floyd

There's nothing more painful to the ear than the prolonged sound of a ringing bell. And that's exactly what my poor ears suffered through every single day for twelve straight months. It got to the point that, whenever I heard the ding of the bell, a Pavlovian roll of my eyes would follow.

"Castor! Oh, Castor!" I heard after one morning's earliest jingles.

With an exaggerated sigh, I shook my head, walked sluggishly to my brother's room, and peeked my head inside. "Yes, Kevin?"

"Can you fetch me some grapes from the fridge, please?" he asked. His fingers waved regally at the door, signaling me to hurry.

"It's been a year. You're fine now. I'm not taking care of you any longer."

Kevin had actually been fine for the past nine months, but

I'd played along with his malingering act and taken care of him anyway. A part of me enjoyed it.

"I think we should ask my kidneys if I'm fine. Oh, wait—I meant kid-*ney!*" He dragged out the last syllable to overdramatize the singular.

I had gone through a year of Kevin's ringing bell, which I called "the hell-bell," and his onerous grape requests. For the first few months after the shooting, I made meals, dispensed medicine, and washed his still-fresh wounds. It had been a 24-7 undertaking then, so I didn't mind the simple things he requested of me now. It was the least I could do, considering he had sort of given up a kidney for me.

But lately, Kevin had become a little too comfortable requesting my services, and was treating me more like an indentured servant than a brother. Plus, he was fine now. The doctors said he'd healed beautifully and could resume normal daily activities. I didn't even think he needed to keep taking his pain medication anymore.

Kevin had been prescribed Vicodin after his surgery. He had started off taking half a pill, but after three months, he'd begun taking more than the recommended dosage, tripling the original amount to a pill and a half. He was noticeably loopy all the time, so I told him he should try to cut back—but he always said he was in pain and needed the medicine to take the edge off. Then he would call his doctor, who would refill his prescriptions with no questions asked. That would make my concern melt away. I figured that if it was a problem, his doctor would be the one to know, and he'd handle it.

Mom had envisioned her escape to Newman's house changing

her life for the better—but she drank more living there than she had when she was living with us. She did seem a little different, though—a little less edgy. She began smiling her way through conversations, and her laugh became chirpy, like a cricket playing a violin. She was like a prisoner whose remaining jail time has just been commuted, after he had already served several years in prison. She didn't know what to do with her sudden freedom, or how she'd survive on the outside alone; but she knew that freedom felt good, and she wanted to celebrate it.

"Have you talked to Mom lately?" I asked Kevin one day.

"Why would I talk to her?" he responded sourly.

He still wasn't sure how to feel about Mom leaving us. She was still living at Newman's house—even though when she'd left, she had said she was only going to stay there for a short while, until she found a place of her own. It was obvious she and Newman were in a romantic relationship of some sort, but they weren't sharing anything with us. Kevin had developed a marked resentment about the whole thing, but he wouldn't talk about it with anyone.

"I don't know," I said. "She left a message telling me to call her. She said it was urgent."

It wasn't unusual for Mom to call and claim an emergency, only for us to find out later that she had been drunk-dialing. We never worried anymore when she claimed chaos. But I went to my room and called her anyway.

"Hello?" she answered sleepily.

"Mom, did I wake you up? It's four in the afternoon."

"No. No, I was sitting here watching my shows. How are you?"

"I'm good. You called and said it was urgent. What's up?"

"Oh, yeah!" she said suddenly, as if she'd forgotten her happiness. "I have a question to ask you."

"Okay."

She stuttered as she began. "Um, well, my and Dean's divorce was finalized last week, and Newman and I are, uh, thinking about going up to the courthouse to, um . . . to get married. Would you want to come with us to be a witness?"

I was silent as I tried to catch the words still floating in the space around me.

"Sam? Are you there?"

I didn't know what to say. Honestly, I was sickened by what I'd heard, and I blurted out the first thing that came to mind. "I can't today, Mom. I have to go wash my hair." It was nonsensical, but it was all my brain could muster.

"Oh, okay," Mom said uneasily. "Then I guess I'll just talk to you later." She hung up without waiting for a goodbye.

I walked to Kevin's room in disbelief.

"That was one of the strangest calls I've ever experienced!"

Kevin looked at me with a curious uncertainty. I went on. "Mom just told me that she and Newman are going to the courthouse this afternoon to get married."

Contempt contorted Kevin's flushed face. "Remember all the time she and Newman spent together when she was still with Dad? I bet she was cheating on Dad with Newman that whole time. She's over thirty years younger than him. She has problems!"

It was the most Kevin had ever discussed the situation with me. I sat beside him on his bed and could see the disgust dripping from his face like teardrops.

"I'm not going to argue with you there. But Dad didn't exactly make it easy for her. Remember the purse incident? When you accidently leave your purse at Walmart and get a shotgun held to your head as punishment, you start to reevaluate the health of your relationship."

Kevin laughed awkwardly. We always laughed at our dysfunctional family stuff.

"I know, I know. But the way she did it, it's still not right. Plus, to me, it's basically an act of incest. It's gross!"

I shook my head, repulsed. "You're right, you're right. I guess she's just searching for shelter or something."

➤

I left Kevin's room and drove to a convenience store for a soft drink and to have a moment to think.

As I walked back to my truck on that sunny afternoon, a cool, familiar breeze brushed against my face, and reflections of Ryan visited my thoughts. She and I had walked through that very same parking lot together on many occasions, holding hands and laughing freely. The quiet memory of her still popped up occasionally, like a rain shower on a clear day, and in my mind, I'd be with her, innocent again and falling. Like an old movie echoing in time, I could see her shiny black hair fluttering in the wind and feel the warm, comforting touch of her skin against mine.

Suddenly, I heard a familiar voice call out, awakening me from the daydream. "Sam!"

I turned around—and there she was. The real Ryan was there, in physical, flesh-and-blood form.

I squinted to ensure I wasn't still daydreaming. But it *was* her, looking as lovely as I remembered—even though she was much changed. Her hair was longer and wrapped around her shoulders, accentuating the sharp outline of her thinner face. No longer the young, naïve girl I had known, she had grown into a stunning woman. She wore makeup elegantly now, in a mature way, and it made her green eyes pop against her smooth tan skin. A short orange sundress accented her soft and supple curves.

Orange was my favorite color.

Like muscle memory, my body began to thirst for her as it had two years ago, the last time I'd seen her.

"Hi," was all I could manage to force out.

There was a short silence while the past whispered between us.

"It's good to see you, Sam," she said softly. "It's been a long time."

In an instant, I felt myself slipping loose and becoming captive in her eyes again—those damn green eyes that had haunted me for so long, or maybe cursed me.

I quickly glanced away. *Stop*, I told myself. *It's not real.*

"Yeah, you too; it has been a long time," I said aloud, trying to focus on her forehead. "You look great, Ryan! You're so . . ." I paused to find the right words. "Independent-looking. And grown-up."

"Thanks," she said, smiling like a schoolgirl on a first date.

She touched her fingers gently to my face, sending a charge to every nerve in my body. "The facial hair makes you look so much older," she said, smiling.

"Yeah, I just haven't shaved."

There was another pause that flowed like running water as we both looked down gracelessly.

"I don't really know what to say." Her words were tinged with pain and sentimentality, but her eyes danced.

"Yeah, me neither," I said.

"I've thought about you so much over the last couple years. I wish . . ." She paused as if she was having difficulty dragging herself to her next words. "I wish things would have been different. I'm so sorry."

Carelessly, I allowed my eyes to descend from her forehead and meet hers. "Me too, Ryan. Me too."

Her eyes could still make my heart flutter. Whenever I was seized by them, I wouldn't see her as she was in the moment. I wouldn't see the pain or the grief she had brought me with her thoughtless behavior. I would see her as I had seen her on that warm summer night when we met.

"Is there somewhere we could go to talk?" she asked, twirling a strand of hair in her fingers.

I thought about all the bad decisions I'd made in my life. What was one more? "Sure," I said. "You want to follow me back to the house?"

"Yes, definitely," she said, grinning.

She turned, and walked confidently to her car.

⁂

When we pulled into my driveway, the gravel dust from our vehicles rose into the air and joined like an old silvery spirit. She climbed out of her car and walked toward me as she gazed into the distance.

"I always loved those dogwoods," she said as she reached me. "They're so beautiful. Whenever I see one, I think of us."

We walked into the house, and her scent mixed again with the smell of home. It was both strangely familiar and intoxicating. We headed silently for my room, and I watched from behind as she carefully climbed the steps. Her hips swayed in a slow, steady rhythm.

When we reached my room, I closed the door behind us and turned around, tentative and unsettled, to face her. Tears filled her green eyes, and her bottom lip quivered.

"What's wrong?" I asked, not wanting to hear the answer.

"Sam, I love you," she said. "I'm so sorry. I still love you."

Those words. What is it about those three words? They're like casting a forgotten spell. What brings them that magic? They made me feel alive again, while at the same time, they stabbed painfully at an old wound deep inside of me. But oddly, it was also like fresh blood running through my veins, erasing the loneliness and numbing a recurring pain. Love and pain—somehow they're so inexplicably entwined, like two underground roots nourishing the same mystical tree.

I reached for her hands and guided her to the bed. We sat down slowly on the edge and stared eagerly at one another. She leaned in and kissed the back of my neck, and chill bumps dotted my arms.

I glanced at the mirror above my dresser beside us and caught our reflections. My head rested on her right shoulder as if I were trying to bury myself inside her chest. Her dark hair spread wildly all around me, like a vine overcoming my body, and for the first time I noticed that it was highlighted with red streaks.

She continued to kiss the back of my neck, slowly moving toward my ear. In the mirror, she resembled a starved vampire feeding at a vein. I backed away from her and looked deeply into her eager eyes.

I pulled her close to me again, and my suffering lips met hers with a force. Like some kind of voodoo, with her words of love and her venomous kiss, she now had me under her control.

"I love you too," I said. And all at once, the hollowness I had been feeling inside myself filled up in that moment. Sadness, that awful poison, had gone away, and I felt a warm light glowing again within me.

And it *was* the truth. I did love her. Being "in love" had dried up long ago, but love was what replaced it.

She unbuckled my belt as I slipped off her orange dress, and in a dying breath, we were both impassioned, going down a long and familiar old road.

We never got dressed or let go of one another that hungry night. As she slept, I wrapped her body closely in my arms. I felt so safe when I had her lying next to me. Her presence had always kept those ghostly shadows at bay.

The light in the room slowly changed from a shaded glow into the gray of dusk, until eventually, night's blackness embraced us. I was still awake, watching her sleep peacefully as a faint glimmer of moonlight kissed her face, when the three a.m. train roared faithfully by.

—

Ryan awoke the next morning in a fluster.

"What time is it?" she asked as she grabbed her clothes.

"It's seven thirty. You want to grab some breakfast?"

"I can't. I have to get back. My boyfriend's going to kill me!"

My heart sank, leaving me breathless for a moment. "Your boyfriend?"

Fumbling to put on her pants, she said, "Yeah. I don't know how I'm going to explain this one!"

I smiled uncomfortably. All along, something inside of me had secretly hoped Ryan and I would get back together one day and live happily ever after. Humans need hope; without it, we die.

But in that moment, I realized that the Ryan of my dreams was just an illusion. That person had never existed—and certainly didn't exist now.

We fool the past until it's a reflection of our own desires. Nostalgia is always sweeter than reality, the present seeming sour in comparison. Awe had always clouded over all the badness of our relationship, but now it was all coming into focus—*she* was coming into focus. And it was in that moment that the wonder of that first love began to fade.

"Let me walk you to your car," I said calmly, trying to hide my hurt and surprise.

We walked outside without saying a word. There was nothing to say, really. I remember feeling sorry for whomever her new boyfriend was. I knew the sting of Ryan's awful poison intimately. Any man who chose to spend life with her would have to spend it anxious that his flower was blooming elsewhere.

"Goodbye, Sam," she said as she opened her car door and started the car. "It was amazing!"

"Goodbye, Ryan," I said, thoughts of the past filling my head. "Yes, it was."

After Ryan left, I drove back to the convenience store and used my brother's expired driver's license to buy a twelve-pack of beer. I raced home and quickly opened the first one. Its coldness pressed familiarly against my warm lips. A comfort came with the feel of the bottle's kiss, and I disappeared into that lovely oblivion where your mind forgets and pain sleeps in a low-hanging fog.

—

Alcohol became my new companion in life. I came to love drinking in the moment. I became so infatuated that I even loved the simple weight of a drink resting in my hand.

But like some of the people in my life, I'd regret each morning after I allowed the intoxicant back in. The truth comes with the early morning sunlight, and the pleasantness turns bitter. You realize that as you empty the bottle, the bottle empties you.

But somehow, by midday, that thought wouldn't matter anymore. When the night fell anew, the familiar shadows would rise up and peer at me with their stony eyes; and when I realized that I wasn't alone in the room anymore, I'd crack open another bottle and wash those spirits away, adrift on a sea of intoxication.

I descended into my own reality. Alcohol makes you forget people exist, makes you forget you need people. Your dreams lie dormant, and you begin to wonder what your place in the universe has become. You're like a comet shooting through the cosmos, a cold light searching for a purpose in what feels like an expanding void.

"What have I become?" I began to ask myself. "This isn't me. I'm not me anymore."

Alcohol is like a weed that wraps slowly around you. At first you feel it embracing you comfortably, but eventually it overtakes everything. It intrudes on your deepest roots and your sweetest fruits. It comes to believe that your space is its own. Even when you try to pull it up, it soon comes back—forcefully, and with a vengeance.

—

Kevin eventually retired the hell-bell and began going out with his friends again. His life went back to the way it had been before the shooting: partying late into the night, sometimes coming home, sometimes not. He was healthy again, though he always seemed sluggish. Sometimes, he'd even nod off in the middle of a conversation. But I chalked it all up to his late nights.

Kevin never had money, but he never wanted a real job either. We talked about his views on work all the time. If he had a buzz going, he became particularly emotional about the issue.

"Americans have been duped!" he'd rant. "How were we convinced that happiness comes from having the biggest house, the highest promotions, or the fanciest things? It's like no matter what kind of evil you do to your neighbor, it's justified if you live in a huge mansion. I won't become part of that sick game!"

"But what about the American Dream?" I'd say, to get him riled up. "That's what America is all about! You work hard, and you get rewarded!"

"The American Dream? Bullshit! The American Dream I believed existed when we were kids only applies to the richest of rich kids now. Sixty percent of America's wealth is inherited, meaning those people never worked for anything. Don't get me started on this, Sam!"

Sometimes, out of the blue, he'd produce a wad of cash, and I'd ask him where it had come from.

"I won a couple of poker tournaments," he'd always say. Eventually, I stopped asking.

Kevin also grew his hair long and stopped shaving. I asked him why, and he shot me an impudent smile. "I want to look more like Jesus!"

It wasn't all fun, though. He also became as moody as my dad. I had to gauge his temperament some days to decide if I even wanted to talk to him. Occasionally, it was too draining for me even to be around him. He danced a fandango between humor and tragedy, sometimes shifting from one to the other within seconds. He developed two distinct personalities. One was an energetic conversationalist who always had a goofy smile on his face. The other rarely spoke and was uncomfortably stone-faced.

He seemed particularly out of it one day, and I asked if he was feeling okay. He looked at the ground and took a deep breath.

"Yeah, I just feel like . . . I feel like I'm exhausted," he said, letting out a loud yawn.

"Well, rest," I said.

He took a breath that seemed to come from way down in the bottom of his stomach. "It's not that simple."

"I assure you it is," I said. He stared blankly in my direction, without seeing me.

―――

My days and nights were all messed up at this point. I stayed up into the wee morning hours, and slept in late.

I thought it would be good for me to get on some kind of a schedule, so I decided to get a job. I knew they were always looking for help hauling trash at the local dump. The only requirement was that you had to bring your own work boots—which I didn't have.

Kevin was out somewhere, so I searched his closet for something that would pass for work boots. As I pushed aside the shoes and clothes that littered the closet floor, a gallon-sized plastic bag drew my attention. It was full of what looked like tiny white Tic Tacs.

I picked up the bag and studied the small pellets. The word "Vicodin" was imprinted in the center of each tablet. There had to be at least a thousand pills in the bag!

I never confronted Kevin about them. I didn't want him to think I had been snooping around his room, and it never occurred to me that prescription pills were dangerous. I figured he was buying them in bulk because they were cheaper that way.

Two weeks later, I would find out just how wrong I was.

$$\Longrightarrow$$

It was around noon on a Thursday that I heard a loud *thump* outside my bedroom door.

I looked down the hall and didn't see anything out of place, so I walked to Kevin's door and knocked a couple times. Usually, Kevin answered right away, shouting for me to come in; but this time there was no response.

"Kevin?" I asked as I gently pushed the door open. I saw him bent over his bed as if he was tying his shoes. "You going out?"

As I inched closer, I noticed his lips were faintly blue, and his eyes were half-open, vacant. I ran to him, grabbed his arms, and laid him down carefully on the bed. His skin felt like a cold fish at the market. I put my ear to his mouth and made out faint, gurgling breaths.

Instinctively, I felt his neck for a pulse. If he had one at that point, it was so weak I couldn't detect it.

Panic set in, and my heart began to pound like a jackhammer. I picked up the phone and dialed 911, and they answered before there was even a ring.

The dispatcher asked if Kevin had taken anything before losing consciousness. I quickly glanced around the room, and saw three empty beer cans and a handful of pills on his nightstand.

"I don't know," I said honestly. "At least a couple drinks. But there are pills here too."

"I have paramedics en route," the dispatcher said.

$$\Longrightarrow$$

I rode in the ambulance to the hospital and watched as a

paramedic administered Narcan to Kevin intravenously. I had never seen someone being hooked up to an IV before. The paramedic had trouble finding Kevin's vein, and blood dripped down his arm and onto the white sheet beneath him. The sight made me feel sick to my stomach.

"He's overdosing, son," said the paramedic. "This will help block the effects of the Vicodin."

Kevin's shirt was pulled up to his chest, and I could see the ten-inch maroon surgical scar that ran along the side of his belly. A dull, horrible moan came from his mouth, and his eyes were crossed and rested without moving. His breaths rattled like water running through a clogged tube.

Is this my fault? I thought. *He never would have started taking Vicodin if he hadn't been shot. And why didn't I say something when I found the pills?*

The paramedics tied Kevin's hands tightly to the stretcher. They must have realized I was troubled by it, because one of them said, "Many patients who overdose come out fighting after we give them the Narcan. This keeps them and us safe. I know it looks traumatic, but sometimes things like that are needed before we can bring them back."

Kevin suddenly came to—but he looked like absolute death. Even though he had chill bumps on his arms, sweat dripped down the sides of his gray face. His hands shook, and his skin looked dry and ghostly. Leathery bumps splotched his face and arms like small, rashy tents. I thought he looked better before they gave him the Narcan.

"You probably don't get a lot of calls like this, huh?" I asked a paramedic uncomfortably.

"Actually, we get about two or three of these types of calls a day," he said, seeming weary.

"Seriously? I can't believe that! Probably only on this side of the tracks, though, right?"

"Not really," the paramedic said as he checked Kevin's pulse. "Actually, most of the calls have been coming from the other side of the tracks. People tend to view these opioids as harmless because they're prescribed by doctors, not realizing they're as dangerous as hard drugs like heroin, and as addictive too."

"I had no idea," I said.

"Yep. In fact, a lot of people start on these damn pills and then move right on to heroin. It gives them the same high at a cheaper price. The hospital has a full-time addiction nurse because it's become such a big problem. I'm sure you'll get to meet her tonight."

———

Sure enough, as we waited in the hospital room with Kevin as he recovered later that evening, the addiction nurse visited with information on where to seek help for an opioid addiction. She handed each of us a small pamphlet with the words "Hope: Heroin and Opioid Prevention Education" in bold blue letters on the cover. Kevin didn't say a word to her at first. He was scared he'd end up in jail if he said anything, but she assured him anything he shared would be kept confidential.

"We can offer you a drug called Suboxone that curtails opiate cravings, but you really need to enter a drug counseling program to have any real chance of beating an addiction like this," she told Kevin.

"I need to do something," Kevin whined. "This is a real beast. I can't stop taking these pills! They've taken over my entire life, and I feel like I can't stop."

I couldn't believe what I was hearing. A veil of guilt blanketed me. I had been so busy getting drunk all the time, I hadn't even noticed Kevin was struggling.

"You're not alone," the nurse said. "Over one hundred people die from opioid overdoses each day. This is a serious problem, and you need to be open to receiving help."

"I had no idea this was even a thing," I said.

"Oh, yes; it's become a huge problem. Americans are consuming eighty-five percent of the world's opioids. Drugmakers have gone as far as paying tens of millions of dollars to advocacy groups to promote their use. They're getting filthy rich!"

"How is that even possible?" I asked.

"You're not the only one unaware of how big a problem it's become. Even doctors, the people who *should* know, haven't really been trained in opioid addiction. The problem really starts there. Drug companies weren't making a profit on opioids in the old days because they were mainly used on patients suffering from intense pain due to terminal illnesses." She stopped for a moment as the blood pressure cuff around Kevin's arm automatically started tightening, making a loud sucking sound like a running vacuum cleaner. "They began marketing to doctors, and convinced them to prescribe opioids for ailments like common back pain. At the same time, they dropped the price of the pills. That helped create an incentive for doctors to offer opioids to patients from all economic backgrounds to combat pain that might have been better alleviated with things like physical therapy or aspirin."

She shook her head and frowned. "People quickly became addicted and needed more and more pills to achieve the same high. What people didn't realize is that it doesn't take much to

OD on these things. Fast-forward a couple of years, and now we have this huge problem on our hands."

"Why doesn't someone do something about it?" I asked.

"This is America. Curing patients isn't a sustainable business model."

I looked at Kevin, who was dozing off.

"He needs his rest," the nurse said. "Could I talk to you in the hallway?"

She opened the door, and we walked out. I flipped off the light switch as we left the room.

"I hate the smell of hospital rooms," I said as we walked out the door.

"It's the hand sanitizer," she said. "I hate it too. Listen, we need to talk about something very serious you have to keep a lookout for."

"Okay," I said, intrigued.

"Three-fourths of heroin addicts start out by taking the same pills your brother is taking. Nearly half of the people who inject heroin abused prescription opioids before they started injecting. Most addicts switch to heroin because it's cheaper and easier to obtain than prescription pills."

"I hear what you're saying," I said a little too smugly, "but I can assure you, Kevin would never take a drug like heroin." In my mind, heroin addicts were unintelligent, dirty deadbeats who passed out in alleys somewhere with needles stuck in their arms. Kevin wasn't like that at all.

"That's what they all say," she said. "All I ask is that you be on the lookout."

She handed me more brochures. "Get him into this rehab facility if you want to save his life. I have to go. I have another one that just came in down the hall."

"Okay. Thank you so much for your help," I said. "You've been great."

I began walking back to Kevin's room.

"Oh, hey! One more thing," she called out. "Don't you take any of his pills for any reason! A huge reason people get addicted to these things is because they take a pill from a family member like it's an aspirin or something."

"Got it," I called with a thumb in the air. "Don't worry. I want no part of them after today. Thanks again!"

"Good luck to you, Sam! Come find me if you need me," she said as we parted ways.

The next morning, I woke up with a sore back on a hospital sofa—more like a bench, really—beside Kevin's bed. He was already awake, flipping nervously through one of the rehab brochures.

I stood up, stretched my aching back, and rubbed my still-tired eyes.

"What do you think?" I asked.

He smiled clumsily but didn't respond. I leaned over his shoulder so we could look at the brochures together.

"Wow, it says we wouldn't have to pay for anything," I said. "Medicaid will cover the detox, addiction meds, and inpatient services." Fortunately, Kevin had been able to receive Medicaid when Mom's insurance company had kicked him off her health-care plan for being over eighteen.

"I know I can beat this by myself if I put my mind to it," he whispered.

"This is kind of rock bottom, don't you think? Don't you feel like a puppet pulled by its strings? You should give it a shot. What do you have to lose?"

"Do I even want to stop? I mean, you only live once."

"What you're doing isn't living. And I don't want to go through what happened yesterday ever again. Do you realize that was almost your last day on earth?"

Kevin slid his hand through his hair and closed the brochure. "I know I have demons. Real demons. I honestly don't know if rehab is going to fix that."

There was a sweet honesty in his voice that made me want to reach out and hug him. "I understand your past more than anyone," I told him. "There's nothing to lose in giving rehab a chance. Maybe there's some magical trick they can teach you that will make the demons disappear," I said clumsily. "Then you can teach it to me!"

He looked achingly ahead, searching the blank space in front of him for an answer. "I'll make you a deal. I'm going to try to defeat this beast on my own." He looked fiercely in my direction. "If it doesn't work, and I mess up just once, I'll let you drive me straight to the rehab facility yourself."

"I don't think that's a good idea. I think you should go now. You have a great opportunity to really change your life."

"I know I can do this! I need somebody to believe in me, Sam."

That comment was the dagger, and he used it with the precision of a pro. Even without it, it was obvious there was no changing his mind.

"One mess-up, and you're there," I said, waving my pointer finger in the air. "One!"

It wasn't a week later that I got a desperate midnight phone call from Kevin. He was at a friend's house and asked if I could come pick him up right away.

"What's wrong?"

"It's not good. I'll show you when you get here."

When I pulled into his friend's driveway, Kevin appeared at my truck, materializing from the darkness as if he'd been hiding in the bushes.

"Go down Tammi Lane and take a left," he said, his words washing around sloppily in his mouth.

It wasn't long before I saw two police cars, one on each side of the road, their lights screaming at the night.

"Go slow," he said. "Look down there."

He pointed with his right thumb toward the side of the road. I looked and saw broken branches giving way to a small ravine with walls so steep they were almost vertical. At the bottom of the ravine sat my brother's truck, upside down in a shallow creek bed. The front of the truck was smashed in like an accordion, and the windshield was completely shattered.

I smacked Kevin hard on the arm. "What the hell did you do?"

"I was on my way to Eric's house, and as I turned on that sharp curve, a kind of devil force pulled me over the edge. The next thing I know, I'm upside down in the water! I banged my head on the steering wheel pretty hard too."

As we drove away from the scene, I noticed Kevin's forehead wore a huge, dark hematoma that looked like it was fighting to burst out of his skin.

"You're just going to leave?" I asked. "Are you not worried

about the damage you're leaving behind? Why didn't you stay with your truck?"

"Why do you think?" he said. "I crawled out the window on the passenger's side and ran to Eric's. He let me hide behind his gate until you got there."

"Kevin, the cops will be waiting for you at our house. They're probably there right now!"

"I know, but I can't go home until I get this shit out of my system. I already called Joe. Drive me to the Nieds' house, and I'll stay with him tonight. Can you pick me up in the morning?"

I glared at him, scowling. "Yes, but you know what this means, right?"

"What?" he asked as if he was confused.

"Don't play stupid. Pack your bags! We're calling tomorrow and getting you into that rehab facility. Do you have a problem with that?"

"Yes, I have a problem with that! I have stuff I have to do, Sam. I can't just go and interrupt my entire life. I only had a couple drinks."

I slowed down, methodically and calmly, and then made a sharp U-turn.

"What are you doing?" Kevin howled.

"You have no humility about your addiction," I said, my jaw tightening. "You think you're too good for help. Well, you're wrong! Humble yourself and go to this rehab place, or I'm going to drop you off in front of the cops and tell them the truck is yours, and you can rehab in jail."

His eyes studied me like a poker player ascertaining a bluff. "Okay, okay," he said, seeming outmaneuvered. "Stop the truck. You're right. I promised, and a promise is a promise. I'll go."

"Good!" I forced a grin. "Listen, when I get home, I'll call the police and say your truck was stolen from our driveway. They'll think some kids took it on a joyride and dumped it here. Sound good?"

"Sounds good! I hope it works." He paused stiffly for a moment, rubbing the back of his neck, and weakly said, "Thanks."

I pulled up to the Nieds' house and turned off the headlights. Kevin got out of the truck and walked over to my window, and I rolled it down.

"Thanks again, Sam," he said as he looked down sheepishly.

"No problem. You going to be okay? That bump on your head looks awful."

"Yeah, I'll be alright," he said, scratching the back of his head. "I'm sorry about all this."

"Don't worry about it. You'd do the same for me! I'll see you tomorrow, okay?"

He walked toward the Nieds' front door as I backed out of the driveway and turned the headlights back on. As I drove away, I thought about how I used to think that Kevin was superhuman, even mythological. He had long since been knocked off that big-brother pedestal. But I yearned for those days again, when my brother was larger than life to me. I used to be so sure of everything with Kevin. Now I wasn't even sure if I could help him.

⇌

Early the next morning, I pulled out the brochures the addiction nurse had given us and called the rehab facility. They said they could have a bed ready for Kevin that morning. I packed some of his clothes and a few toiletries so there would be no excuses about having to come home to get his things, and headed to the Nieds' to pick him up. I knew if he didn't go straight to the facility, he'd never make it there.

Kevin hopped in the truck as soon as I pulled in. The first thing he saw was his suitcase overstuffed with clothes. His eyes widened.

"You ready?" I asked, smiling. "I called them and made all the arrangements. They're waiting on you!"

"Damn it, Sam," he said quietly, shaking his head as if trying to force a thought out of his ears. "Yes, I'm ready."

After a mostly silent trip, we pulled up to an immaculately manicured property on at least five bright-green acres. An old mansion that looked like it had been built in the 1800s sat regally atop a hill in the center of the property. Large oak trees lined walking paths all around the estate.

It was one of the most beautiful scenes I had ever encountered. It seemed so peaceful and relaxing, it reminded me of the time I'd visited Monticello on a school field trip when I was younger.

A Hispanic man in a short-sleeved pink polo was standing at the top of the driveway, waving to us.

"Hello!" he said as I pulled up, a warm smile on his face. "You must be Kevin. Very nice to meet you. Congratulations on making it here. That takes so much courage! I'm Dr. Hernandez, the director here at Garrett's Wellness."

Kevin looked at him nervously and forced a spastic smile.

"You must be his keeper," the director joked.

"Yes, I guess I am. Nice to meet you. I'm Sam."

"Kevin, do you mind taking your bag and meeting me at the front gate up there? I'll introduce you to Jennifer, our intake officer." Dr. Hernandez pointed in the direction of a large white gate in front of the building.

"Sure, no problem," Kevin said as he picked up a bag, threw it over his shoulder, and began to walk away. "Sam!" he called from a short distance. "Take care of yourself." He turned and took a couple of steps before spinning around. "Hey, are you coming back to get me?"

I walked over to him without saying a word and hugged him a little too tightly and for a little too long. "You know I am," I said. "Good luck, brother. Give it an honest chance."

"I will," he said. "I will."

I turned around quickly, feeling tears build behind my nose. Dr. Hernandez put his arm around me and walked me to my truck.

"Sam, great job getting him here. That's the first step," he said. "But this will be a long journey. Once someone takes an opioid, a switch is flipped in their brain that makes them start craving more. It can take five years to get that button switched back to normal. Our rehab program only lasts for twenty-eight days." Dr. Hernandez stopped and grabbed me by the shoulders. "You understand what I'm saying? Are you in this for the long haul? Rehab is only the beginning of the journey; he won't reach the destination here. He'll need you to help get him to the goal line."

"Of course," I said. "I understand. I'll be there for him in the long haul."

We shook hands. "Good, my friend," Dr. Hernandez said. "Don't worry: bad gets okay, okay gets good, and good gets better! I'll see you in twenty-eight days!"

I reached my truck and looked out to my brother as I grabbed the door handle. He watched me from a distance. Tall trees surrounded him and danced slowly in the wind. His expression seemed lost, worn-out and confused, defined by fear.

I waved to him as memories hung soundlessly between us. He waved back, but seemed anxious and concerned, gnawing on the insides of his cheeks. I had never seen him look so fragile before—as if he could break at any moment.

Then something happened that I hadn't seen since we were kids in Mr. Franks' church, on that day so long ago: Kevin openly wept.

"I've done what I can to fix you, big brother," I whispered to the wind as I watched Kevin turn and walk away. "Now it's up to you."

7

Against the Wind

"Wish I didn't know now what I didn't know then."

—Bob Seger

"Where's your brother been?" my dad asked. "I haven't seen him in weeks. Is he on another drunken bender?"

I hesitated momentarily. *Should I tell him?* I wondered. *Will he just use Kevin's situation as an excuse to be an asshole again? Would it make him contemplate the damage he's done if I told him the truth? Maybe he'd show a little remorse.*

Reluctantly, I muttered, "He's in a rehab program."

"Rehab? What a loser!" Dad said, with a vulture-like laugh. "A *man* can handle his alcohol."

"Not alcohol—pills. Vicodin, actually. He got hooked on them after the surgery." I walked away before he could respond.

Without Kevin at home, the house felt more hollow than usual. I didn't sleep well with him gone, either. In fact, I'd started having a recurring nightmare. It happened so frequently that on some nights, I was scared to go to sleep.

In the dream, I was alone on a small vessel in the middle

of an ocean. I wore a long white burka and a captain's hat as I attempted to navigate my way home by the stars. A blood moon hung in the sky until storm clouds captured it, producing an enraged thunderstorm.

The storm quickly became so powerful that it threatened to capsize my tiny boat. I fought to keep the ship steady until a huge wave blindsided me, knocking me helplessly into the cold water below. My body became heavy as the long burka soaked up the icy sea around me.

But then, a small break appeared in the clouds to the east, revealing a star that shone brightly through the darkness and twinkled like the Christmas Star. I became so captivated by its light that I stopped fighting, resigned to slowly sinking into another world below the ocean's surface. Once I was under the water, the burka formed an image of wings as I floated gently in the reverse sky.

But peace soon gave way to fear as I began to panic for the world above—the only world I knew, the only one that made sense to me. Suddenly, a marine air horn blew. I could hear its low, cello-like call from under the water. The muffled sound convinced me to swim vigorously for the surface, summoning from within me a fighting instinct to live.

As I broke through the water's exterior, gasping for air, a life preserver flew through the blackness and landed within reach of my water-wrinkled hands. Overjoyed, I grasped for it, believing I was finally rescued from the nightmare my voyage had become. But as I gripped the circular lifeline, it disintegrated into tiny pieces between my wet fingers, until it was completely eaten away by the ocean water. Hope had been a lie, and I didn't have the strength to fight anymore.

I bobbed violently in the sea, swallowing the salty liquid, choking desperately. I looked up for that shining star, only to realize the sky had clouded over, and the light was gone. Glancing toward my ship, I saw my father, shaking his head in disappointment, his arms crossed in a perfect X.

"Why have you ignored me?" I cried out in anguish.

"Worthless!" his voice roared like thunder as I awoke.

In my waking hours, I realized I wasn't doing well. I was covered in self-pity like a pall covers a casket. As I drew more inside of myself, cynicism toward the world and the people in it seeped through the cracks of my pain. I began to despise others, mostly for their potential to hurt me, and pushed anyone away who tried to get close to me. It seemed natural to project the way I felt about myself onto the world.

Memories acted as emotional formaldehyde, preserving my pain. The week Ryan and I had spent together during the snowstorm replayed in my head like an old-time silent movie. Lynn's "We are brothers" lie echoed whenever I glanced at the tailgate of my truck. My brother, covered in blood on the floor, would call to me in terror as my dad's screaming made thunder outside.

I wanted something to take it all away. *I could only be happy without my pain,* I thought.

My drinking became more frequent. It tempered the void and made the badness feel like nothing more than a dream.

But somehow that wasn't enough. One night, I took a sharp knife from my bureau and sliced thin, bright red lines into my arm. The slits of blood pooled and dripped rose-colored tears down my arm. There was a strange comfort in releasing the pain I was feeling into the world.

Like mud struck by a celestial bolt of lightning and becoming man, my pain soon began expressing itself in the form of anxiety. Chronic anxiety is cruel. It takes away all your happy associations and cleverly morphs them into fear. It visits you during the most mundane of life experiences, like walking, driving, or socializing with friends. Imagine a thousand-pound lion straddling you, roaring and displaying its massive blood-stained teeth. Now imagine the lion disappears, but you remain in that fear as you drink coffee in a restaurant or work at your desk.

Calm didn't exist for me anymore. I couldn't think straight, couldn't stop my heart from pounding—and the more I chose not to confront the anxiety, the greedier it became.

I came to avoid every situation in which I'd previously been anxious. It got to the point that I couldn't go anywhere, because every place I'd been was associated with that irrational fear in some way.

＝

With Kevin still in rehab, I stopped by Newman's house to bring Mom some pictures she had left at home. In her rush to leave, she'd overlooked them while packing, and had recently asked me to drop them off for her.

When I arrived at the house, I knocked gently on the front door. It felt strange having to knock on my own mother's door. It was as if a new barrier had been permanently placed between us.

No one answered. I tested the knob, and it was unlocked, so I cautiously poked my head inside. "Hey, Mom!" I hollered.

"Hey, Sam! I'm in the kitchen."

My stomach growled as I walked into the kitchen and saw

Mom drinking coffee at the table. For some reason, I always seemed to feel empty when I was around her. "Do you have anything I could eat?"

"Sure," she said. "Get yourself something from the fridge."

I opened the refrigerator door and looked around. There were only a few items, and they were all expired or moldy.

"I can't eat any of this," I moaned. "It's all gone bad!"

"Sorry," she said. "I haven't made it to the grocery store this week."

My hunger pains would have to wait. "It's okay," I said as I shut the door.

While I was there, I talked to Newman about how I had been feeling. I told him everything—things I had kept to myself, things I'd been ashamed of. I have no idea why I chose him—maybe because the wrinkles on his face evoked wisdom and harmlessness. But I was right to choose him. He listened intently, as only an old man can, not saying a word until he was sure I had finished.

When I was done, Newman took a low, troubled breath and looked softly at me with his sky-blue eyes, life-worn around the edges.

"Sam, I'm so sorry for everything you've been through. I really am. I've been in that place before, where you're tormented by the words from someone else's song. I wish I could do something to make that hurt go away. But I think the only way I can help is if you allow me to be honest with you. Can you handle some honesty?"

"Of course," I said, half-lying. I was horrible at taking criticism, much too fragile for it.

"Well, I'm going to give it to you frankly," he said, straightening himself as if preparing for battle. His old back cracked like a slow-bending twig. "I think you're putting too much stock in two things. First—" He pulled one pointer finger tightly back with the other. "You're defining every person and every experience you come across with something negative from your past. You have to stop doing that."

"What do you mean?" I asked.

"Well, it's like this." He spoke slowly, stressing the words he thought most important. "In two separate minds, the exact same world can be Heaven or Hell. The only difference between the two minds is their thought process, the way each defines its experiences. You're caught up in the habit of associating everything in life with something negative. You have to switch that around. That's how you travel from Hell to Heaven—just by thinking positive, accentuating everything with something good. It's kind of like reverse anxiety. Instead of fearing everything, you come to love it all. Trust me, I know. I've done it!"

He paused, looking out the living room window to the sky as if begging it to give him the right words to say. "You know, some people have this defeated feeling inside of 'em, no matter whether they're winning or losing. Truth is, whether you win or lose doesn't matter much. It's how you define the outcome that matters."

I looked at him, exhausted, feeling as if my brain battery had drained to one percent. "Newman, my whole life has been about suffering. Where am I supposed to find these positive things to think about?"

"They're there. They're everywhere! Even if you don't see 'em right now. And if your whole life has been about suffering, then you're blessed, kid! You're further along than most!"

My brow furrowed. "How am I further along?"

"Without some suffering, happiness isn't really possible. Happiness comes from gratitude, from being thankful for the simple things around you."

"Happiness comes from gratitude?" I asked. "It's that uncomplicated?"

"Trust me, if you're grateful, little else matters." He laughed loudly. "Of course, if you're not grateful, little else matters too! It's all about the way you frame things."

His words swam chaotically through my head until understanding began to float to the surface. "So, what's the second thing?" I asked.

Newman scratched the side of his chin. "Second thing?"

"You said I was putting too much stock in *two* things."

"Of course!" He smiled thoughtfully. "I almost forgot! The second thing is this: you're too worried about the way the world defines *you*. You're under the impression that you have to own things or have a special label to be a success, because that's all you've been told by this world. You believe you're a failure if you don't have those things. But that's all nonsense. *You* have to be the definer of you! *You* define the world, not the other way around. Don't give that gift away to anyone or anything. You're trying to make yourself into an idea of what you believe others want you to be, instead of just being happy being you. And that's really how the door opens to things like anxiety, depression, and substance abuse."

"You're right. Sometimes I don't even recognize myself when I'm talking to people. I guess I just want to be special, or maybe loved, and I'm willing to sacrifice my own self for that."

"That's your ego talking." His face looked as sure as rain in

November. "You're already special if you're being you! You don't need to chase someone else's definition of happiness. If you look closely enough at those people who are trying to tell *you* how to be happy, you'll see they aren't so happy themselves."

"That's true," I said.

"Do you know who Ralph Waldo Emerson is?" Newman asked.

"'Self-Reliance,' right?" We had talked about Emerson in school.

"That's right! Good!" His smile was like a priest's smile at a wedding. "Emerson said, 'To be yourself in a world that is constantly trying to make you something else is the greatest accomplishment.' Man, I love that quote! It's something I try to live by every day. A lot of people think they'll find meaning to their lives in the next promotion or the next paycheck. Human beings all yearn to be fulfilled, but we don't understand what we need to be filling ourselves with. Our misguided world tells us that titles and wealth are the answers, so we become ambitious for those things and change who we are to achieve them. Corrupted ambition can be fiercely destructive to your humanity. What's really needed to make you feel whole is authenticity."

My mom burst into the room with a glass of chardonnay in hand. "What in the hell are you two nerds talking about?"

"We're talking, sweetheart, about truths," Newman responded.

"Well, you guys need to relax. Have a drink!"

Mom plopped down on the couch beside Newman as a splash of wine spilled onto her lap, and placed her hand on his knee.

"No beer today, Mom?" I asked. I rarely saw her without one in hand.

"I stopped drinking beer and started drinking chardonnay! I

feel a bit more sophisticated," she said, one eye wider than the other. "It has a higher alcohol percentage, too, so you get a better buzz going! There's something mystical about a good chardonnay, really. It's almost like I can see the world more clearly when I drink it."

"Is that because you have to look at things with one eye closed?" I asked.

Newman laughed and shook his head disapprovingly.

I stood and began walking toward the front door. "Newman, thanks for the talk. I mean that. It really helped."

"No problem, Sam," he said with his head held high. "I'm glad we could do it!"

I looked down at my mom. "Bye, Mom," I said hopelessly.

"Bye, Sam," she mumbled without looking away from her chardonnay.

I walked out the front door and out to my truck. It was a mild, crisp, clear day, the kind of day when you can sit outside for hours and not have to worry about taking off a piece of clothing or putting one on.

"Sam!" Newman called out from the front porch when I was halfway to my truck. "Look at that magnificent sky."

I squinted at the blue canopy, not yet ready for the shining gold light of the sun after being inside so long.

"Some people look at that radiant sky and see all the beauty that this world has to offer, all the beauty they need." His face became serious as he pointed at dark shadows moving bleakly in the distance. "Others look at that same sky and only see those ravenous buzzards circling overhead."

He turned back to face me, satisfied in his metaphor. "Choose to see the beauty, Sam. Feast your eyes on it!"

I looked up and studied the wondrous sky above. Too often I'd taken its simple, awe-inspiring presence for granted. I smiled and waved gratefully to Newman.

"I will! I have a lot to work on, but I will."

On the way home, traffic was backed up due to a car accident. I sat completely still in my truck for what seemed like hours while police and firefighters attended to the crash ahead.

"God, how long will I be on this road?" I griped. An ambulance quickly screamed by, making me cover my ears as it bellowed loudly. *Why am I complaining about a small inconvenience like this?* I thought. *There could be someone hurt up there.*

I put my truck in park and waited contentedly, listening to the radio. One of my favorite songs began to play, so I turned up the volume and sang quietly along with it, thankful in that moment for the simple healing gift of music.

By the time I made it home, the sky had turned coal-black. Clouds blocked even the slightest illumination of stars. I walked into the house through the side door and noticed my dad on the couch in the living room, staring at me snake-eyed as I entered.

"Where you been?" he asked. His tone made a thick lump form in the back of my throat. As I came closer, I noticed his fists were clenched.

"Nowhere. Just out."

"You were at your mother's, weren't you?" he asked, his voice slithering louder.

There was a hostile silence. I could see anger building in his face. A vein along his throat ballooned out, making his skin go purplish-red from the neck up. His normally blue eyes turned an absolute shade of pearly black.

"No, I was just riding around," I told him with a feigned, barely perceptible smile.

"You're a piece-of-shit liar!" he screamed. He sprang up quickly and, in a blink, his face was within an inch of mine.

"What? What's wrong?" I asked, backing away.

"Where are the pictures she left? Did you take them to her?"

I knew I was caught. "Oh, yeah," I stuttered as if I'd forgotten, scratching the back of my head. "I did drop those off for her earlier today."

A light flashed, and all I saw was black.

⇌

I awoke lying on the floor without knowing how I had gotten there. A loud sound like church bells rang in my ears. I could see my dad screaming above me, but I couldn't make out what he was saying because of the ringing. Small globs of sticky white spit flew out of his mouth as he screamed. I tasted the bitter, metallic flavor of blood on my tongue, and mechanically touched my mouth with a finger. When I looked down, it was saturated with what looked like thin, ruby-red raspberry juice.

It took me a second to fully come to. As I did, I instinctively placed my hands in front of my face, anticipating another blow.

"Why can't I see Mom? What's wrong with that?"

I wanted to cry, but I fought it like hell. Instead, I feigned anger, not wanting him to know he could still hurt me.

"Because she's a cheating bitch, and you're just like her! All you want to do is take advantage of me. You want to see her? Go live with her then. I don't want you here anyway! You're a worthless, freeloading bastard."

"I'm sorry!" I shouted. "I didn't know you felt that way! It won't happen again, okay? I promise!"

He ignored me, deaf in his anger. "Oh, wait, that's right! She doesn't want you either! Nobody does! She left the two of you here! Think about that! You're why she's gone in the first place!"

He placed his fist flat against my face, staining his knuckles with my heart's blood. "If it happens again, I swear you'll be sorry! You hear me?" His booming voice changed into a faint, toneless murmur. "I don't care if you live or die—remember that."

He walked away. I stumbled up the stairs like a wounded animal and looked in the mirror that hung on my closet door. A large knot had formed under my left eye. It looked like a chicken egg was trying to pop through my cheekbone.

"I look like the elephant boy," I said to the mirror.

I couldn't see any of the pink on my lips. They were covered in in a mix of dry and wet blood that dripped in parallel lines from each of my nostrils and painted my chin bright red.

Before attempting to clean myself up, I went to pour myself a drink from a bottle of vodka that I kept under my bed.

Damn it, I thought. *I need ice for my drink . . . and my face.* I wasn't sure it was worth the risk, though. I didn't want to pass my dad on the way to get it. I knew just the sight of me could launch him into round two. But I couldn't think clearly, and I needed my drink cold, so I decided ice was a necessity. I'd have to roll the dice.

I snuck down the stairs and heard the muffled sound of a television. Dad was in his room with the door closed. I was safe!

I put ice in a glass and filled a large Ziploc bag with ice as well. As I tiptoed past the dining room table, a familiar face on the front page of our local newspaper caught my attention. I snatched the paper and slid it under my armpit as I hurried back to my room.

Once upstairs, I sat on my bed and stared at the grayscale image of a young man on the front page. It was Lynn, someone I had once loved and wished I still did, decked out in a crisp suit and tie, with a big, fake smile on his face. People who didn't know him wouldn't be able to tell that his smile was fake, but I knew all his expressions well. It was the same smile he used to show his dad when he was asked whether he was going to attend Yale. He was finally playing the role his father had laid out for him, but he appeared dead inside. I wondered if he could feel anything anymore.

Just seeing his picture brought back an ocean of memories. I still resented Lynn for everything that had happened. Not long after Kevin had been shot, I found out Lynn was the one who had told Ramsay about Becky and me. Lynn couldn't foresee everything that would have happened as a result of him exposing that private information, but it was still an awful thing for a friend to do.

I read the article with blood crusting over my swelling face and making it itch. The article reported that Lynn's dad had appointed him vice president of his company. Lynn had received a healthy signing bonus, a six-figure salary with benefits, and opportunities for special compensation based on performance. He was twenty years old.

I could almost see Lynn in my head, dancing like a fly on shit over his new promotion. "Looks like you won the Yale argument," I sighed to the page. "At least you won't have to worry about college. Look how the stars sparkle for you, old friend."

With the paper still in my trembling hands, my arms fell to the bed. Something about the taste of my own blood and seeing Lynn's familiar face suddenly made me feel terribly alone.

I hung my head and closed my eyes as long-hidden, homesick tears began to drip onto my knees.

I soon forced myself to stop. "Not on the inside," I said, the final drops burning the puffy skin around my eyelids. "Don't let them get on the inside."

I thought about what Newman had said earlier that day. "Choose to see the goodness! Positive thinking! Positive thinking!" I attempted to convince the image of myself in the mirror to think positively as my tears dried.

I tried, I really did. But I just couldn't bring myself to think of anything positive. Not in that moment, and not in that place.

—

It was finally day twenty-eight, and time to pick up Kevin from rehab. I was looking forward to seeing him and hearing about all the things he'd experienced. I had missed him considerably while he was away. He was a puzzle piece of my past, and without him around, my life felt less complete.

I left the house an hour and a half early, even though the facility was only thirty minutes away. When I arrived, I saw Kevin in the distance, sitting on the ground with his packed bags flanking him. I could tell he'd been working out—his oval-shaped face was slimmer and his body appeared more defined. He was clean-shaven now and wore black flip-flops with silver basketball shorts and a light blue T-shirt. His face was fresh and vibrant, like a room that's just received a new coat of paint. His eyes glistened cheerfully with a luster I hadn't seen since we were kids.

I hugged him as I got out of my truck, squeezing so tightly that he winced. His smile was honest and genuine. I couldn't remember the last time I had seen an authentic smile on his face.

"Wow, you look great!" I said.

He smacked me playfully on the shoulder. "Thanks, bro; I feel great!"

"How'd you get so big?" I asked, pinching his enlarged bicep.

"Eating well and working out! They have a fantastic gym here. I'm going to join Mount of Olympics Gym when I get home."

"That's awesome!" I said, reaching for one of his bags. "Maybe I'll join too, and we can work out together."

"That'd be great." He looked around like a nervous child. "Sam, let's get out of this place."

He glanced back at the grounds and the buildings around us.

"You going to miss it?"

He gazed silently at me as if struggling to determine his answer. "No," he finally said, reaching for the handle on the door of my truck. "Let's go!"

On the ride home, Kevin told me that one of the best things about being at the facility had been how peaceful the environment was. He said the lack of chaos was unusual at first, but he'd quickly come to embrace it. Every morning, he walked the trails all around the property. It reminded him of walking the tracks behind our house.

"So many memories from the past lingered during those walks—things I hadn't thought about in years," he said. "It was hard to encounter some of it."

After his walks, Kevin would go to the gym and work out for half an hour on good days, and an hour on bad ones. He'd had a lot of downtime, which, he explained, was an important part of the wellness process.

"I'd go to group therapy sessions in the afternoon, and in the evening, I'd do one-on-one treatment."

"What'd you talk about? If you don't mind me being nosy."

He looked out at the road ahead. "Mostly about factors contributing to addiction, like family issues and stuff. We also talked a lot about addiction's impact on your body, mind, and spirit. I've never learned so much about myself in such a short amount of time. They taught us more about philosophy than I initially thought they would, too, which I enjoyed. It changed my perspective on some things."

I nodded and flashed an impressed, upside-down smile. "Was it difficult?"

"I stopped drinking and taking the pills cold turkey, and on the second or third day, the feelings I'd been suppressing with them began to creep to the surface." He placed his hands at his neck as if he was about to choke himself. "I felt like there was something alive inside my chest, scratching my insides to get out, and the only way to stop it was to get a drink. That was the hardest thing for me to deal with. I wanted a beer so bad, I could hardly stand it. Just so I wouldn't have to face those things."

A barely noticeable rainbow appeared in the distance. Surprised by its unexpected arrival, I pointed to it, and Kevin smiled. We sat quietly in thought for a moment.

"I know this is weird," I said, "but that right there is something that always makes me think of Ryan."

He glanced at me like I had worms crawling out of my ears. "What?"

"The rainbow." I looked at the open road ahead.

"The rainbow? Yeah, it's beautiful, I guess," he said, squirming uncomfortably in his seat.

"I hate rainbows. They remind me of how I felt when I was with Ryan, before—"

"You really loved her, huh?" Kevin interrupted, sounding genuinely surprised.

"Oh, yeah. She was my first love," I said softly. "It was like a fairy tale or something. I was wrapped around her little finger. She made the world bearable, more hopeful, gave it beauty or something—just like that stupid rainbow."

"A rainbow's just an illusion. Just refraction of light, not actual light. The sun and the rain are what's real." Kevin straightened up in his seat. "You know what I learned back there?"

"What?"

"You have to love yourself first. Then you won't need someone so desperately. When you forget about finding love from others and focus on discovering it in yourself, that's when the right person will come along. It will be even better than anything you've ever imagined. And it'll be real, not an illusion, because it will be for the right reasons."

"Damn, Kevin! You really did get all philosophical, huh?" I joked. "How'd you learn all this stuff?"

"They assigned me a mindfulness coach too," he said, laughing. "Deepest dude I ever met!"

"What's that, a mindfulness coach?"

"They show you how to focus your thoughts on what's around you without creating judgment in a negative way. And how to focus on the present moment rather than rehashing the past or imagining the future," he said as we pulled into our driveway.

I helped him grab his bags from the truck bed. A train passed by the house and blew its whistle as if to welcome Kevin home.

"Here we go!" he said with a nervous smile. Then he froze, staring at the house.

"You okay?"

"Dad," he answered. "They said this would be the hardest part of coming back."

We walked through the door—and there he was, standing in the living room, watching TV. The blackout shades were all closed, and it was dark in the room. Dad's body reflected the pale blue tint of the television screen. He glanced over his shoulder as we walked in.

"Well, you're back!" he announced, laughing wildly. "Want some Vicodin?"

All Kevin could muster was a brisk, "Hey." He scurried up the stairs, and I followed.

We walked into his room together and threw his bags on his bed.

"Don't listen to him. He can burn in hell."

"Have you ever thought about why everybody thinks of Hell as hot?" Kevin asked with a vacant expression. "An intense cold is worse than extreme heat to me. I envision Hell as a place that's stone-cold."

Kevin did amazingly after returning home. He began working out at the gym on his first day back, and went on long, contemplative walks down the tracks each morning. He ate a lot of sweets—about a whole box of Lucky Charms a day—but he still looked fit and slim. He even said he was searching for a job and thinking about applying to a technical school. It was the most content I'd ever seen him.

The week after Kevin returned from rehab, Dad went out of town for two whole weeks. It was great not having him around. Kevin and I agreed that the house was actually quite pleasant without him in it.

Mom stopped by to see Kevin while Dad was away. When she mentioned she was coming by, I thought she was crazy. I believed my dad would literally kill her, and possibly Kevin and I as well, if he found out she'd been inside his house without his knowledge.

I heard her knocking on Kevin's door when she arrived and went over to join them.

"Hey, Sammy!" she said. It was obvious she'd had a couple of cocktails before coming over—and not just because I had never heard her call me Sammy before. "How are you, my boy?"

A twelve-pack of beer sat beside her feet on the floor.

"What are you doing?" I asked through clenched teeth.

She lifted her drink and hugged my brother clumsily with one arm. "Kevin and I are going to celebrate. He's back!"

Kevin looked in her direction, avoiding eye contact and grinning nervously.

"Mom, are you celebrating Kevin coming back from rehab by bringing him beer?"

She looked at me like I was crazy. "A couple beers isn't going to hurt anybody, Sam!"

I was disgusted at the lack of sensitivity, or even awareness, she showed to his issues. I grabbed her by the arm and pointed to the door with my other hand. "Get out," I said in a low tone.

"Sam, it's okay," Kevin interrupted.

"No, it's not okay. Mom, take your drinks and get the hell out!"

"I am your mother!" she said as if I was joking. "You're supposed to respect your mother."

When someone uses a title, you know they're doing it to manipulate you for their own purposes. Her attempt at this made me even angrier.

A baseball bat leaned against the wall in the corner of Kevin's bedroom. I picked it up and calmly placed it on my shoulder. I had passed normal anger and was now approaching something more like a raging madness, so livid that I couldn't even yell. In a cold, monotone voice, I said, "If you don't get out of here right now, I'm going to take this baseball bat and knock the shit out of you with it."

They both looked at me in shock, unsure whether to laugh or to run. Without taking her eyes off me, Mom slowly stood up, clumsily grabbed her beer, and hurried down the stairs without saying another word. I heard the front door slam shut.

Kevin burst out laughing. "Damn! That was hilarious!"

I erupted in laughter as well. "Well, it worked. What in the hell is wrong with her?"

"She's actually better than before," he said. "I'll say this: Newman makes her happy, and he respects her. She's never experienced something like that before. She's happier than I've ever seen her."

I put the baseball bat back in its place in the corner. "I guess Newman is good for her; or at least he's better than the low bar Dad set. But if she's so happy, why's she still drinking so much?"

Kevin paused for a moment. His eyes drooped apprehensively as he gazed out his window and into a sober sky, as if seeing into some distant future. Almost achingly, he said, "Addiction is a really hard thing to kick, Sam."

8

The Sound of Silence

"'Fools,' said I, 'you do not know, silence like a cancer grows.'"
—Simon & Garfunkel

You never forget your first true love. It becomes a lasting part of the person you become. It attaches a truth onto your heart that acts like some kind of immortal gospel. That first love is like the ocean, and every person you meet after that is like a boat sailing on its surface. All that forever follows is painted purely in the reflection of *the one*.

My mom's first experience with love had been terrible. Her second experience, judged against the first, made Newman look like a knight in shining armor, even if he was thirty years older than her. He was everything my dad wasn't: kind, considerate, supportive, and loving. But the sad facts were there, too. Mom had cheated on my dad with Newman. I had a hard time processing exactly how to feel about it all.

She and I only discussed the affair once.

"Mom, I can't believe you just left us the way you did. That wasn't right." The words burst out of my mouth like a geyser.

"Sam, how long can you go without love before you go looking for it elsewhere? Days, weeks? Years?" she asked.

"That's not the point! The way you did it was dirty."

She shook her head dismissively. "You're too young to understand! There was no intimacy, no mental or emotional support. It was hell!"

"I understand feeling unappreciated. But the way you went about it was all wrong. You should have left Dad a long time ago if you weren't happy, not waited years and then split as soon as someone new showed you a little attention!"

Her words shot out like firecrackers. "There was never a 'thank you,' a 'please,' or even an 'I love you'! Holidays and birthdays came, and I didn't receive a thing, not even a kind word or two!"

"I know," I said, "and that made you feel neglected. I get that. But you're using cheater's logic. The way you left, and how you went about it, was just plain wicked."

A part of me wanted to punish her for leaving Kevin and me alone with Dad. However dysfunctional, we were a family. We were supposed to be in it together. She couldn't see what she'd done as bad because, for her, it had led to something that felt good.

I think Newman recognized how I felt and understood. My feelings were even more confusing because I liked Newman. He was smart, philosophical, insightful—and best of all, a great listener.

Time didn't care about my feelings, though. Life went on. Mom stayed at Newman's, and Kevin and I remained in that sweltering house with Dad.

Kevin was never able to get close to Newman after Mom left. He just stopped talking to them completely. I visited their house from time to time, and even had dinner with them occasion-ally. Sometimes, I'd call their house asking to speak to my mom knowing she wasn't there, just to talk to Newman.

I remember one January conversation like it was yesterday. I had called Newman that day, slyly asking for my mom. He had told me she was at bingo—which I already knew, of course.

"Hey, how are things going?" Newman asked. "That voice in your head saying good things instead of bad?"

"It's actually going pretty slow. Now that I pay more atten-tion to it, I realize how negative I've been about everything all the time—including myself. When I try to switch those thoughts to positive ones, the bad sneak right back in somehow."

"It's great that you've started. I'm so proud of you! Always remember: the greatest forest in the world started as one small seed, and the world's oceans started as a single drop of rain. It will take time and patience, but don't lose hope."

"I know. I guess I just thought it would be simpler."

"You're in the habit of negative self-talk. It took a long time to form that tendency—most likely a lifetime. Now you have to develop a new pattern of thinking. It's going to take a little while, but trust me: one day you'll wake up and realize your whole life has been painted in totally different colors."

I loved the way Newman spoke about things. He was always so optimistic. I wasn't used to adults being that way.

"Newman, were you always so hopeful?" I asked. "You seem eternally positive. Have you always been like that?"

He softly cleared his throat, and his voice weakened. "I went through things similar to what you're going through right now. When I was a kid, my father was an alcoholic. He was kind when he was sober, but when he got drunk, he was mean as hell! One night, he had too much to drink and stumbled out into our garage alone. I heard what I thought was a firecracker go off and went out to investigate it. I found him lying next to our jon boat with a gunshot wound to his head. His walnut-colored Winchester Model 21 shotgun lay beside him on the cold cement floor. It still had smoke rising from its midsection, like an eerie fog. Half his face was gone."

"Wow," was all I could summon.

"I was only twelve years old. My mom had to raise four kids all alone after that, and I was the youngest. A lot of my dreams fell by the wayside. To make matters worse, a couple years after his suicide—when I was about your age actually—I got a girl pregnant."

"What?" I gasped. "I never knew you had a kid."

"It was a one-night stand kind of thing. I was doing bad things and running around with the wrong crowd, and the girl said she didn't want me to have a relationship with the kid. She said she'd already picked out who she wanted the father to be. She left town shortly after that, and I never saw her again. Right now, I have a child out there somewhere who I've never met and who probably doesn't even know I exist. It's heartbreaking."

"I had no idea you'd gone through so much," I said, my voice disbelieving. "How'd you get to where you are now? Most people would have become cynical after . . . after all that."

Newman was quiet for a moment. Then, with a short sigh, he said, "Well, my mom wrote me a letter when I was at my lowest point. That got me started on the right track. But I really began to change after opening my first book. Books opened my eyes to a world I didn't know existed. They showed me I didn't have a monopoly on pain. I'd always hung around people who were similar to me, so I never really grew as a person. You stop improving when you only associate with people who are just like you. Books challenged my thinking about everything and introduced me to people who were very different than I was. They made my life richer and fuller, and helped to heal some broken parts of me that I'd kept hidden. They're like people, in a way. You take a part of them with you, especially the good ones, for the rest of your life. They're the puzzle pieces of who you become. With each new story, I found myself a little bit more, and with every word, I became more comfortable with who I was."

"I wish I read more," I said. "I get so busy that I feel like I just don't have time."

Newman chuckled. "Don't ever get so busy chasing the wrong things that you miss out on enjoying the right things, Sam."

"It had to be more than just reading books that changed you," I insisted. I sat down on my bed and put my feet up.

"Of course; every big thing is just a combination of little things. I also developed a meaningful relationship with God. I was raised Catholic and always considered myself religious, but the rituals became a turnoff for me."

"I feel that way too sometimes," I said.

"The church never made me feel close to God. It seemed more like a social club for humans than a conduit for worship. I didn't like the idea of only acknowledging God one day a week, so I decided to acknowledge Him in every moment of every day."

"How so?"

"Well, if I ate hot dogs, I was as thankful to Him as if I were eating steak. If I was waiting at the DMV, I was as thankful as if I were on a beautiful beach with my toes in the sand. Believe it or not, making that small change in my thinking completely changed my life."

Hearing Newman speak made me think about how different he was from my mom. I decided I'd take the opportunity to ask him a question I'd had since he first came into our lives.

"Can I ask you something without you getting upset?"

"Of course," he said.

"Why are you with my mom? I mean, you had an alcoholic father, and your previous wife was an alcoholic. You seem like a pretty decent guy. What do you see in her?"

He paused and let out a short, uncomfortable snort. "Well, happiness is social as well as personal. As humans, we're happier when we connect with others. I'll admit that part of my initial attraction to your mom was to ward off loneliness. Loneliness is like a predator that stalks you and slowly eats away at your joy in being. But somewhere along the line, I really fell in love with her. Maybe because of my father, I try to save people like her."

"I think we're attracted to what's familiar," I offered.

"That's true." He spoke softer and uneasily now. "That's why I worry about you sometimes. I don't want you to end up attracted to someone who hurts you, because on some level, a part of you finds comfort in the familiarity of that behavior. I want you to find someone who will see how good you are and treat you the way you deserve to be treated."

I was shocked he thought I was a good person. People never told me things like that—especially not adults. His words lit something inside me, warming me from within.

I looked at the clock on my nightstand and realized it was almost two in the afternoon.

"Alright, Newman. I hate to end this, but I have to go. You going to watch the game tonight?"

"I am," he said. "I'll tell your mother you called."

At first I didn't understand what he meant. Then I remembered I had initially called asking to speak to her.

"Okay, thanks! Hey, who are you pulling for tonight?"

"Green Bay, of course!" he said enthusiastically. "You?"

"I'm going with Chicago."

"I'll make you a deal," Newman offered, his voice sounding wily. "If Chicago wins, I'll rent a beach house this summer for just the two of us. We'll leave everybody else at home! What do you say?"

I couldn't believe what I had just heard. I was ecstatic! It felt good to have something big like that to hope for.

"I say that sounds awesome! But what if Green Bay wins? That's a pretty big bet!"

"If Green Bay wins, then you have to read all the books on my bookshelf," he said. "Every last one!"

"Sure! Deal!" I shouted into the phone. "I'm in!"

Newman laughed. "Alright, I'll be watching!"

"Okay! Take care, Newman!" I told him, beaming. "And thanks for everything!"

"Anytime, son."

The way he called me "son" made chill bumps materialize on my arm.

"Bye, Newman!" I said.

I'm pretty sure I heard laughter as Newman closed our time together with, "Goodbye, Sam. Good luck to you!"

⌁

I don't recall what time it was when my mom called me that evening. I figured Newman had told her I had phoned earlier, and she was calling me back.

"Hello?" I said, slightly annoyed that she was interrupting the football game.

"Sam!" Mom screamed so loudly that I had to pull the phone away from my ear. "I think Newman is gone! Can you please come over here?"

"What? What do you mean gone?" I asked. "Gone where?"

"I don't have time! I just—please, come over here! I don't want to be alone in this," she begged.

I jumped up from my sofa, searching for my keys. "Okay, I'm on my way."

I raced to my truck, frantically started it up, and burned tires on the way out of the driveway. I made it quickly to the tracks, and my tires shrieked as I hit my brakes hard. The gate was down, and the tail end of a passenger train was passing slowly by. A bell hanging on the caboose rang loudly in the misty night air.

When the crossing sign stopped blinking and the gate ascended, I sped off again, bouncing wildly over the tracks.

"Thank you, Lord!" I said as I passed over them, the gate still rising.

My stomach growled as I drove feverishly to Mom's house. I looked to the passenger seat for a split second and saw a pack of cheese crackers. I grabbed them, ripped the bag open with my teeth, and threw an entire cracker into my mouth as I drove.

I arrived in my mom's neighborhood in record time. It was dark out, and the absence of the new moon made the night seem blacker than usual. As I reached the final turn, I saw red lights dancing off the still faces of the nearby houses.

My heart sank as I arrived to the sight of an ambulance and two police cars in Mom's driveway.

I parked halfway in the ditch by the mailbox and rushed

through the front door.

A police officer stood beside Mom in the living room. He glanced at me without making eye contact as I walked in, his face awash with empathy.

I turned to face the kitchen and saw three paramedics frantically administering CPR. My view of their patient was blocked by the breakfast island that separated the living room from the kitchen. With all those people moving wildly about in the house, I expected more noise—but in its place, a damp and eerie silence fell like a cold rain.

I need to find Newman's rosary! I thought. I had seen him praying with it many times, and wanted him to have it in that moment. I don't know why—I think I just felt like I had to do something.

As I passed the kitchen to search for the pearly white beads in his room, I glanced back at the paramedics. The bottoms of Newman's huge, bare feet stared at me as I walked by in what felt like slow motion. He was flat on his back, and his pale, bloated stomach was exposed, blowing up like a balloon as the paramedics pushed hard on his chest. A small bottle of orange juice lay near his limp right arm, the liquid spilling across the linoleum floor.

I searched Newman's room and couldn't find the rosary anywhere, so I rushed to the den, where he liked to watch TV. The game flashed on the screen, happy fans screaming wildly as oversized players tried to break one another. I looked around Newman's favorite recliner, noticing its plush rolled arms had worn down so much, they were molded into the shape of Newman's forearms. The rosary, though, was nowhere to be found.

Suddenly, I heard a commotion in the living room, like metal hitting metal.

I walked quickly out of the den to find the paramedics carrying Newman out of the house on a stretcher. Newman's familiar face gaped statically in my direction, his mouth open as if suspended in an endless yawn. Half-open eyes peered at me like black holes. The light that once shone in them was gone, so that they mirrored the new-moon night. Those clever old eyes that had brought me so much peace now stared blankly, fixed in an eerie, mannequin-like gaze.

"Do you want to ride with me or in the ambulance?" I asked my mom.

"With you," she said, grabbing my arm tightly.

We beat the ambulance to the emergency room and rushed through the same slow-moving doors I had rushed through on the night Kevin had been shot. I headed straight to the front desk and told an old lady with purple hair who we were. With the kindest smile I'd ever seen, she asked us to take a seat in the waiting room.

I sat down next to my mom as she looked straight ahead into empty space. "He's gone," she murmured. "He's gone."

"We don't know that yet. Let's let them work on him," I told her softly. "What happened?"

She spoke in a low monotone. "Before I left for bingo, he asked me to pick up some milk on my way home, so I stopped by the grocery store. When I pulled into the driveway, all the lights in the house were off, even though it was dark outside, and I began to worry. He always kept every light on in the house at night. But I told myself I had to stop thinking bad thoughts, that he was probably just in the back room. Then, when I opened the side door, I saw him just lying there in the darkness. I dropped the milk and flipped on the light switch. I knelt by him and shook his arms and called his name. I could feel that he was still warm, so I ran to the phone and dialed 911."

A couple burst through the emergency room doors with a small child in tow. They began speaking in loud Spanish to the purple-haired lady at the front desk.

I turned back to Mom, and she continued. "I couldn't dial the numbers at first, but eventually I got someone. The man who answered said to start administering CPR, and I told him I didn't know how. He talked me through it, but I don't think I was pushing hard enough. I kept telling him, 'Honey, he's gone; honey, he's gone!' I don't know why I called him 'honey.' He kept asking me, over and over, to continue doing the chest compressions. But like I said, though, I don't think I pushed hard enough. As soon as the paramedics arrived, they took over, and that's when I called you. I don't even remember how they got into the house."

Mom was still speaking when a voice called out Newman's last name. We stood up, looking around nervously, and found a young nurse motioning for us to follow her.

We walked down a long, bright hallway filled with free-flowing, incandescent light. A hospital chaplain came out of a side room and trailed awkwardly behind us. My mom looked back at the chaplain as if she were the Grim Reaper.

"See?" she whispered, darkly assured. "He's gone."

"Come on, this way," I said, placing my hand on the small of her back and guiding her forward.

The nurse directed us to a room with a small sign that seemingly announced our fate positioned by the front door—*Family Grieving Room*. The room was dark and shadowy, a sharp contrast to the luminous hallway we'd just traversed. Black tissue boxes stood like sad statues on each table in the room.

After a couple of minutes, a short, bald doctor with a horse face and a serious expression entered the room and sat in front of my mom.

"Are you his daughter?" he asked her.

"His wife," she responded faintly, without looking up.

"Oh, I'm sorry." The doctor paused and glanced uneasily at me. Mom had been right. I heard what the doctor had to say without hearing it. His expression said it all. Newman *was* gone.

The doctor placed his hands together, locked his fingers, and turned back to Mom. "We lost him," he said. "I'm very sorry."

She stared at her knees and said nothing. Most likely, she believed this was just another problem she could ignore, and it would somehow go away.

The doctor asked if Newman had experienced any medical problems in the past. Mom tapped her chest lightly and said almost silently, "Heart."

The doctor looked confidently at us. "It was most likely a massive heart attack. With his age and medical history, I would recommend against it, but would you like an autopsy performed?"

Mom's eyes opened quickly, wide and confused, as if she'd just been stung by a hornet. After a few long seconds, clearly disturbed in thought, she gently shook her head no.

"I'm very sorry for your loss," the doctor said. "Would you like to see him?"

Mom was only capable of a whisper. "Yes."

The chaplain led us to a large, open room that I assumed was the trauma unit. Random, high-pitched beeps echoed through the massive space, sounding like a flock of birds chirping in a field. A group of fatigued-seeming nurses watched silently as we walked toward a sea of blue curtains. The chaplain gently pulled back one of the baby-blue sheets, and there was Newman, lying on a metal hospital bed, his face set in the same half-closed, empty stare as before. A needle had been inserted into his wrist, and a small pool of blood had dripped from it and collected on the chalky-white floor below him.

Couldn't they have cleaned that up at least, or closed his eyes before we came in? I thought.

There was nothing to do but stand there, paralyzed, in naked silence. After a few minutes, the chaplain limply asked, "Would you like me to pray?"

Mom reluctantly rocked her head up and down.

I don't remember what the prayer was about. I remember the nurses talking outside the curtains and laughing at some private joke. I stared into Newman's listless eyes and walked up to him in the middle of the prayer, gently squeezing his stiff, cold hand in mine.

"Thank you, Newman," I muttered. And as if in a dream, I could hear a faraway echo of his voice whisper back: "Thank *you*, son."

I turned and walked out of the room of blue curtains, leaving my mom and the chaplain sedated in prayer.

As I walked through the waiting area, heading for the exit, my attention was captured by a softly glowing television screen suspended from the ceiling. Scrolling across the bottom, a graphic displayed the final score of the playoff football game that night:

Green Bay 21, Chicago Bears 14.

Alone and without warning, under those shining, incandescent lights, tears began to fill my eyes. Newman had won our bet.

I suddenly didn't know what to do or where to go, so I did the first thing that came to my mind. I went fishing.

The days after Newman's sudden death passed by in a cloudy blur—but one strong memory did burn itself solidly into my consciousness, on the morning after he left us. I remember watching a cheerful sun ascend from its usual place in the heavens and questioning indignantly how it had the audacity to show its face at such a sad time. *A light has been taken from our lives, and yet the sun still shines? Doesn't the universe care?*

In hindsight, my response was irrational and egocentric. But in that moment of raw emotion, it seemed logical and justified. My young mind wanted to believe that somehow, the universe was still on my side.

Mom made a mess of her grief, so I did as much as I could for her. I met with the funeral director, who reminded me more of the Crypt Keeper than he did a living, compassionate human being. I picked out the casket: mahogany with a creamy interior. I chose the navy-blue suit in which Newman would be buried. I called the Social Security Administration, Newman's pension provider, and Medicare to notify them of Newman's passing. I also took his death certificate to the bank and had all his finances transferred into my mom's name.

The second day after his passing, Mom asked in a drowsy haze if I would take Newman's clothes away. She said she couldn't bear the smell of them anymore. I think she loved the scent because it somehow kept him there in the house—and she just couldn't handle that.

I took Newman's clothes to the Goodwill in oversized black trash bags with bright yellow drawstrings. As I unpacked them,

I became increasingly uneasy. I worried what Newman would wear if the universe realized what it had done and somehow let him come back. What if Newman's death was just a hallucinogenic dream I was having, and I was giving away all his clothes based on a horrifying illusion? I knew he'd be upset with me if he came back, so I saved a pair of his underwear, a pair of white socks with red stripes at the tops, a pair of cream-colored Nike tennis shoes, a blue shirt with "Jennette's Pier" printed on the front, and a pair of khaki pants. I folded everything and stacked it neatly in a pile on the floor of his closet in anticipation of his possible return.

I slept on the living room floor at Mom's house that first week, and was awoken one night to her shouting in her sleep.

"If you're going to leave, damn it, just go!" she screamed. "Don't you dare think you can just lag around here!"

Each morning, as soon as she woke, Mom began drinking. She'd always had an excuse to drink at night and on the weekends; now she had an excuse to drink in the mornings too. She repeated over and over that she loved Newman, and rambled about how she couldn't believe he was gone. We spent hours acting out morbid scenes of what his final moments must have been like, trying to make sense of the senseless. He must have fallen very hard. We realized that the exact spot where he had fallen was the only place in the house where the wood in the floor creaked. The squeaking, like the sound of a mother sparrow protesting an egg missing from her nest, was a macabre reminder of that sad day which the house would forever hold onto.

The night before the funeral, I sat in Newman's room with the door closed and stared at the multitude of books on his bookshelf. There were all the familiar classics: *The Grapes of Wrath, Adventures of Huckleberry Finn, The Old Man and the Sea,* and *Moby Dick.* But there were also various books on history, psychology, sociology, and religion. I saw the name Ralph Waldo Emerson on the spine of a thick, antique-looking brown book and slid it out. Inside, Newman had underlined multiple passages.

I sat silently on the edge of his bed and read every one of them. As I flipped through the pages, an old, yellowing piece of paper slipped out and gently fell to my lap. On it, Newman had written excerpts from the book. At the top of the paper, he had scribbled the word "Favorites."

I read the ghostly quotes silently to myself, savoring their timeless lessons, almost able to hear Newman's voice reciting each one. Then I stood back and viewed the entire bookshelf.

It was an impressive collection. No doubt each book had been transformative, developing Newman into the man he had become.

"A bet's a bet," I said to myself as I grabbed one from the top shelf to begin my own transformation.

—

The day of Newman's funeral, a gentle snow fell from a dull gray sky. The snow spread out like an endless nothing, making the ground look as if it had pulled a cotton blanket over itself to keep warm.

When we walked into the chapel where Newman rested, I saw that the immense room was filled with people, most of whom I didn't recognize. Flowers were everywhere, each with a distinct scent, all repulsive. Their strong odors bombarded my sinuses and made me nauseous. I'd never understood why people would send someone flowers after his death, but never do the same for the living people they knew. It seemed to me that such a gesture would be more beneficial to the latter.

During the service, the priest boldly asked the congregation to stand to share a memory of Newman—something we had specifically asked him not to do when he brought up the idea the day before. Everyone sat in uncomfortable silence, the monotony of it broken only by a stray cough and the crinkly sound of someone fumbling with a cough drop wrapper. I worried that no one would share anything, so I timidly raised my hand.

"Yes, son. Please, share your memory with us," the priest said, smiling approvingly.

I stood in the pew and turned to view the congregation. I paused and looked down sullenly at my mom. Her expression was heartbreaking, as if she'd just been abandoned by her new puppy. She stared idly at the tissue she held in her lap, her face gray as the sky outside and defined by a tender grief.

"Last night," I began with a nervous stutter, "I read a few pages of a book from the bookshelf in Newman's bedroom. The book was by C.S. Lewis, and Newman had underlined a passage that said, 'Humility is not thinking less of yourself. It's thinking of yourself less.' That's the person Newman was. He showed me what a kind, honest, and unselfish love looks like, and he did it with his actions, not just his words. For that, I am truly and forever grateful to him. When he saw I wasn't feeling good about myself, he thought of himself less and tried to make me see that I was special. He'd listen to me for hours and offer guidance along the way, expecting nothing of material value in return.

"In a book about Teddy Roosevelt, I found he had highlighted a passage that said, 'Do what you can, with what you have, where you are.' Above that highlighted passage, he wrote the words, 'The Key.' On many occasions, he encouraged me to do just that in whatever surroundings I found myself. Newman taught me that I could find goodness anywhere—mostly in the seemingly simplest of things. He taught me there was more value in a child's smile than in any material possession. And if a friend doesn't act like one, they don't deserve that label."

I could feel tears pressing against the bottoms of my eyes, but I continued. "I'm going to miss him a lot. But I'm thankful for the time I got to spend with him. I only wish I'd told him that while he was still here.

"We talked a lot about Ralph Waldo Emerson. Newman absolutely adored him. I found a piece of paper inside one of his books last night with some of his favorite quotes by Emerson written on it. I think they're appropriate for this occasion, and that he'd love for me to share them with you. If you knew Newman, you can almost hear the sound of his voice uttering these words."

I took the yellowed piece of paper from my pocket and read the words written in Newman's own distinct handwriting.

"'It is not length of life, but depth of life that matters. Never lose an opportunity of seeing anything beautiful, for beauty is God's handwriting. With the past, I have nothing to do; nor with the future. I live now. Write it on your heart that every day is the best day in the year. Nobody can bring you peace but yourself.'"

As I closed with those words, I spun awkwardly and took my seat on the hard wooden pew, glancing at my mother. She nodded and smiled as tears dripped down her delicate face.

The night of the funeral, we went back to Mom's house to

sleep. As soon as we got there, she sat at the kitchen table and poured herself a glass of her go-to, chardonnay.

"I had a vivid dream last night," she said as she took her first sip, looking almost frightened. "I was a child again in my parents' old house. I had beautiful butterfly wings, only one was broken, so I couldn't fly like everyone else. My mother had green skin and was dressed head to toe in leathery black clothes. She gave me a cup of hot chocolate and made me mix it with a strong drug, or some type of poison. Then she told me to drink it. I trusted her, so I drank it and fell into a deep sleep.

"I woke up trapped in a small, dark box no bigger than a casket. I banged on the walls, trying to get out, but they closed in on me with each strike.

"Then a tall man with no face arrived on horseback outside the box. I could see him through a small hole near my face. He was dressed in a cloak as white as the snow on the ground today. He was wearing a hood, and where his face should have been, there was nothing but flaky skin. He released me by shooting an ivory arrow into the box's lock. When I opened the lid and stood up, he lifted his hand above his head, and a bright light came out of his palm and shone all around me. It was so bright, I had to close my eyes.

"Eventually the glow faded, and when I opened my eyes, my old life had been completely transformed. I was somewhere new. I can't even fully describe it! It was a place that was pure and beautiful, without any pain, or sickness, or suffering! I could feel a maternal presence there protecting me, but it wasn't my mom. Somehow I knew she was gone forever.

"I started crying. I wasn't sad, though—I was happy. The man with no face came slowly toward me. He wiped away my tears, and then I heard a voice. It was a woman, I think. She called me her dear child, and told me to fly.

I tried to yell that I couldn't. I told them my wing was broken. But the voice told me to look again. It sounded so kind.

"I looked down at my wing. It had a scar, but it had been healed! I started flapping, and rose off the ground. It was so easy. I could finally fly just like everyone else!"

She paused and took a large swallow of her chardonnay. It seemed to burn her throat as she swallowed. Her face scrunched up, and she cleared her throat forcefully after washing the liquid down. "When I woke up, I wanted to go back to sleep. I wanted to live in that place a little longer. Maybe forever. Do you . . ." She paused and looked at me innocently, the way a child looks to a parent for an answer to a magical question. "Do you think the man with no face was Newman?"

I was exhausted. Mentally, physically, and emotionally, I was drained. I liked Newman, but I didn't want to hear any more about how much Mom loved him or how great he was. Especially since I never heard her say those things about us.

Without thinking, I snapped. "No, Mom, I don't think it was Newman! I think it was Death. We all have death on our minds from everything we've been through in the past week. The no-faced man taking you to that place was Death!"

I could see my words pierce her like a sword. She held back tears as she focused her eyes on her wineglass in front of her.

"I'm sorry," I said. "I didn't mean that. My brain is fried with all this darkness."

"It's okay. I understand," she said, taking another swallow. "You've been great. Thanks for being with me through this whole thing. I just loved him so much." She sounded hopeless.

"Who's going to love me now?"

"Mom, we love you. We've always loved you!"

She took another slow sip of her cold wine. "Everything keeps changing," she said softly into her glass. Then, even softer, she said, "I hate change."

A nostalgic smile came to my face. "You know what Newman once told me about change?"

Her face lit up like a Christmas tree. "What?"

Performing my best Newman imitation, I said, "'The objective isn't to block the waves of change; that's impossible! The goal is to learn to surf its waves. Turn change into moments of opportunity, and fall in love with the ride.'"

She smiled as if she could hear Newman speaking the words right there in the room with us. "Aw. That sounds just like him," she said.

"Yes, it does."

Her expression quickly faded back to sorrow. "It's bittersweet, though, isn't it?"

"What?" I asked.

"Change."

Mom believed that as long as nothing changed in her life, she couldn't be hurt by it. "Yes, it is," I said thoughtfully. "It gives you hope, though, you know? Hope to hold onto. Right when you get pushed to the edge, there's the comfort that you can always choose a new road, no matter how long the night's been."

"Even when everything seems wrong?" she asked behind dark, charcoal-like eyes.

"Even when everything seems wrong."

She banged both fists on the table. "I should have known

this would happen, with his age. I should have avoided him. I didn't know it would be this hard."

I placed my hand on one of her closed fists. "I know. I'm sorry, I really am. But you had to give it a try, right? If we're afraid to fall, what good is there in even being here?"

She finished her drink in a final swig, as if trying to kill an aching pain inside of her. "It's been a long day, Sam. Let's go to sleep."

"I'm too tired to sleep," I said, my eyes raw with fatigue.

Mom smiled. "Me too."

She breathed in, pushed herself up, and without saying another word, began to walk to her bedroom.

"Mom!" I called out.

She slowly rotated and looked at me solemnly, with disheartened eyes, as if she were a child and her favorite toy had been taken from her. "Yes?"

"We love you. You're not alone. Give time a chance. It'll help."

She nodded, and then peered down at the spot where Newman had fallen. "I know. Thank you. Goodnight."

I could tell, though, that she didn't *really* know. It was like I was light-years away from her. Her expression betrayed her true thoughts. Anytime my brother and I told her we loved her, anytime we said anything positive, for whatever unknown, destructive reason, all she heard was an empty silence.

I went home early the next day, before Mom woke up. It was time to get back to our normal lives—or get to creating a new normal.

When I arrived home, I noticed Dad's car wasn't in the driveway. I went straight to Kevin's room to find out why.

"Where's Dad?" I asked.

"He's out of town for two weeks!"

I felt as if we'd just won the lottery. "Two weeks?!" I shouted.

Kevin's arms shot up, his fingers in Vs in a Nixonian victory celebration. "Yep!"

"Awesome!" I reveled. Then I asked, "Did you tell him about Newman?"

The joy drained from his triumphant face. "Yeah, I told him. He laughed and said he was glad the piece of shit was gone. Said he'd wished for it to happen."

"That was sweet of him."

"He also said he hopes Mom is next."

"Good ole Dad!" I said. "A heart paved with rubies and sapphires!"

"More like fire and brimstone," Kevin replied.

I'd believed even Dad couldn't go as low as saying hateful things about a man who had just paid life's ultimate price, but Kevin and I tried to make a joke out of the situation, like always. Humor was our hearts' defense mechanism. If we could laugh at the misery around us, then we weren't its victims.

—

I called Mom that night to check on her. I could tell she was very drunk. She slurred her words and spoke slowly, repeating bizarre, mumbled thoughts. At one point in the conversation, I let slip that Dad would be out of town for two weeks.

"The times when he would go out of town were the best in the house," she stuttered. "It was like a fog lifting off a meadow."

She reminded me how much she missed Newman and how wonderful he was. Then she reminded me again, and after that, once more. I was annoyed, both with her strange canonization of him and with her drunkenness, but I told her I missed him too.

"I'm going to try to dream about the man with no face tonight," she said before we ended our conversation.

"That's good," I replied. "Whatever you have to do."

The next morning, I awoke and walked straight to the tracks. The morning felt cool and fresh, like a dive into cold water on a hot summer day. The sky was as blue as a jaybird's wings, and the sound of nature sung a wondrous psalm around me. I looked to the horizon and could almost hear Newman say, "Enjoy it, Sam! 'The sky's the daily bread of the eyes.'" It was one of his favorite Emerson quotes.

Something tickled my leg, and I looked down. A pretty little ladybug was wobbling toward my knee. I reached down and grabbed her, letting her crawl happily around my hand before she soon stopped and decided it was time to go. And as quickly as she had come, she spread her celestial wings and flew away into that wonderful blue sky, becoming a part of its beauty.

I heard the side door smack shut against the house behind me, and turned to see Kevin walking slowly in my direction. He reached me and stood for a moment beside me, looking up in admiration at the still tips of the trees.

"Wow, what a perfect morning," he said.

"It's gorgeous."

"You okay?" he asked quietly.

"Yeah, I'm good. I'm going to go shopping for a little while. When I get back, I think I'll just sit out here and admire this amazing gift."

I didn't really need to go shopping. I just wanted to go somewhere unfamiliar and be alone with my thoughts for a while.

"I'm going to hang around here, but I think I'll join you when you get back," Kevin said, smiling.

I returned home that afternoon after wandering around the edges of our little town. It had been a long day of contemplation and directionless driving.

I stopped on my way back and picked up a pizza for Kevin and me to share. When I pulled up to the house, Mom's car was in the driveway.

"She better not have brought him alcohol!" I said angrily to myself.

I walked upstairs, feet heavy, and didn't even knock on Kevin's door. I just barged right in.

"What the hell?" Kevin howled as I entered. He was alone, sitting on the edge of his bed and watching TV.

I looked at him in awkward confusion. "Sorry. Where's Mom?"

"What do you mean?"

"Her car's in the driveway," I said, pointing to the doorway with my thumb.

"I haven't seen her." He paused, and then said, "I thought I heard someone go into your room earlier, and I assumed you were back."

I turned around to check my bedroom for Mom. When I opened the door, I immediately noticed an out-of-place pink object lying on the edge of my bed. It was a folded note with a smiley face drawn on the outside cover. A hidden cricket chirped somewhere in the room, breaking the thick silence as I unfolded the piece of paper and began to read.

Boys,

I'm so sorry to do this to you. Please understand that it was the only way. I can't stay here without Newman any longer. I loved him so much, and I can't live in this place without him. Since my childhood, emptiness has consumed me. Newman took that away for a little while. The sound of his voice drove away the fears and pain I've carried with me for so long. But I know time won't heal me this time, and nothing will fill this gaping hole I have inside me.

When I'm sober and my mind is clear, I sometimes close my eyes and can see the two of you as children. I remember holding each of your tiny little hands when you were still just babies. I so wanted to protect you from this frightening world, but I was too busy protecting myself from it, and I became blind to what you desperately needed from me. It haunts me every second of every day that I didn't shield your precious innocence from Dean's hate. I know you needed your mommy to keep you safe, and I'm so sorry I wasn't there for you. I was scared, selfishly, of what he'd do to me. Your mommy wasn't as brave as her little boys. I know it destroyed something we should've had. I wish I'd have been a better mom to you. This world has been so painful for me, and I'm finally ready for that pain to end. Please forgive me, and never blame yourselves! Sometimes, the people in our lives just leave, and there's no real answer for why. Know that I'm in a better place.

Mom,
xoxoxo

"Kevin!" I screamed without looking up from the letter.

He rushed through the doorway. "What?"

"It's Mom. I think she's going to try to hurt herself or something!"

He glanced at the letter in my hands. "How? What are you talking about?"

Close by, a powerful train whistle resonated. It wasn't the one or two gentle blows we were used to hearing. This whistle was blowing uncontrolled and frantic.

Something was terribly wrong.

"Oh, God!" I cried out.

We charged down the stairs and out the front door. Once outside, we stopped and looked around frantically. In the distance, we saw Mom's silhouette walking calmly down the railroad tracks, her back to the oncoming train.

Adrenaline burned through my veins. We took off running in her direction.

"Mom! Mom!" we cried at the tops of our lungs. The train whistle screamed.

She walked gracefully in the distance, like a ghostly apparition, her white dress snapping in the air like a butterfly's wings. Above her, the sun hung indifferently in the placid sky.

I heard Kevin trip and fall to the ground behind me as we ran. I suddenly became aware that I was the only one who could save Mom.

I ran desperately, and soon made it to within thirty yards of her. I could see her long milky-white dress clearly, and for the first time I noticed a white wire dangling at her side. She was wearing my headphones and listening to music as she walked, singing serenely as she went.

"Mom! Please!"

The whistle drowned out the sound of my voice. The train's brakes squeaked like a rusty hinge.

And then it all stopped.

I closed my eyes. Blackness hit like a hammer on stone. For one absurd moment, there was only silence.

Her body made no sound upon impact. There was no dull thump as you'd expect, no agonizing scream. Her passing appeared to be instantaneous. As a shiny chrysalis breaks open, she was gone.

I don't believe she felt any pain. But my brother and I felt a sea of pain—a pain that broke us, a pain that took our dreams and stole who we had been just earlier that morning. And there at the tracks, we collapsed to our knees and cried tears that only a mother's child can cry into the gorgeous, clear-blue afternoon sky.

—

I couldn't watch as the firefighters removed Mom's body. I was sure her white dress was now a mangled pink mess. The thought of that bloodstained dress would haunt me for the rest of my life.

I overheard a firefighter say she was wrapped up like a salted pretzel. A police captain standing next to me told him to shut the hell up.

I didn't mind his joke, though. I knew it served the same purpose for him as my tears did for me. They helped him deal with an extremely stressful situation. His mind would cannibalize itself without that humor. It was his way of coping with his own pain at seeing another human being in such a grotesque condition. Where there is tragedy like that, humor is there showing its absurdity, and somehow that helps to bring healing. It wasn't fair that Mom had put that man in the position of having to see her in such a horrible state, so I couldn't blame him for dealing with his feelings in his own way.

Besides, I had bigger worries. I was more concerned about where Mom was going. *Will she go to Heaven?* I wondered. *Will I ever see her again? Will I only see her now in my sleep?*

But my questions didn't slow the anger bubbling from the bitterness I felt at her leaving me alone again.

When someone commits suicide, they never die alone. There is always someone with them in their death. Sometimes it's the person closest to them, or a person who they didn't realize cared so much. Sometimes it's someone they didn't even know, or someone who tried to save them in the end.

We never realize how much our lives are intertwined, and how much we can secretly affect one another.

꠸

After a horrendous day filled with police officers and fire-fighters, Kevin and I simply walked back home. Once inside, we stood silently in the living room under the painting of the girl in the house with the knobless doors, and wondered how we'd erase the gruesome memories of what we had witnessed that day.

The pizza I had brought home earlier sat where I had dropped it on the dining room table, and the smell of pepperoni and cheese hung densely in air. The moment seemed so ridiculously ironic and unreal.

The police had made a copy of the suicide letter and given me the original back in a clear plastic bag. Now I opened the bag and removed the pink note Mom had written as her final good-bye to us. As I unfolded it, the paper's thin edge cut a burning slice through the side of my finger.

I silently read the note again and shook my head as I took a deep, frustrated breath.

Kevin raised an eyebrow and focused his stern blue eyes on mine. "What?"

I showed him the note, where Mom had written "xoxoxo."

"Even at the end, she couldn't bring herself to write out the words, 'I love you,'" I said darkly. "Why was it so hard for her to feel love?"

9

Change

"So, I wanna write my words on the face of today,
and then, they'll paint it."
—Blind Melon

A death paralyzes a person's ability to communicate effectively or think clearly. After my mom died, anywhere I went, people spoke to me nervously, in short, nonsensical sentences, unsure what to say or how to say it. All of a sudden, people I'd known for years didn't know how to talk to me anymore. They spoke low and mournfully, bringing no comfort whatsoever—only anxious faces.

Some said, "Your mom's in a better place."

In my head, I thought, *A better place than with me?* But instead of saying so, I smiled and politely said, "Thank you."

One or two people even made me feel worse, butchering their attempts to console. One neighbor, an old woman with a wolf-gray beehive on her head and wrinkles that would make a Bullmastiff jealous, brought over comfort food and said, "That poor girl! You know, it's not Christian to kill yourself. Our church wouldn't even allow her to be buried in their graveyard."

"I'd think someone like her, afflicted and long-suffering, would need the church's compassion the most," I'd said. "I guess grace just isn't *en vogue* in the church nowadays."

Others repeated that we were in their prayers. Some ignored the situation completely, as if Mom had never existed.

The inability of people to communicate with me in a normal way made me feel more alone in my grief. Even Kevin kept saying, "You know, death always comes in threes." As if death needed companions.

I began drinking a lot after Mom's death. I needed something to numb what I was feeling and help me escape reality for a little while. I was desperate to forget, even if only for a short time.

The night after Mom died, I had a vivid dream. I couldn't get it out of my head. It felt so real. Ryan, Lynn, Mom, and Dad were all sitting around an oversized dining room table on top of the train tracks at night. Heat lightning danced chaotically in the dark sky behind them. They laughed cheerfully, as if at a festive celebration.

The table was laden with food, and black balloons rose high from the back of each chair, resembling dark, somber moons from a distance. Ryan, Lynn, and my parents gorged on the feast like ravenous animals, their messy faces smeared with bits of food and gristle.

As I moved closer to the table, I saw what they were eating. It was my body that they were devouring, spread across the table as they happily carved out chunks with a butcher knife. The large knife reflected a blinding silver light as it moved from slice to slice.

I startled awake from the dream when the eyes on my half-eaten body opened statically—just as Newman's had on the day he died—and stared back at me, paralyzed and helpless.

＊

By the time Dad finally returned home from his trip, Mom had been buried for over a week. We told him what had happened as soon as he arrived. He was uncharacteristically attentive, and kept asking for specific details.

I watched him walk out to where she had died. The wind blew his black hair chaotically as he stood over the rails, where dark red stains still lingered.

As he leaned over those discolored tracks, I witnessed him again becoming the young man she had met at the Halloween party on Brooklyn Park Boulevard so many years ago. Ghosts haunted his dark, lonely eyes with dreams he'd carelessly burned away during his wasted years. Then I saw something that amazed me: he wiped away tears from his cheeks.

This man had wished for my mother's death not even a month earlier, but now, he appeared heartbroken over it. I'd never seen my father show this kind of emotion before. I'd always believed he was the embodiment of pure evil. But watching his pale face on that cold February day made me question whether good and evil were so binary. Now, I couldn't help but think that maybe, most people existed in a messy gray space, somewhere in between those two places.

＊

Kevin and I went to Mom's house early one Sunday morning to take her belongings to the Goodwill. As I was cleaning out Newman's room, I discovered a Korean jewelry box on the bottom shelf of his nightstand. When I opened it, a melody began to play. In the box, I found the picture Newman had taken of me on the day we went fishing together.

Under the picture was a crinkled note, yellowed with age, that looked like it had been opened thousands of times. Written at the top in Newman's distinct handwriting were the words: *Note from Mother, 1948.*

I sat on his bed and read the letter silently to myself.

To my dearest son Newman,

I am so very sorry that at your tender age you had to go through such a horrible event with your father. Some people choose to use adversity in their lives as an excuse to destroy themselves. I hope you use this experience and the memory of your father as inspiration to make yourself better each and every day in some small way. I hope you use this experience to empower yourself! I have some recommendations for you, and if you adopt them into your life, they will surely help you on your journey.

First, live in the moment! The only thing you have the power to change is the present. There is nothing you can do about the past or the future. So, live every present moment in a positive, kind, forgiving, and fun way, always with an eye toward self-improvement. If you make that a habit, over time, your past and present will be so full of joy and hope that you'll have no choice but to look at life with a grateful heart and see the future as a beautiful, unopened gift.

The next most important thing is to always have fun! When I say to have fun, I don't mean drinking or taking drugs. Those things don't improve the self—they take away from it. I mean finding someone you love and giving that person all your attention and care. If it isn't a person, give your all to an activity that interests you! This will bring a deeper and more meaningful "fun" into your life than any substance ever could.

"Do you love me?" were words I heard from your father for more years than you have walked this planet. Be sure not to let a day go by without the people around you knowing how much you love them. The words "I love you" are only secondary to the actions of showing your love. The act is more important than the words—though both are essential.

I tried to convince your father, as I am trying to convince you now, that the only way to genuinely love this world, to honestly love others, and to gratefully love God, is to first love yourself. You are unique! Every second of every day, remember how wonderful you are. Treat yourself, and thank God in every moment that he made such an awesome human being—you! Take a class to improve yourself in some small way, or go for a degree or a job you think you could never get. Do something you're scared of or something that seems impossible to you. Then bask in the pride you feel each time you complete one of these new goals you originally thought you'd never accomplish. Attaining goals like this has an incredible effect. Building your self-esteem helps you see how special you truly are. It transforms over time into a virtuous cycle of feeling good about yourself that then gives you the ability to be good to others in an honest way.

There is only one downside to all of this. No one can do the work for you. You have to want to achieve good things in life. You have to want to love yourself and the people around you. You have to want to be thankful for every moment. It takes work—no one can give you this gift. It's up to you to take accountability for it all! I, and others, will be here to help along the way—if you choose to accept help—but only you can make it happen.

My hope is that you choose empowerment in your life to honor your father. I looked up "empowerment" in a thesaurus, and the first synonym that popped up for it was "blessing." Your father would like that. And he would want you to honor him by being a blessing to yourself, and in the lives of others.

I'll love you forever, my dear son,

Mother

It was obvious whence Newman had inherited his great outlook on life. When I finished reading the letter, I had tears in my eyes. The same tender words could have been written to me about my own mother's death. I didn't want to let that awful experience with my mom, or any experience, negatively define my life.

For some people, it's easier to take up residence in grief. It makes you feel like you're holding onto that loved possession in some way. But that keeps you from healing and moving forward. I didn't want that for myself. Something inside me wanted to be better than my life's circumstances.

Where do I begin? I thought.

And then I heard Newman's voice, laughing joyfully and saying, "I won the bet, son! Start there!"

"That's it!" I said out loud.

I looked at Newman's bookshelf and realized I hadn't started the first book I had picked out the night before his funeral. I'd start simply, just by reading the books our bet had indicated I should! I'd follow their lead and see where they'd take me.

Instead of locking myself in my room and drinking, I locked myself in my room and read. I began with Newman's books on Emerson, since he was Newman's favorite author. I became a pioneer in search of truth. I began to thirst for it, as the Sahara Desert thirsts for rain. I read inspirational passages that seemed they were written directly to me. On the back cover of the book, Newman had seemingly summarized a bit of Emerson's philosophy. Newman wrote, "When it is dark enough, you can see the stars."

Emerson began to wake the cold and broken pieces of my soul that I'd kept locked inside me. He taught me that the secret to success really was work, but not just any work—working on yourself. Committing every day to becoming a little better, a little smarter, a little kinder. He also reminded me of the wonders I'd seen so often all around me, but had stopped noticing. The sky, a friend, a meal, a spouse, a child—all were miracles I needed to appreciate in every precious moment. Emerson revealed that those are the things you truly don't want to live without; and with his help, I began to see the world with the wonder of a child seeing it for the first time.

Emerson also showed me Newman was right: your thoughts *do* make you who you are, so you have to focus them on what you want to become. Our lives are born of our thoughts. If your thoughts are constantly negative and self-critical, that's what you'll be. If they're uplifting and positive, on the other hand, you'll become uplifting and positive as well.

I realized the life I'd been living had really been a mirage, an insidious lie—and as I had this revelation, I sensed for the first time that I was truly starting to blossom, or at least unravel.

The first fruits of this new way of thinking bloomed one day as I was rereading the letter Newman's mom had written. Right then and there, I decided I'd do something I never thought possible before: I was going to go to college!

The idea of going to college had never entered my mind when I was in high school. It seemed like a monumental task, and I just wasn't up to it. The only way kids on my side of the tracks got into college was through athletic scholarships, and that just wasn't in the cards for me. But now, instead of accepting the status quo, I committed to doing something that had escaped me. I went one step at a time, researching what I needed to do to be accepted into the nearest school, and I did it all. I filled out forms, wrote essays, took tests, and sent off an application package.

Months later, to my surprise, I received a letter in the mail informing me I had been accepted to a local college: Virginia Commonwealth University! It seemed so simple in hindsight. I even received a generous financial aid package that covered some of my educational costs. The one thing it didn't cover was room and board, so I was thankful the university was within driving distance.

At some point, the thought dawned on me that being accepted into college was something that would finally make my dad proud of me. *This is it*, I told myself. *A new beginning for us!*

But when I told him what I'd achieved, he didn't care. In fact, he responded as if he hadn't even heard a word I'd said.

"I met a woman," he said sourly, "and she's going to stay here for a while."

"Oh, cool," I responded, feeling a little disheartened that he didn't seem to care about my good news.

He looked at me indifferently. "Yeah, it is. She has a son with special needs, though."

I'd thought he hated kids. I couldn't believe he'd want to date someone with children.

"That's really great," I said, forcing a half-smile.

He peered at me with a blank look on his face. "So, when are you moving out?" he asked.

At first, I was confused, instinctively shaking my head. "What do you mean?"

"The boy, he's moving in too."

"And he's taking my room?"

"Yeah, where else would he stay?"

I wanted to punish him. I wanted to hit him right in the face. It wasn't a surprise that he didn't give a shit about me; he'd said so on many occasions. It was that I hadn't received financial aid for housing. I wouldn't be able to go to college without a place to live. My hopes quickly began to fade.

"Did you hear what I said about college?" I asked.

He burst into his slimy, stinging laugh. "Yeah, you won't make it. You might as well not even go!"

I walked upstairs with my shoulders slumped and my head tilted toward the ground. Was he right? Maybe I was destined to be a failure.

As soon as the negativity began to creep in, though, I heard Newman's voice again. "Find a positive way out!" I could hear him say.

I sat on my bed and stopped to think it over. Maybe it would be good for me to get out of the house and away from Dean. All

I was doing there was collecting scars. A new place to live might be just what I needed, even if I couldn't go to college anymore.

"Screw him!" I said to myself. "I'll find another way."

Everything Mom had inherited from Newman was now mine and my brother's. Kevin and I were initially going to sell Mom's house and split any profits. After I told him what Dean had said to me, though, I asked if he wanted to live in Mom's house with me while I attended college. Kevin responded that he wasn't ready to move into her house just yet, but told me I should live there while I started school.

"I'm sorry he did that to you, Sam. Who does he think he is?" he asked. "I hope you weren't hurt."

"My heart isn't hurt," I snapped. "I don't have a heart anymore when it comes to Dean."

Kevin looked down and rubbed his fingers along his chin.

"I'm sorry, Kevin. I didn't mean to pop off at you like that."

"It's okay," he said, expressionless, staring at his feet.

I could sense Kevin had other things on his mind. "Can I ask you something?" he said in a subdued voice.

"Sure, what's up?" I asked, sitting down beside him on his bed.

Kevin's voice was soaked with pain, as if his troubled mind fought some unseen enemy. "Do you think, if Mom would've stopped for a second to think about how what she did was going to affect us, she would have reconsidered?"

I had thought about the same question a lot since her death. "I don't know. She saw no value in life. She couldn't figure out what brought her happiness. It certainly wasn't us. Her thoughts betrayed her, made her believe there was no hope in the world. If somebody doesn't have any hope left, watch out—they're going to do something. Hope for humans is like sun for plants. Without it we shrivel away, but with it we grow strong and fruitful. The opposite of living isn't really death, in my opinion; it's hopelessness. That's what really killed her."

"Well, what else could she do?" he asked sadly.

"What could she do? When this house seemed suffocating to her, she had a choice to make. She could stay, or she could go. The door was always open, and she knew she had options. She made the choice to walk out the door and leave. No one can force you to do that. The choice was hers."

"Choice? What choice did she have?" he asked. The words came from some untouched place deep inside him.

"The choice to do whatever it took to make life worth living. If for nothing else, for us! We were her children, for God's sake! When people are hurting over someone's death, it's hard for them to blame the person they loved; they have to find a boogeyman to project responsibility onto. But the truth is that she gets the blame on this one."

I could see my words marinating in his wounded mind.

"You're right," he said finally. "You sound angry."

I really wasn't sure how I felt. I had mixed emotions, and it was hard to put my feelings into words.

"I think I'm not so much angry as resentful. Like you said, she didn't consider how her leaving would affect us—as always. There are two kinds of people: those who allow themselves to heal from their wounds as time passes, and those who hold tightly to their wounds as if they're some kind of cruel security blanket. That's what Mom did. Instead of walking away from her pain, she walked into it."

"You know, in the middle of my addiction, I seriously thought about killing myself," Kevin said unexpectedly.

His words unsettled me. "I would have killed you!" I said ironically. Then, more calmly, I asked, "What stopped you?"

"I decided to go to Starbucks instead. I got a grande latte. Thank God it was good that day! It changed my outlook completely," he said, smirking.

I couldn't help but laugh. "It was that simple, huh?"

He smiled before a solemn look appeared on his face again. "I'm just sad she felt forced to do what she did. We were right beside her, literally running to save her life. How could she not understand that we cared?" Pain afflicted his face as he spoke, and I noticed little white hairs I had never seen before speckling his head, blending right in with the brown. Crow's feet outlined his young eyes. Mom's death had hurt him much more than I'd realized.

"You know what, Kevin? We'll come out of this stronger somehow; you'll see. You know, I read today that the strongest animals are those that are hit continually by the heaviest waves."

"You sound like my old counselor," Kevin said, smiling. Again, he quietly processed his thoughts, looking as if two warriors were fighting out opposing ideas inside his head. "Do you think she went to Heaven?" he asked.

"I honestly don't know. Hell isn't just filled with loudmouths, murderers, and rapists. It's also filled with people who think of themselves as decent, but who stood by and allowed evil to be done without confronting it."

"I know; I thought about that too," he said. His shoulders slumped as if gravity were pulling too hard on them, and his voice sounded weak. "Dad did some horrible things, and she just stood by and let them happen."

"I once read a quote that has always stuck with me. I can't remember who wrote it, but it was something like, 'Silence in the face of evil is itself evil. God will not hold us guiltless. Not to speak is to speak. Not to act is to act.' When someone reveals what they are and you stand silently by, you reveal in your silence what *you* are."

"I get it," Kevin said as he stood. "If you stand by, you're just as culpable. If you ignore it to protect yourself, you become a part of it. I just feel bad for her."

I paused in thought and could almost see Mom standing in the room with us, chardonnay in hand. "I do feel guilty, though," I said softly.

"You do?"

"Yeah. I knew she was fragile. I could have been more sensitive. She was like a wineglass that could be easily broken. I guess I chose to handle that glass irresponsibly, knowing its frailty."

Kevin looked down sadly and put his hands deep in his pockets. "I feel that way too, to be honest."

I shook my head, silently thinking of how my carelessness had now led me to be cut by that glass's sharp, broken pieces.

⟶

I didn't even say goodbye to Dean before I left the house for the last time. I just packed my few belongings, told Kevin I'd see him soon, and headed for a new start.

On the way out the side door, I walked past the eerie painting of the sad girl trapped in her small house. I took a sharp knife out of a drawer in the kitchen, cut her out of the canvas, and took her with me.

"We'll make it together, away from here," I said, smiling at the picture.

I left the rest of the picture hanging on the wall with a hole through it, now just an empty house with two stupid doors that were missing their handles.

Before I got into my truck, I went out to the tracks one last time to say goodbye. The wind blew gently, kissing my face with memories of what I was leaving behind. I took a deep breath as I looked around, closed my eyes, and whispered, "Thank you," secretly to the tracks. They'd always been there, and I knew they'd exist inside me forever, a piece of everything I'd ever touch and every place I'd ever be.

My eyes were soon drawn to the spot where Mom had died. As they lingered sadly on the discolored rail, a part of me didn't want to leave. I felt as if the rail had become a piece of her, or as if her spirit lived along the tracks, and I was somehow leaving her behind.

***

But I did leave; and once I did, my life transformed. Having Dean out of my life was like a rebirth. Without him getting in the way, I could feel good about myself every day. I didn't have to walk on eggshells when I came home either. It was all very liberating. The world turned out to be so different than I had always believed it to be. When Kevin told me the woman Dean had met moved out two weeks after she'd moved in, I didn't even give a thought to going back to that house.

On top of that, going to college was like finding an oasis in the middle of a desert. It was as if I'd been using black and white crayons my entire life, and had suddenly discovered a multitude of bright colors existed from which I could choose. I didn't love that I had to work full-time to pay my bills while my friends partied, but it was what it was.

Education helped me to go outside the edges of Verities. I realized that the more you know about someone, the less you fear them. You can relate to anyone's life in some way, no matter how different they seem; and relating is what brings people together.

My friends skipped class all the time; but I loved the lectures. The old, musty professors weren't used to their students questioning them, so I didn't have a great relationship with some of them. They just couldn't understand that in my eyes, they weren't my benefactors; I was theirs—or rather, we were each other's. The debates I had with some of them were legendary and put me on more than one shit-list. One professor told me I wasn't popular with the faculty because I didn't flatter them.

"I guess I'm an outside-the-box kind of person," I said.

"You want to be more liked, more respected? Stay comfortably inside the box while you're here," was the curt reply. "The less boat rocking you do, the further you'll go. Don't you know anything?"

I listened to the professors' ideas, but not blindly. I was on a search for wisdom, truth, and creativity—not stale, regurgitated theories. Sometimes you have to siphon truth out of the platelets of your own blood, rather than someone else's. I was determined to make up my own mind on issues, and some professors hated me for that. They were used to being hero-worshipped by their students. Like many in positions of authority, or anyone trying to control you in some way, they got upset and labeled me arrogant or argumentative if I challenged their reasoning.

In one class, a professor tried to advocate the benefits of appeasing dictators instead of fighting against them. This was a concept with which I felt personally familiar. Mom's appeasement of Dean had never been beneficial. I shared my thoughts with the professor.

"Appeasement only makes someone more brutal and encourages a ruthlessness to grow inside them. Ignoring small aggressions only leads to bigger ones," I told him confidently. "It might seem like you're taming the animal in the moment, but it'll attack you more ferociously in the future. The aggression isn't buried away or diverted, but put aside to wait patiently for the next opportunity."

The professor wasn't impressed with my contribution, and moved on without responding.

Once, another dispassionate educator who never smiled said that our society was biased toward males, and this was an existential problem for the survival of our country. While I agreed with some of what she was saying, I decided to share an opposing thought. By this time, professors wouldn't call on me if I raised my hand, so I just began speaking.

"Professor, females are shown preference throughout their primary education because most teachers are women. Characteristics associated with masculinity are frowned upon or even framed negatively in the classroom because of that fact. This puts males at a serious educational disadvantage right out of the gate. It's why more women than men are receiving college degrees today. And there are now more female medical students than men. That's never been the case in the history of our nation." The professor tried to interject, but I continued. "Boys also have an especially difficult journey in their emotional development. For girls, it's okay to cry or just have simple feelings. It's okay to talk about those feelings with peers or trusted adults. But from birth, society tries to circumcise boys' hearts along with their manhoods. They're not allowed to have feelings or cry without being labeled weak. It's considered unmanly for them to ask for help if a burden in life becomes too heavy to bear. It's probably why most people who commit crimes are male. There's no outlet for them to express their pain in normal life, and they lose their cool. Even Jesus wept after being betrayed. If the most powerful man in history can openly weep, surely we can give young men a break."

She studied me with a stunned but bubbling rage. Aggravation dripped from her face like icicles melting in a warm sun.

But I didn't let their reactions bother me. I actually loved it all. Getting out on my own and exploring new ideas became a daily pleasure for me.

———

A couple months into my sophomore year, I went to grab the next book from Newman's bookshelf and realized something extraordinary: I had read every work in his collection.

"Newman, I did it!" I said out loud. "I fulfilled my end of the bet!"

I stared at all the books I had read, and thought about Newman and the life-changing wager I had made with him on that cold January day.

He set me up for a win-win with that bet, I thought. *What they say is true: sometimes you have to lose to win.*

I looked down at the bare bottom shelf of the bookcase. I hadn't noticed before that Newman had left it empty. *He did that on purpose,* I said to myself. It made me realize it was time for me to take the next step and begin contributing books of my own. Newman had provided me with a fantastic foundation, but now it was time to cut my own path. I decided to go to the school bookstore and search for a new book with which to begin the next journey.

As I browsed the mathematics section's books on probability, I accidently bumped into someone searching the shelves behind me.

"I'm so sorry!" I quickly turned to see a familiar face.

"Hi!" the girl said sweetly.

"Hi! Don't I know you from somewhere?" I asked. *Wow, she's beautiful!* I thought.

"You're Sam, right?"

"Yeah. Where do I know you from?"

"I'm Denise. I'm in your Race and Gender class. You really pissed off Professor Hagadorn."

I laughed and said, "Yeah, they don't like when you question them, but I can't help it. I love a good debate!"

"I'm aware," she said, smiling. Two dimples dotted her cheeks.

"What are you up to now?" Denise asked. "Want to grab a coffee or something?"

"Sure," I said, turning back to the shelves. "I was actually trying to find a good book to read, but I'm not having any luck."

Denise scanned the books on her side of the aisle. I glanced down quickly and saw she was wearing tie-dyed pink Vans skate shoes.

"Here!" she said, pulling out a small, brightly colored book. "You should read this. It's one of my favorites!"

I studied the cover. "*The Four Agreements*, Don Miguel Ruiz. What's it about?"

"It kind of teaches you how to love yourself, and then how to pass that love out into the world. This book really changed my thinking about stuff."

"Sounds perfect! Thanks." And with a smile that that could

rival that of a small child with an exceptionally large Christmas present, I said, "Let's go get that coffee."

We ordered from the bookstore cafe. I got a large coffee with an exotic name I couldn't pronounce, and she ordered a small latte. They served our drinks in beautiful blue ceramic cups with funny faces on them. My cup's face was cross-eyed and only had one tooth that looked like a large marshmallow. Her cup had googly eyes and a big, goofy smile.

We sat down on a long dark blue sofa that smelled like burnt cardboard, she on the mushy middle cushion and I to her left. Her delicate hands danced like a conductor's when she spoke, occasionally brushing against my arm and making chill bumps. I was distracted by her beautifully unkempt hair. It was long and chestnut-brown, with faint champagne-blonde streaks, and she'd done it up into a rare combination of wavy, rippling curl. A bright orange bandana tied tightly around her head completed the exotic look, and she smelled like fresh strawberries and cotton candy. I was finding it difficult to think about what I wanted to say.

"So, what're you trying to get out of it?" I began.

"'It'?" Denise wondered.

"College. I mean, like, what do you hope to take from it?"

"Oh," she said oddly, as if she'd never thought about the question before. "I guess I hope to get a job and make some money."

"Really?" I said. I could feel the disappointment wrinkling my forehead before it occurred to me to hide it.

"Yeah, why? What else is there? What are you searching for?"

"I think I'm just searching for whatever the opposite of being full of shit is."

"Be serious!" she said, smacking me hard on the arm.

I shrugged. "I guess I'm trying to understand who I am, you know? And where I'm going, where we've been—all those kinds of existential things."

Denise's eyes opened wide. "That's too deep for me! I'm just trying to get a job that will make me feel like I'm somebody."

"Your worth isn't defined by a title ordained by another human being. That's not how you become somebody. You're someone special right now."

"Oh, you think I'm special?" she asked as she leaned close and playfully smacked my knee.

"It doesn't matter what I think. What do you think?"

She laughed. "You know, you aren't very good on a first date."

"Are we on a date?" I asked. The thought hadn't occurred to me. I'd always thought you had to ask for dates.

"Of course we are!"

As she said the last word, her coffee cup slipped from her hand and crashed to the floor. People around us jerked to look in the direction of the sudden sound before slowly starting to clap.

Denise looked cynically at the chaos. The wooden floor was covered in small blue fragments. She had barely taken a sip of her drink, and liquid spread in all directions.

Exasperated, she threw up her hands. "Of course! That's my life right there."

I smiled as we both bent down and helped one another clean up the mess. A couple sitting nearby handed us their napkins to help soak it all up. After I threw away the last broken piece of the coffee cup, I said, "Wait here. I'll be right back!"

"I'm going to go wash my hands and I'll be back," I heard her call out as I walked briskly out the front of the store and into the warmth of the weightless night. An old man with a flower cart was set up outside, and I purchased an orange tulip to match Denise's bright bandana before hurrying back inside.

She must have finished washing her hands, because I found her on the sofa.

"If we're on a date, I want you to have this!" I said, handing her the cup-shaped flower.

"Aww, I thought I had chased you away! How'd you know that tulips are my favorite?"

"Just a lucky guess." I paused in thought. "Now, what were we talking about?"

"College goals," she said, dragging out the words as if she was bored.

"Oh, yeah! You said you didn't have any," I joked.

"No, it's not that. I guess I just figured a college degree was the only road to that proverbial big house and fancy car."

"Have you ever thought about why people live in gigantic houses that only get them further away from the people they love?" I asked.

Her forehead creased like the skin of a raisin. "Do you mean that?" she asked, her voice high. "Or is that a BS question?"

"Yes, I mean it! Give me a little house with big love over a big house with little love any day. After all, a home is only as good as the people in it."

As we continued to talk, it was as if our words embraced in the open space between us. She made me feel things just by looking at her, like seeing Niagara Falls for the first time. She wore little to no makeup, but her face seemed to glow. A mischievous smile peeked out when she was amused, revealing white teeth that had probably been straightened by braces in her teen years. Her nails were bitten down to the nail beds.

"So, tell me about your family," she said, throwing me an unexpected curveball.

I looked down sheepishly at the black coffee in my cup, trying to hide the thorny feelings her question aroused. "There's not a lot to tell, really."

"Come on! Tell me something," she pressed. "What's your mom like?"

"She passed," I said quietly.

"Oh, I'm so sorry." She touched my hand gently and looked deep into my eyes, as if trying to heal me with her gaze. There was an innocent beauty about Denise, like sand formed into sculptures by the wind.

"That's okay. Thank you," I said softly.

"What about your dad?"

"He's awful," I blurted without even thinking. I immediately regretted it, thinking she might be turned off by someone who had such harsh words to say about their father.

But to my relief, she said, "Yeah, I have one of those too. I haven't talked to my dad in years."

"Are you mad at him or something?"

She hesitated for a moment, then skeptically asked, "You really want to know?"

"Yeah. I'm curious."

"Well, yeah. I guess I was angry with him for a long time. But one day I asked myself who I was hurting more by hating him—him, or me? I realized that hate was like drinking poison. It was making *me* sicker than it was making *him*."

"So what'd you do?"

"This will probably sound weird," she said as she cocked her head to the left and looked down at her knees, "but I prayed for him. No one ever says prayers for the worst people. We pray for good all day long, but no one prays for the bastards. Praying for him made my anger slowly recede. It's hard to keep hating someone you pray for each night."

She paused and studied me intently, maybe to gauge whether I was still interested in her story. Eventually, she kept talking. "At some point, you start to become what you don't forgive. Once I forgave him and let it all go, it was like a weight lifted off my shoulders. I still wasn't talking to him, and I still didn't think everything he did was great, but it didn't matter anymore. I was free of the illusion of him."

I nodded, stuck in a trance, and thought about Dean. I scooted forward uncomfortably on the edge of my seat.

"So that makes sense to you?" she asked, awakening me.

"One hundred percent. I've been through things like that before. Sometimes there's no difference between illusion and reality. What's he do for a living, your dad?"

"He's a lawyer," she said hesitantly. "He works at Marcel Law Firm." For the first time that night, she couldn't look me in the eyes.

"Oh, got it. That explains it."

"What do you mean?"

"No offense, but I feel like today's lawyers have lost their sense of purpose. They're willing to lie, mislead, or manipulate the truth just to win cases. They aren't motivated to fight for justice, but to win, unconcerned about the lives affected in the process. If they prosecute an innocent man and the jury rules in his favor, they're unhappy because they lost what was a game to them."

"That's my dad, alright. He wants to win at any cost. And the means are justified as long as he wins."

"Do people really believe God won't judge them for the means?" I asked in a sharp tone. "That's what the Nazis thought at Nuremberg—'It's my professional duty, so I'm not personally responsible,' they said. I think it's going to be a big surprise to a lot of people that there's no distinction between personal life and work life in the eyes of God. It's *all* duty in His view, duty to *Him*."

She nodded and crossed her arms. "That's very true. Something else I've never understood about my dad is why he worries so much about how others view him, but has never cared how his own family sees him."

"That's so ridiculous and shortsighted," I griped.

I felt so comfortable talking with Denise. I think we recognized broken pieces in one other. There was an inward understanding that built a connection between us. We spoke intimately, as if we'd known each other for years; and we were only a couple hours into our first date—or whatever it was.

Eventually, a booming voice from the loudspeaker announced that the bookstore was closing.

"Gosh! Where's the time gone?" Denise asked.

"I don't want the night to end." I immediately regretted saying it. I didn't want to seem too desperate. But like wax on a burning candle, my worries quickly melted away when she smiled and said, "Me neither."

With a bubbly feeling in my stomach, I asked, "Would you like to continue this over dinner tomorrow night?"

"I would," she said easily. She wrote her number on a napkin and kissed me softly on the cheek. "Enjoy the book!"

As I watched her walk away, I felt warmth consume me, like when the sun pokes unexpectedly through the clouds, warming your skin and driving away a chill in the air. It had been a long time since I'd felt that way for anyone—or any*thing*, really.

I stayed up all night reading *The Four Agreements* so I could talk to Denise about it on our dinner date the next day. I finished it a little before four in the morning.

⇁

It didn't take long for Denise and me to become an official couple. Soon after that first dinner, she began to sleep at my house almost every night. I knew it was getting serious when she showed up at my house with her toothbrush.

Having Denise around was healing to me. She chased away some of the madness and made me feel like I was better than I really was. Either she didn't pay attention to my scars, or she just didn't notice them. After the first time we made love, she told me she could feel the loneliness inside me. That was the moment I fell in love with her.

Even my dreams transformed themselves. I began dreaming of a golden field that stretched as far as I could see over a yellow horizon. There were no shadows in that field; it was too bright for them, and they hid along its edges, sulking. The smell of honeysuckles and mint perfumed the air.

Tired, I lay in the middle of the field and rested, as a silent breeze blew gently across my face and the warmth of the sun kissed my skin. I could feel love all around me, as if it was tangible. Whenever I woke from this dream, I smiled and thought, *Life is good.*

Somehow, through old wounds, sunlight was getting in. Opening myself again to the people around me was therapeutic. I could feel something inside of me was truly changing. Sure, pain still found ways to seep in, like water through the tiniest of cracks—but I knew I could get through it. My scars no longer crippled me or reminded me of the wounds I had suffered. They were proof that no matter what, I had survived; and that even in the most desperate of times, there had always been healing.

10

No Son of Mine

"You're no son, you're no son of mine."
—Genesis

One day, Professor Hunt, my eccentric academic advisor, left me a message asking me to stop by his office. He didn't say what it was about, but the request was odd, if only because he'd never contacted me by phone before. I was curious what he might want, so I swung by his office the first chance I got.

The door was open when I arrived, and I cautiously poked my head in. Professor Hunt's office smelled like a musty old cigar box. Pictures of famous people and exotic places lined the walls in crooked, angular patterns. There were so many frames, I couldn't even see an inch of wall space, and Professor Hunt was featured in each one. Papers and books were stacked everywhere in the manner of a professional hoarder, and the cadence of an old grandfather clock's ticking drifted through the air in the small room.

"Hi, Professor Hunt," I said. "You left a message that you wanted to see me?"

Professor Hunt was a cheerful, short, and chunky man with a lengthy, salt-and-pepper beard and light brown skin. His black hair, speckled with strands of eggshell white, was receding, and a shiny bald spot sat atop the round dome. His intelligent, earthy brown eyes that always seemed bloodshot were hung below thick, burly eyebrows—or, I should say, his eye*brow*. It was really one long, meandering caterpillar, and Professor Hunt proudly proclaimed it was his trademark.

"Sam, my boy! Come in and have a seat," he said warmly. "How are you?" His voice was gravelly, but wondrously lyrical.

"I'm doing well, sir. How about yourself?"

"Oh, I'm great." He glanced at me, his eyes worried. "I heard you've had a rough go of it lately. I had no idea how much you'd been through these last few years. I wanted to check on you and see how you're holding up."

I wondered how he'd heard anything about my personal life, and what exactly he'd heard. I assumed he was referring to my mom.

"Thank you. That's nice of you," I said as I sat down. "I'm doing pretty well."

He stepped toward me. "Do you need anything from me?"

"That's very kind of you, but I'm good. It's been a while now. Actually, the best thing for me was diving into the books."

"Oh, I understand that completely," Professor Hunt replied. "But if you change your mind, you let me know, okay?"

"I will. Thanks again!" I smiled—but then I twisted uncomfortably in my seat. "Before I go," I added more quietly, "there *is* something I've been wanting to talk to you about, if you have time."

Professor Hunt's face lit up like a lighthouse, and a huge

smile overtook it. "Absolutely!" He closed his office door, wobbled back to his desk, and sat in his upholstered, oversized brown vinyl desk chair. Its high back rose two feet above his head, making it look as if the seat were swallowing him. "How can I help you, Sam?"

"It's about my future." I began to bounce my right knee against my hand. "I know we talked once about me possibly teaching. I think I'd really love teaching; I'm just worried I won't be able to survive on that salary. I've heard teachers don't make a lot of money."

Professor Hunt bounced up again and walked over to a coffeepot in the corner of his office. "Would you like some?" he asked, picking up the glass carafe and thoughtfully tipping an empty mug in my direction.

"No thank you, sir."

Professor Hunt sat down again. "You have a four-point-oh GPA. You can pretty much do anything you want. The sky's the limit, really!"

"I guess I'm asking what you suggest for someone like me."

He smiled thoughtfully. "I can give you my opinion, but that doesn't mean it's what's best for you. You have to decide what's right for yourself."

I nodded with an appreciative smile. "Of course. I understand."

"For me personally, I think it's absurd that people spend their short time on this tiny rock in pursuit of things that don't bring their lives meaning. My advice would be to figure out what you truly value in life and pursue that."

"What if what I value isn't profitable financially?"

Professor Hunt slurped his coffee. A wispy cloud of twirling steam rose from its surface and disappeared, becoming part of the room. I noticed his mug had the words "World's Best Professor" stamped on it in thick strawberry-red lettering.

"If there's one thing I've learned in my years, it's that money isn't going to buy you happiness."

"Yeah, only power can do that!" I joked.

He chuckled. "Don't get me started! As you know, I'm writing a research paper on that very subject right now. I fear power—it's the worst of all drugs! It has to be the most intoxicating substance known to man. It changes a person for the worst, transforms him into an appalling version of himself. I've seen it happen a million times. I'd even be willing to bet that more people are in Hell for chasing power than money!"

I leaned far back in my leather seat. "I grew up with a close friend whose family was one of the richest and most powerful in our town, and they never seemed to have a true sense of happiness."

"That's what I've been finding in my research. People become frustrated when they realize they can't find what they're looking for in a bank account or a boardroom. If your number one desire is money or reputation, you'll spend your whole life feeling unfulfilled. Those things just aren't where you find happiness."

"So, what do you do, then?" I asked, placing my hand on my chin and studying Professor Hunt closely.

"What do you do?" Professor Hunt asked. "You live in the moment, work for your own interests! The money will come."

"I feel the same, but isn't it good to make money? I mean, it's hard to do anything without it."

He laughed in a high-pitched squeal, sounding like a

drowning guinea pig. "Yes, it's definitely good! But if we do things that we don't enjoy just to make money, we use up the most precious gift we have."

Slowly, I sat forward. "What's that?"

He paused and packed tobacco into the chamber of a long Sherlock pipe made of dark brown wood. Holding the stem, he lit a match, moving it in short, circular motions across the bowl like a familiar dance as he breathed in shallow puffs. He leaned back comfortably in his chair as spicy clouds of smoke drifted peacefully to the ceiling.

"Time," he said, holding the pipe's bowl firmly. "Once it goes, it's gone, and you'll never get it back."

I looked out his office window at the tips of the trees as they rocked back and forth in the wind, seeming so content.

Professor Hunt snapped his thumb and middle finger together. "Hey! Hello? What world are you in right now? What're you thinking about?"

"I'm trying to think about what I value most in life."

"You don't have to figure it out right now. You have plenty of time. But think about this: what would you do if you knew tomorrow was your last day on earth?" He knocked his fist twice against his desk. "When you can answer that question honestly, you'll come closer to knowing what you value most. People don't usually respond to that question by saying things like 'I'd work late,' 'I'd shoot for that next promotion,' or 'I'd pick my kids up late from day care.' Usually, they say they'd spend time with their families, or finally take a trip to the Grand Canyon, or watch a last sunset over the ocean."

It's strange, but I remember that simple conversation as one of the most formative of my young life. It was as if Professor

Hunt had given me a compass that pointed to my true north whenever I felt lost. I decided right then that at the end of my time on earth, I wanted my laugh lines to be deeper than the frown lines on my old, crinkly face. I didn't want to look back and find I'd been so worried about foolish things that I'd forgotten to live honestly.

As our separations lengthened, I found myself worrying about Kevin a lot. Between college, working, and Denise, I rarely got a chance to see him. I'd call him sometimes just to see if he was high or out of sorts. Each time we spoke, I brought up how refreshing it had been to get away from Dean, and asked Kevin if he was ready to move in with me. I even attempted emotional extortion here and there, saying I really missed him and needed him around. But he always became reserved and said it wasn't the right time.

I wondered what kept him fastened to that lonely house. It never made sense to me that he didn't seem to want to escape its callous embrace. But for some reason, he just couldn't give himself permission to leave. It was like he was a prisoner fearing freedom after a lifetime of incarceration. He couldn't conceive what life would look like for him outside of that house.

Early one morning, Kevin called and asked if I could come over and help load a tiller into his truck. He said Dean was dressed like he was going to a funeral, so Kevin assumed he wouldn't be home. "Probably a gambling trip," he said happily.

I told him I was busy in the morning, but would come by later that night.

The sky was darkening by the time I made it out to help Kevin, but there was still a faint glow of sunlight in the west. As I crossed the familiar tracks, I saw two cars parked in the driveway. One was Dean's, but I'd never seen the other before.

I had hoped Kevin would be right and Dean wouldn't be there when I arrived, but it looked like Kevin's optimism had been misplaced. I stepped out of my vehicle and into the driveway as a dark cloud in the distance crept slowly toward the house and consumed the last bit of sunlight.

The wind picked up, beginning to howl through the see-sawing treetops. Hesitantly, I walked to the side door.

Upon entering the house, I was greeted immediately by an angry commotion.

"You son of a bitch! What the hell are you two doing?" Dean screamed from upstairs.

A loud rumble shook the entire house, and in the next instant, Joe Nied came rushing down the stairs. He wore only his boxer briefs and a terrified expression, and was clutching his clothes in his hands. He didn't even acknowledge my presence as he shot by and straight out the door, his belt clanging as he went. Before I could process what had happened, I heard his car peeling out of the driveway before the sound quickly faded into the distance.

"You're not my son!" Dean shouted from upstairs.

Oh, God, I thought to myself. *What have I walked into?*

Suddenly, another loud rumbling came from the stairs. This time Kevin rounded the corner, he too in boxer briefs, with Dean close behind him in pursuit, bearing the face of an angry hunter. Without looking at me, he chased Kevin out the side door and into the driveway, and I followed quickly behind.

"Stop!" I screamed. "What the hell is going on?"

The air stole my breath as I stepped outside. The night had turned stone cold, still as a shadow behind a grave. Dean caught up with Kevin within a few feet of the door and reached out as their bodies fell violently to the gravel.

"You fag!" Dean yelled as he pinned Kevin to the ground. His hands moved wildly toward Kevin's face. "You're no son of mine, you piece of shit!"

Dean clasped his hands around Kevin's neck, his fingertips and thumbs meeting at Kevin's spine and throat. Kevin's mouth opened awkwardly, and he gasped for air.

"Dean! Let him go!" I shouted. "You're choking him!"

Kevin tried to fight back, writhing and twisting, but Dean's bulk on top of him kept him pinned. He squirmed and kicked in a valiant effort, but the weight was just too much of a burden.

Fight, Kevin! I said to myself. *You can do this!*

A strong wind blew as if from nowhere. The trees whistled, a foreboding, low-pitched wail that descended around us.

"Piece of shit!" Dean shouted as he clutched Kevin's neck more tightly, his fingertips blanching. Kevin struggled silently for air. His face turned a dark, unnatural red.

"You're going to kill him, Dean! That's enough; let him go!"

The wind swelled, battering everything it touched. A light rain had begun to fall. Kevin's lips turned from pink to purplish, and his cheeks became beet-red. His eyes protruded so much, I feared they'd pop out of their sockets. He kicked and wriggled his arms, but he was noticeably weakening, losing consciousness.

I glanced around and saw a brick stamped with a black "3"

on the ground near me. I bent and picked it up, staring into its past as it rested hard in my hand. Standing tall behind Dean, I shouted a final warning as the cold rain trickled down my face.

"Let him go, Dean! Now!"

Dean only clutched Kevin's pale throat more tightly. His face had a sour, acerbic expression, as if he could taste death on his tongue.

The rain poured now in sheets. The wind blew so strongly, the tree branches crackled like lightning.

I raised the old, murderous brick high above Dean's head. Light-filled flashes of memories played in my mind's eye. Like an out-of-control movie projector, an orgy of impressions flared wildly: Dad asking me what I was looking at in the church. The sign that read AND HE SHALL SMITE THE WICKED. Dean screaming at the top of his lungs. Jessie licking my face. Dean pushing Mom through a glass door. Blood drawn from my face.

Then a deafening sound cut through the wind and rain, bringing me back. The ghostly whistle of a passing train wailed in the darkness. And what flashed now was my brother, dying at Dean's unforgiving hands.

I'd been frightened until that moment. Now, in an instant, my fear became rage.

I swung the brick with all my strength. It struck Dean squarely on the back of his head, tearing off a portion of meat. His body slumped off Kevin and fell face-first to the earth.

All I could hear was Kevin wheezing, gasping desperately for air. I quickly knelt and held him in my arms. His shoulder leaned against my chest.

"Are you okay?"

Kevin looked stunned. His eyes opened wide.

"Hey! You alright?" I shouted as I shook him.

He nodded and pushed me away. Coughing loudly, he got slowly to his feet. Then he bent and put his hands on his knees, absorbing the horror of the scene.

I looked at Dean's lifeless body where it lay on the muddy ground. For the first time since I had arrived at the house that night, strangely, I felt safe.

"What'd you do, Sam?" Kevin panted. His voice strained, harsh with anger.

"He wouldn't let you go!"

Kevin wobbled, taking short, sharp breaths. "Is he dead?" he asked. He seemed unable to look in Dean's direction.

"I don't know."

The wind whispered, and I noticed the rain had stopped falling. I bent and turned Dean's face toward mine. He lay still as the brick that rested beside him. Blood trickled out of his nostrils. His face was wet and smeared with dirt. The earth drank the blood that leaked from his ears.

I felt for a pulse at his neck, then his wrist. I leaned down and placed my ear to his mouth. There was nothing. He lay motionless, eyes half-open, looking blankly past me toward the lit dots that decorated the night sky. As I stared down at his frozen, lifeless face, a startling and confusing feeling drifted into my awareness—the feeling that I'd never seen the man in front of me before.

"He's dead," I said somberly. Then, softly so that Kevin wouldn't hear me, I added, "Quiet at last."

"Damn it!" Kevin shouted. He grabbed at his face. His eyebrows came together, and his eyes widened with grief. With this one look, my indifference transformed into apprehension.

Abandon all hope, ye who enter here.

The words echoed darkly in my head, and I felt sick to my stomach. Heaving, I ran behind a pine tree and threw up.

When I'd finished, I held onto the tree for support. I heard Kevin come up behind me.

"They're going to lock you up for the rest of your life—maybe kill you, Sam!" he said. I turned to see him grabbing chunks of his hair with both hands.

I could hardly speak. "I had to save you! Kevin, he was going to kill you. I wasn't going to let him murder you!"

"It doesn't matter. They're going to fry you for this!"

The severity of the situation began to reveal itself. Obscure thoughts raced through my head. *Will I be charged with patricide? I've heard that's the worst of all crimes. What will people say? What will Denise think? But what about filicide? Isn't what he's doing worse? We're his children. We're the innocents!*

"Okay. Okay," Kevin said. He stood tall, seemingly trying to steady his shaking body. "This is what we're going to do."

He pointed. "Look at the dogwood tree over there."

I looked, and saw that the wind had snapped a large branch off the tree. The broken limb rested on the ground. "Yeah?"

"Grab Dean," Kevin ordered.

"What?" I asked. "What if someone's watching us? We've already made a ton of noise."

"Just do it! Drag him over here!"

I pulled at Dean's ankles, dragging him foot by foot to the broken tree limb as I glanced furtively at the surrounding houses. I was surprised how easy he was to move. He had always seemed so massive; but pulling his body was almost as simple as lugging a full bag of trash.

"Make sure his head is under it," Kevin said, pointing at the branch.

"Are you serious?"

"Sam, now!"

I tried lifting the branch but couldn't get it up on my own.

"It's too heavy," I said.

Kevin hurried to help me hoist it up. "Can you hold it for a second by yourself?" he asked as sweat dripped down his face.

"Yea, go ahead."

As I struggled to keep the tree limb on my shoulder, Kevin positioned Dean's body underneath it, then helped me lower the branch back down.

"We're going to call the police and tell them it fell on him during the storm."

"They're never going to buy that," I groaned.

"They will. They have to! You have a better idea?"

I stared at the fallen branch. Dean's legs protruded from beneath it. "Actually, it's not the worst idea," I finally said.

"Alright, get your game face on." Kevin grabbed me by the shoulders. "I'm going to call 911. Are you okay? Can you do this?"

"I can do this," I said.

I looked at my watch to see what time it was, and realized I'd hit Dean so hard, my watch had broken. The glass face was shattered, and I couldn't see the hands. The moment would be timeless.

A few minutes after Kevin made the call, paramedics, police, and firefighters showed up. Though it was immediately obvious Dean was beyond resuscitation, they worked on his body in vain. I think they wanted to make it seem like they were trying to do something, believing it would make us feel better.

To my surprise, they never questioned our story. When he had finished taking our statements, the police officer in charge looked soberly at Kevin and I and said, "Boys, this is the second death we've had tonight from that damn storm. Same exact thing happened over on Sunset Drive. A tree fell on a woman. See all the ivy growing around that tree?" He pointed at the dogwood, and I looked at the trunk and branches. For the first time, I noticed a green weed wrapped around them. "All that growth adds weight and torque during a windstorm like that. It can make a limb snap like a twig. That wind came out of nowhere. It was almost biblical! The meteorologist called it a freak storm. You don't usually see stuff like that when it's this cold. Weather service said it spurred four different tornadoes in the area! Your dad was just in the wrong place at the wrong time. My pop died when I was about y'alls' age too. I'm so sorry for your loss."

I turned to Kevin and saw that he was crying. Tears streamed down his puffy red cheeks. The officer studied Kevin's face, then turned away, wiping tears from his own eyes.

⇌

As the last of the emergency vehicles disappeared into the distance, I glanced anxiously at Kevin, then turned back to the road. We tried to avoid catching each other's glances as a heavy silence settled over us.

"So, Dean's gone," I finally said, still in shock at all that had transpired.

"Yep," he answered as if in a heavy daze. "We're officially orphans."

"Are you okay?"

Kevin looked down and took a long breath. "Yeah, I'm okay."

"Also," I asked awkwardly, scratching above my right eyebrow. "You're gay?"

"Sam!" Kevin snapped. "You can never talk about what happened tonight. You understand? You don't tell anyone!"

I didn't know if he was referring to what had happened with Dean, or himself.

"I'm not judging. It actually explains a lot. I'm glad I know now."

"It means God hates me," he said sharply. "You heard what that preacher said when we were kids."

I frowned as I watched sadness overtake his face. "It doesn't mean that."

"They hate me, Sam," he said softly. "They all hate me."

"Being a gay Christian isn't contradictory. Being a hateful Christian is. I can't imagine God wouldn't be proud of you for being yourself, just the way He created you."

"Now you see why I don't pray," he said. He turned his back to me and looked at the ground as sadly as an old man missing his last sunset.

"Why?"

"I'm not going to send up a hypocritical prayer. I'd just as well stay silent."

"God doesn't think you're a hypocrite because of the way you feel." I placed my hand on his shoulder. "What you're feeling is guilt from Man, not God. It's Man using God to express his own prejudices and fears."

"I don't want to talk about it anymore!"

"You shouldn't feel ashamed. You're not doing anything wrong. You don't have to hide anymore. He's gone!"

He glared at me as seriously as a tax collector. "I said I don't want to talk about it!"

"Okay, okay."

I paused to look up at the sky, and unexpectedly began to laugh.

"What could possibly be funny?" Kevin asked.

"Dean always thought the Nieds were the perfect red-blooded conservative family. He wanted so much for us to emulate them." My laughter became loud, convulsive. "And all the while, you were banging their son, the quarterback!"

A smile crept through Kevin's anger, but his face quickly tensed and grew pensive as the gravity of the moment overshadowed it.

"What are we going to do?" I asked, running trembling fingers through my hair.

"Plan a funeral," he said, turning his back to me. His voice held no hint of doubt.

"It's that simple?"

"Yep," he assured me. "It's that simple."

He turned again, and looked me straight in the eyes. His voice seemed haunted. "You're not going down for this, Sam."

Shaken, we walked back to the house, Kevin biting his nails and me wringing my hands the whole way. We walked past the spot where the broken limb still touched the earth as the sun was slowly rising.

I looked at the gravel driveway where Dean had originally fallen. The brick lay on the ground where I'd left it, the naked orange glow of the morning sun shining on its surface. *So much power, in such a seemingly unimportant thing*, I thought.

I slowly walked over and picked it up. I studied its surface, mesmerized by the quiet, lurid tales it had to tell

"You go ahead," I said to Kevin. "I'll catch up."

He nodded, and walked away.

I carried the brick to the small shed that stood near where Jessie rested. I turned the brick over so that the black "3" faced away from me. My hands were still shaking as I opened a can of paint and painted the words "My Best Friend" in green letters on the brick's blank maroon exterior.

Blowing gently on the letters to help them dry, I walked over to Jessie's grave. The mound of dirt had long since grown yellow-brown patches of grass and weeds. Placing the brick on the ground to mark where my beloved friend rested, I said, "Love you, Jessie. I haven't forgotten—never."

I somehow slept peacefully that night, tucked under the protection of two warm covers. While I did, I had a dream that seemed more real than reality.

I was back in the dark forest, and three familiar beasts were circling me like vultures circle dead meat. The white reflections of their catlike eyes glowed brightly in the night sky. This time, though, I looked to my sides and saw Denise, Kevin, and Jessie walking with me.

We were unsure of the way out of the forest—until a glittering star in the sky shone unexpectedly through the thick, woody canopy. We followed the star to the boundary of the forest, where the darkness gradually faded into a bright yellow glow, and gazed beyond the edge of the forest into a field of flowering golden dandelions that shone as brilliantly as the sun.

To my left, a calm, crystal-clear pool of water reflected the perfect night sky above. I bent down and washed my hands in its fresh, warm water. When I looked up, fluffy white seed-heads from white dandelions blew softly like feathery snow across the sky as, in a high-pitched chorus, the clouds sang a song from *The Wizard of Oz:*

You're out of the woods,
You're out of the dark,
You're out of the night.
Step into the sun,
Step into the light.

Glancing behind me, I suddenly noticed an ivory casket resting back in the forest, about thirty yards away. It sat atop a dais made of purple stone. At the same time, I noticed a figure dressed in black perched atop a tall Grecian column on a hill to my left. He was looking down at me. The figure had a wormy parasite wriggling around its left milk-colored eyeball. His cloak had loose-fitting arms like wings, and he gestured in the direction of the box.

Yellow petals danced in the air around me as I walked slowly in the direction of the creamy white casket. Next to it, a fiery sign read, "Pork BBQ – $3.99." When I got there, I saw my mom having a picnic on the ground next to it.

Suddenly I found myself standing over the casket. A pig, rotting from the inside out, lay against a bright red silk lining inside. Worms fed on its flesh, and large mosquito-like insects with human hair fought over space on its skin. Rust-like decay speckled the creature's mouth and chest. Its eyes were like petrified wood, staring blankly ahead at nothing. It had human eyes— blue, just like mine.

As the figure in black laughed maniacally behind me, one

of the pig's hooves rose and slowly pulled down the casket lid above it. With a loud click, a lock engaged, and the black figure's crowing stopped. The angry pig had locked itself inside the box, walled up in its blindness!

After the pig's death-door shut, the ground beneath me began to shake violently. Distressed and frightened, I looked to my mom for help; but she seemed undisturbed by the tremor.

"Sam! Come get you something to eat, honey!" she called calmly.

Kevin planned the funeral. He arranged for all of Dean's assets, including the house, to be put in his name. He said it was his duty as Dean's son to take care of things.

He also said he wanted to continue living in Dean's house. I thought that was a horrible idea. I didn't want him to be trapped in that house forever, like some troubled ghost.

"The house feels like death now. Don't you want to get out of here?" I begged him. He ignored my pleading and walked away.

I even tried to convince Kevin I didn't need to go to the funeral—but Kevin was adamant I go. "What image would it portray if you didn't attend your own father's funeral?" he asked.

I decided not to fight him on it. But it turned out I was right: I didn't need to go. Kevin and I were the only attendees. Outside the two of us, the only thing there to keep Dean company was his casket.

At one point, Kevin left me alone in the cold, miserable funeral home visitation room. I reluctantly walked up to Dean's body and stared at his face, which had been plastered in layers of beige makeup. The morticians had parted his hair the wrong way. His eyes were sunken unnaturally into his skull. Even though

I knew he was gone, I was still uneasy in his presence, as if he might jump out at any time and grab me. My eyes began to water, not out of sadness exactly, but because of the tragedy of knowing I would never experience the love of a father for his son.

"Dean, I guess you've paid your dues. I'm going to do something I never thought I'd do. I'm going to forgive you for everything you did to us." I paused to clarify: "I'll forgive you for everything you did to *me*. I'm going to let you take the anger along with you to wherever you're heading. Thank you for letting me stay at your house as long as you did. And thank you for the food and clothes you bought me."

With those words, I closed the casket and let him go. Forgiveness had snuffed out hate like a strong wind snuffs a candle flame. I felt Dean's heavy presence gently leaving some shallow, outward part of me. I didn't suddenly forget the things he'd done; I just no longer wanted to punish him for them.

I turned around to realize Kevin had been in the room, watching me.

"How long have you been standing there?" I asked.

"Long enough to be a proud brother," he said.

Since Kevin and I were the only ones at the funeral, we didn't bother going to the burial site. We sent the old black Cadillac-style hearse to the cemetery alone. We'd been through enough, and it was time for us to rest.

"Told you I'd get you a Cadillac," I whispered to the vehicle as it pulled slowly away.

On the way to what was now Kevin's house, I asked him how he felt about everything. He said he was upset Dean had been disappointed in him at the end.

I tilted my head in confusion. "What?" I cried out. "Why do

you care so much about what he thought about you?"

Father-and-son bonds can be complicated—a blend of heartache and desire that you dream about while awake.

Kevin swallowed deeply. In a voice laced with uncertainty, he said, "He was my dad, Sam."

When we arrived at the house, an unfamiliar car was waiting in the driveway. A young woman stepped out. Like a feather caught in the wind, her dark silhouette drifted steadily toward our vehicle.

"Oh, shit," Kevin said, alarmed. "Is that Ryan?"

I looked closely at the mysterious figure. "It is her," I said in disbelief.

Kevin got out and walked straight into the house without even looking in Ryan's direction. I walked over timidly with my hands in my pockets. She wrapped her arms around me and hugged me tightly. She smelled like cigarettes and vanilla hair spray.

"I heard about your dad," she said, her face crumpling. "I'm so sorry."

"How long have you been waiting here?" I asked.

"An hour or so. I felt like I needed to see you. I heard about what happened to your mom, too. It's all so awful. How are you holding up?"

"I'm as good as can be expected, I guess. Thank you for coming by. That was very thoughtful of you." I reluctantly fabricated a smile and asked, "How are your folks?"

"My mom's doing okay. My dad actually passed a couple months back, too." Ryan looked sadly at the ground.

"What!? What happened?" I asked.

"Heart attack. He died at his desk."

I shook my head sadly. "I'm so sorry to hear that. I didn't know."

"It's okay. I know. No one from his work even came to the funeral. He had stomach ulcers that gave him pain all the time, and he couldn't sleep. He was so big that his knees were always hurting. I think he realized his soul was sick in the end. It's just sad that it took him so long."

"I hope your mom is okay."

We walked slowly toward the tracks, looking outward. "They divorced a while back. He became way more successful after the divorce—lonelier, but successful. He settled into his long career like a corpse into his casket. Looking back, I think he worked all those hours out of loneliness."

We stopped and looked at one another as a familiar breeze blew between us. "He never understood that we'd have been there if he would have just taken the time to see us. He said to me once near the end, 'I kept trying to make it meaningful, but it never was.' It was sad to see his life end that way, in the futility of ambition."

There was a guarded silence. I didn't know what to say to her anymore, outside of the usual small talk. The last leaf of feelings I'd had for her had fallen without my noticing. She was now only a someone, and I had only a cold friendliness toward her.

Finally, she smiled, breaking the awkwardness of the moment, and said, "You look great, Sam."

"Thanks," I said cautiously, feeling as if I were talking to a stranger. Then, out of obligation, I offered, "You look good, too."

"We should go upstairs," she said, smirking, "for old times' sake. We were always so incredible, remember?"

In that moment, I could have told her she was a horrible human being. I could have said she'd broken my heart, and that I was never the same after what she'd done to me. In that moment, I finally had the sole power between us. I could have made her feel a tiny bit of the awful pain she'd caused me.

But the truth was, it wasn't worth it to me anymore. I didn't care. I realized Ryan was like a chameleon. She made herself into whatever the person in front of her wanted her to be, like an empty shell for others to paint on. And empty shells aren't safe for others. They suck what's good out of the people around them in an attempt to fill their own emptiness. But they can never take enough, and like a deer tick, they eventually move on, still thirsty, to their next host.

"I'm sorry, Ryan. I actually have to go. You're too late. I'm going to have to say no this time."

For a moment she looked as if she'd just been struck by a bolt of lightning. Maybe it was understanding that struck her—a sudden realization of how careless she'd been with something that had once been so magical.

"Okay. I understand," she said uneasily as she began to back away. "I guess I'll just move on, then. I'm so sorry about everything. It was great seeing you."

I feigned a smile. "You too. Take care of yourself."

Ryan walked slowly to her car, her long black hair snapping like a whip as she went. Right before she grabbed for the door handle, she turned around. Smiling, she looked with glazed eyes into the distance as a warm old wind blew, caressing her face. A mockingbird sang in a tree high above.

"I still love those dogwoods," she said. "Even when they're not in bloom."

My mind drifted back to days of honeysuckles and daffodils the color of the sun. I remembered how desperately I had once wished for Ryan and me to be together. Sometimes, not getting what you want is the best kind of luck you can ask for.

"The memories are for keeps," I said, pressing my palm to my heart, "even if we're not anymore."

She smiled without saying a word. I waved gracelessly as she started her car and fluttered, like a strong and unexpected wind, out of my life forever.

⟶

A week after Dean's funeral, I stopped by Professor Hunt's office. Since Dean's death, I'd been struggling with conflicting feelings over whether killing my father was justifiable. I wondered if I'd have to pay for it when I too inevitably met my night.

I didn't like what I'd done. If you enjoy killing, there's something decaying inside of you; but a part of me was glad he was gone.

When I walked into Professor Hunt's office, he immediately stood and hugged me.

"I heard about what happened, and I'm so sorry," he said.

"Thanks, Professor," I replied, forcing a smile.

"Do you want to talk about it?" he asked. "Come; sit down." He gestured toward the leather chair across from his desk.

"Actually, I do. I wanted to ask you something, if you don't mind. It's a little uncomfortable, but I need some answers."

He smiled and said, "Of course."

I sat and looked at my feet. After a short pause, I said, "I don't think I feel bad that he's gone." Taking a deep breath, I continued, "In fact, I think I'm relieved. He was horrible to me, to all of us. He only brought chaos into our lives."

"I see," Professor Hunt said. He stood up and stared out his office window, scratching his chin.

With my voice cracking, I asked, "Am I a horrible person?"

"Horrible? Horrible for what?"

"For not being more upset."

Professor Hunt shook his head and turned to face me. "You should do whatever produces the most happiness in your world, Sam. All you need to worry about is maximizing the actions that create the most good."

For a moment, the old anger took hold of me. "I think I wanted him dead. I wanted to kill him myself sometimes."

His face contracted, as if he was deep in thought. "I know this is hard to hear, but sometimes closing the curtain is better. Let me put it another way. Do you think it's moral for a soldier to kill another soldier in war?"

"I guess," I said, "since both sides are aware of the potential consequences."

"Well, it sounds like your father waged a war against you your entire life. He was like a soldier in a self-created conflict against his family, and that makes him guilty. That's probably why you're having trouble with your feelings about his passing. For some reason, a lot of people think that when the war ends, the wounds stop hurting. But a soldier takes injuries with them long after the fight is over."

"I think he was responsible for my mom's death, in a lot of ways. At the very least, he helped introduce her to some demons. Once, he tried to choke my brother to death with his bare hands. And when I was a little kid . . ." I squeezed my hands together, and the corners of my lips tightened. "Believe it or not, he killed my dog."

Professor Hunt's eyes seemed to glisten with moisture. "Then you don't need to feel guilty about wanting him erased from your world; that's just part of the debts of war. You're probably relieved no one else has to sacrifice."

I let out a long breath and leaned back in my seat. "Thank you for talking to me, Professor Hunt. That all makes a lot of sense, and helps. I've been thinking about this all week. It's really been bothering me."

"Who really knows what's right or wrong, anyway? The right things can lead to bad outcomes, and the wrong things can lead to good ones. Don't lose sleep over ending a war you didn't start, or over debts that are now paid in full. Rest peacefully, Sam."

11

Bitter Sweet Symphony

"I let the melody shine, let it cleanse my mind,
I feel free now."

—The Verve

The time has passed as quickly as those trains once passed by my childhood home in Verities. I'm no longer a young man, and the gray stones before me remind me of the specks of gray now flecking my thinning, receding hair.

I can't believe I'm turning forty-five today. It's been over twenty years since I said goodbye to Dean. Back in those days, I never even imagined I'd make it to forty-five.

In front of me, the local cemetery lies silent and empty, bordered by familiar trees. I love the dogwoods in this hallowed place this time of year. They spread out so regally across the sacred grounds. Some are adorned with beautiful snow-white blossoms. Others are stained pink. The mixture of white and pink flowers contrasting with the texture of the tree's scale-like bark along the skyline is breathtaking, if not a bit heartbreaking.

Newman had once told me that the cross on which Jesus was

crucified had been constructed from the wood of a dogwood tree. In those ancient days, dogwoods grew larger than oak trees and produced only white blossoms. God was so angry at the cruelty of the dogwoods' use that He transformed the once tall trees into tiny ones to prevent similar misuse of their wood. Today, dogwoods rarely grow taller than twelve feet. God also commanded the trees' blossoms be arranged in the form of a cross and stained bright red in remembrance of the innocent blood shed that day.

Some people are nervous in cemeteries, but sitting here beneath one of those dogwood trees, I feel at peace. Sometimes I stay for hours, listening to the stones whisper under this bent and twisted tree. The gray dots of the graves against the backdrop of manicured, rich green grass reveal a beautiful sermon.

I close my eyes. A familiar breeze blows sweetly against my face, and I am reminded of a passage I love to quote from First Kings, in the Bible. In this passage, Elijah takes refuge on the mountain on the Sinai Peninsula where God revealed Herself to Moses. A powerful storm comes through, shattering the rocks on the mountain—but God isn't in that mighty storm. Then an earthquake shakes the ground, destroying everything it touches—but the Lord isn't in that, either. The earthquake ignites a fire that rages and turns everything black around Elijah—but even in that fire, She is not to be found. But after the chaos of all that magnificent power settles, a gentle wind comes and kisses Elijah's face—and there, in a tender, almost silent breeze, Elijah finally finds God.

That story's message has always made sense to me: God and Her love can be found only in the whispering moments of life. Many wanderers search for Her in the wrong places, believing they must wait for some awe-inspiring event to find themselves in Her presence. But I believe She reveals Herself quietly, in mundane things like a soft, gentle wind.

The dogwood trees, the wind, the color of the grass, and this damn awful heat make my mind sail back through many yesterdays. Childhood memories come, as vivid as if they happened only a week ago. I hear the faint and familiar sound of a train whistle blowing in the far distance, and I know exactly where it's crossing.

Denise walks up to me, holding the hands of our nine-year-old daughter and our four-year-old son. Cadence, our daughter, is giggling at little Brooks because he's sticking his tongue out at her. Cadence asks Denise whether she and Brooks can go play.

Denise tells them they can, but reminds them to be respectful of the graves. Then, sitting down next to me, she puts her soft hands firmly in mine.

"I can't believe he's been gone this long," she says.

I stare at the stone, remembering the face of the man who now rests beneath it, and whisper, "Me neither."

I look at the headstone that bears my brother's name. It's been hard for me to talk to anyone about his death. I was supposed to be his keeper, but the only person I couldn't save him from was himself.

"You know," I say, "I don't blame that young girl, but when she pulled out in front of him, it was the beginning of the end for Kevin." I sniff and wipe my nose with my sleeve. "Before they took him back for surgery, I told the doctor about his past addictions."

Denise looks at me, her eyes heavy. "I know, baby."

But there's a kind of catharsis in repeating old stories. "I knew the anesthesia they used could cause a relapse. I knew it contained opioids. I begged them to find another way. But the doctor didn't take me seriously. And then they prescribed Kevin Vicodin after the surgery. Of course they did; they always do.

"After that, it only took a month. One month later, and Kevin was dead of a heroin overdose."

"It happened so quickly," Denise whispers.

"He was only twenty-eight years old."

"I still can't believe he's gone," Denise says, her eyes misting.

"We had planned a trip to DC for the weekend after he died. We were going to meet there and check out the monuments. The last thing he said to me was, 'I'll see you up there.'"

"I'm so sorry," she says, laying her head on my shoulder.

"Right after he died, I visited the old house we grew up in. The dogwoods had bloomed early that year. The weather was unseasonably warm for days, and then a cold front came. It chilled the air like a spirit."

The kids' laughter echoes around me as they chase one another. "I snapped a branch off one of the dogwoods out front. Kevin and I had grown up with that tree. We'd played catch under it. We'd climbed on it. Imagined on it. It had white flowers with bits of red on them, four petals around a bright yellow center—one petal for each person in our family."

I take a deep breath. "For better or worse, we were all bound together on the same branch, just like those petals. The same roots nourished us and gave us life. They defined the world around us, made us who we were, and who we would become.

"I put the branch on Kevin's grave. It was just a mound of freshly dug dirt then. Brown and dark red, just like Kevin's hair." I pause for a moment, and can see Kevin in my mind's eye, with his blue eyes smiling at me. "When I visited the next morning, it was so cold out, I was shivering. The branch I'd left had frozen, so the whole thing looked like a diamond in the sun. I stared at it the way you'd stare at a sky full of stars. The red in the petals had faded, and they'd gone white, like freshly washed bedsheets."

I pause, and look into the distant blue sky.

"To the world, he became just another of the tens of thousands of lives taken every year by opioid overdoses. But to me, there was something beautiful about him—something I loved. I hate that he became just another statistic."

"I don't even know how you got through it all."

"I had no choice. I was the only one left. I had to keep surviving. That's what it's all about. You have to drown in all that crap, and if you make it back to the surface, you somehow emerge a better version of yourself. I guess some of the ego and selfishness can wash off during your struggles, and that's when change can happen.

"Anyway, one positive thing did come out of it all. His death made me realize I wasn't just *his* keeper. I was everyone's, in a way. I found out real love is about seeing yourself in others."

"I wish he could have beat it," Denise whispers lowly.

"You know what I think was his ultimate undoing?" She glances at me for the answer. "His insatiable need to capture our father's love. Lots of abused children develop a sick form of Stockholm syndrome as a survival strategy, and he was one of them."

After contemplating those words, Denise says, "I really loved what you said that day."

"What do you mean?"

"At his funeral, the words you recited. Do you remember them?"

"The Aeschylus quote?" I say softly. "By heart."

"After all these years?"

"'And even in our sleep, pain that cannot forget falls drop by drop upon the heart, and in our own despair, against our will, comes wisdom to us by the awful grace of God.'"

Denise stands up, pretending she's checking on the kids. She doesn't want me to see the tears falling down her face. She thinks it'll upset me. She's still as beautiful as she was on the day I met her, and always in good spirits. Her beauty hasn't waxed or waned with time; it's transcended the foolish definition of beauty I possessed in my youth. I don't know how I ever existed apart from her. Anything in life not connected to her in some way doesn't seem to bring as much joy as the things that are.

"Can we stop somewhere on the way home?" I ask her.

"Whatever you want," she says. "It's your day."

"Kids," I yell. "Get in the car! I want to show you something."

I kiss my fingers and touch Kevin's cool headstone. "Happy birthday, brother," I say quietly.

⌐

As we cross the tracks, the car jumps into the air, and Brooks and Cadence laugh. We pull into the driveway of my old childhood home. The dogwoods are blooming here too, just as beautifully and contentedly as I remember. As I step out of the car, I feel a strange impulse, as I do every time I'm here, to glance at the spot where Mom died.

"Where are we?" Cadence asks.

The haunting symphony of cicadas fills the air. They fly aimlessly, wandering through the summer day and filling the warm silence with their love song. Sometimes, it seems as if all of Earth's creatures are drifting, aimlessly seeking love.

"This is the house I grew up in."

"Wow!" she says.

Looking at the house is like looking at a star in the night sky—one long since burnt out and powerless, but still transmitting its light as a reminder of what once was. Thick green vines grow halfway up its sides.

I walk over to the dogwood tree that still stands with a large scar on its trunk—a scar with a precious secret.

"Look!" Denise calls, pointing at the top of the tree.

Orange-and-red butterflies—hundreds of them—cover the trunk above the scar, making the tree seem as if it's been wrapped in a silky butterfly dress. More of the insects flutter past, dancing in the air between us. It's a breathtaking sight.

"They must have migrated," I say.

"It's absolutely beautiful!" she says, smiling with childlike wonder at the scene.

I've come a long way too, I think to myself, looking at the butterflies. *I was old too soon and smart too late.*

But in some ways, I feel there's been something magical about my life. The melody has been more beautiful than the lyrics. Maybe Newman *was* right: "You can't truly see the stars until it's dark enough." I had to descend into the depths to appreciate the heights.

On clear nights, I look up at the sky in awe and watch the stars sing a silent song in the same heavens my ancestors came to know from the beginning of the world. There's wonder in observing the vastness of space. It makes me feel my smallness.

Few people pay attention to the blackness between the stars—but I do. I wonder what's between the light, and why light is always associated with goodness. To me, the nothingness among the specks of light melds a childlike fear with serenity. Maybe life's beauty can actually be found somewhere in the darkness.

When he was alive, Newman used to make wonderful carvings from some of the trees on his property. I'll never forget the time he took me to his workshop. When I walked in and looked around, I told him I'd never seen such beauty before.

Newman had said that the first thing my mom had noticed when she walked into the workshop were the shavings all over the floor. She couldn't see past those scraps of wood to find the beauty in his creations; she only saw a horrible mess.

I thought both the shavings and the art were marvels. After all, you couldn't have the latter without the former.

Far off in the distance, a dog barks. The kids run around the backyard, playing by the tracks and singing. When I was their age, I never imagined this place could be fun.

I walk in their direction and notice a brick lying on the ground near the tracks, the words I painted on them faded to just a couple of indecipherable green dots.

"What's that?" Denise asks.

"That was a tribute to my first dog, Jessie, the best dog ever! I buried him there."

She smiles knowingly. Our hearts hold some secrets that even those closest to us never see.

I hold Denise's hand as we walk toward the tracks. Crouching, I touch the steel rail tenderly.

"Think about all the metaphors about life that relate to trains," I say. "I don't think that's a coincidence."

"True." Denise smiles. "You're on the right track there."

I laugh and say, "I'm just letting off steam!"

She fires right back, "But you're on the wrong side of the tracks!"

"Yes! But don't worry; there's light at the end of the tunnel!"

She throws up her arms. "This is a train wreck!"

"Because my plans got derailed?"

"Yes, but you're still chugging along."

We both laugh, and I reach out and hug Denise. As I'm holding her, I look uneasily at the house behind us, and then at the rails again.

"I know this is weird to say, but I feel like these tracks were always with me, guiding me somehow."

Denise smiles and says, "Your life's been one crazy story, that's for sure. You could almost write a book about it."

"You know? Maybe I will one day. I'm not really a writer; I'm a reader. But maybe I'll try to put it all on paper sometime."

Denise looks to the rails and then back at me, and smiles thoughtfully. "We better get going," she says reluctantly. "You have an afternoon class."

"I almost forgot." I call to the children. "Time to go, guys!"

Just before I climb into the car, I turn and take a last look at the tracks and the house I grew up in. It held so many memories, so many things left unsaid. I wonder what might have been if a few cards in all our lives had come up kings. I envision my brother, mom, and dad all playing in the yard by the side porch in the sun. I see Mom pick up my brother and twirl him in the sweet air as the dogwoods loom, envious of our love.

But as soon as it arises, the vision quickly begins to fade. It's all an illusion; it just wasn't meant to be. The mirage flees like a lost ghost in the sun as Cadence runs to me and jumps into my arms.

Holding Brooks, Denise leans over and kisses Cadence on the cheek.

I smile, thankful that the past doesn't have to determine the present. Those steel tracks and that blessed whistle sang in a season that now seems like another lifetime. And they wrapped their haunting sound around a broken and scared child, carrying him gracefully ahead.

My life has been utterly mad and malicious, but also fortunate and fantastic. And when I hear a whistle scream against yesterday's wind, I remember; and for the preciousness of the moment, I am so very grateful.

<hr />

After dropping off Denise and the kids, I arrive at class right on time. As I enter the large lecture hall, my students greet me.

"Good afternoon, Professor!"

"Good afternoon, everyone!" I respond. "We're going to jump right back into last week's discussion. . ."

Final Track
Everybody Knows
by Leonard Cohen

Everybody knows that the dice are loaded
Everybody rolls with their fingers crossed
Everybody knows the war is over
Everybody knows the good guys lost
Everybody knows the fight was fixed
The poor stay poor, the rich get rich
That's how it goes
Everybody knows

Everybody knows that the boat is leaking
Everybody knows that the captain lied
Everybody got this broken feeling
Like their father or their dog just died
Everybody talking to their pockets
Everybody wants a box of chocolates
And a long-stem rose
Everybody knows

Everybody knows that you love me baby
Everybody knows that you really do
Everybody knows that you've been faithful
Ah, give or take a night or two
Everybody knows you've been discreet
But there were so many people you just had to meet
Without your clothes
And everybody knows

Everybody knows, everybody knows
That's how it goes
Everybody knows

Everybody knows, everybody knows
That's how it goes
Everybody knows

And everybody knows that it's now or never
Everybody knows that it's me or you
And everybody knows that you live forever
Ah, when you've done a line or two
Everybody knows the deal is rotten
Old Black Joe's still pickin' cotton
For your ribbons and bows
And everybody knows

And everybody knows that the Plague is coming
Everybody knows that it's moving fast
Everybody knows that the naked man and woman
Are just a shining artifact of the past
Everybody knows the scene is dead
But there's gonna be a meter on your bed
That will disclose
What everybody knows

And everybody knows that you're in trouble
Everybody knows what you've been through
From the bloody cross on top of Calvary
To the beach of Malibu
Everybody knows it's coming apart
Take one last look at this Sacred Heart
Before it blows
And everybody knows

Everybody knows, everybody knows
That's how it goes
Everybody knows

Everybody knows, everybody knows
That's how it goes
Everybody knows

Everybody knows, everybody knows
That's how it goes
Everybody knows

Everybody knows

About the Author

 **Randy White** founded and serves as executive director of Love of Learning, a nonprofit that hosts read-alouds and donates high-quality children's books to low-income kids in central Virginia. He has received numerous Making a Difference awards for his work promoting literacy opportunities for disadvantaged children. Before founding his nonprofit organization, Mr. White spent ten years as a public school teacher in a suburb of Richmond, Virginia. He holds a master's degree in teaching and a bachelor's degree in sociology from Virginia Commonwealth University, as well as an associate's degree in social sciences. A native of Richmond, Mr. White currently lives in the city with his wife, Christin, their two young children, and two adorable boxers.

CPSIA information can be obtained
at www.ICGtesting.com
Printed in the USA
FFHW020732081119
56016078-61901FF